Dual Footsteps in the Fog

by Helen Reardon

Other Helen Reardon Novels

Strands Across the Sea

A Long Time Dead

Man of Vision

Dual footsteps in the fog

The small child stirred in her cot. She half opened her eyes and reached out, her fingers opening and closing. She cried for a time then fell into an unsettled sleep.

Madeline Bennett had woken at the first sound on the intercom. She was about to get out of bed but her husband Steve gently restrained her. "She'll go back to sleep. She always does."

"You're probably right, but I wonder what makes her so restless. It's as though she is always reaching out for someone."

"The only thing we can do for her is to let her know that we love her as much as our own son." Steve settled back to sleep but Madeline remained awake, remembering the day they had brought the baby home. The day they met their precious daughter.

Chapter 1

"You should have some breakfast Joanne. How will you be able to concentrate if you don't have some food?" Madeline fussed in the kitchen as her daughter came down the stairs. Luckily they lived just a short distance from the bus stop where she could catch a ride to the teachers' college a few miles from where they lived.

"I'll eat this on the way." Joanne grabbed a slice of toast and a sachet of flavoured milk. "Thanks Mum. See you tonight."

"Sure. Have a great day." Madeline watched her daughter until she disappeared from view, then poured a cup of tea and sat down to browse through the morning paper. Her husband Steve had left earlier after a substantial feed of bacon and eggs. As supervisor on a building site it would be some time before he could take a break.

She had showered and changed into a loose summer dress. Now the hours stretched out before her. It was her day off from the grocery store where she worked part-time stacking the shelves. The extra cash helped out while Joanne was completing her teacher training.

Madeline smiled as she thought of the happiness their daughter had brought them. Bradin's birth had been a difficult one and left her with little chance of becoming pregnant again. With all the other play group mothers producing their second and third child, Madeline felt isolated as though she was not fulfilling her woman's role.

She was devastated that she may not be able to produce a sibling for young Bradin. She didn't want him to grow up as an only child.

Her doctor was the first person to suggest adoption. "Often when someone adopts a child, another pregnancy follows naturally, although in your case I don't think that will happen. I'll give you a contact for an agency and recommend you get in touch.

It was a few days before she showed the paper work to her husband. "The doctor thinks we should try to adopt a baby. Would you object to raising a child who was not your own?"

Steve gave her a hug and said to go for it. A small baby would soon seem like their own child.

It had taken almost a year before the good news came. A little girl had been born who would be perfect for them. "How does a mother feel about giving up her child? It must be incredibly difficult whatever the circumstances." Madeline was overjoyed but felt sorry for the mother of the child.

The girl from the agency was kind, but businesslike. She had brought the papers to the house and asked a few questions, making notes on a typed document.

"I'll leave a copy of this here and you can discuss the details with your husband when he comes home tonight. If all is well, you should be able to collect the baby in just over a week."

After agreeing to the adoption, Madeline was in a whirl for the next few days. The baby crib which had been stored away for the past three years was brought out, along with the baby clothes that Madeline had saved. She would need to buy some new night gowns, matinee jackets and napkins. Then there were baby creams, powder and feeding bottles.

It was surprising how much baby gear turned up in such a short time. Knitted jackets and booties, lace trimmed sheets and frilled pillow cases. All the play group mums seemed to have something to contribute.

Young Bradin was quite puzzled at all the activity. "You are going to have a little sister. You will be able to help us take care of her." Madeline gave him a hug.

It was a sunny day in early summer when they pulled up outside the nursing home. Steve was surprised at the palatial surroundings. "It must have cost an arm and a leg to have a baby here. The family must be really wealthy."

Madeline was a little overwhelmed, but she took Steve's arm as they walked into the spacious entry foyer. "We'll do our best to provide the child with everything she needs. She will not want for anything in our care."

They sat nervously in the brightly coloured waiting room with chrome chairs and a black leather couch. Lush green pot plants and an ornate floral arrangement were set on small wrought iron tables.

An older woman wearing a smart green uniform came into the room and smiled at them. "Come with me and meet your new daughter," she said, and led them into another small room where a baby lay sleeping in a cane bassinette.

A tiny face and a shock of black hair was all Madeline could see as the baby was wrapped firmly in a white napkin. Her eyes filled with tears as she handed over the bag of clothing she had brought with her.

Soon the baby was unwrapped and the woman looked her over carefully. She examined the navel and seemed satisfied then quickly dressed the child in the little garments which Madeline had lovingly prepared.

"There you are. All fingers and toes accounted for and she is feeding well. She's just a little soul but has already reached her birth weight." She handed Steve a sheet of paper with all the important details. Date of birth, weight and the milk formula.

The woman wrapped the baby in the fine wool shawl, gave her a hug and handed her to Madeline. "Here you are Mrs Bennett. She's all yours. You will need to arrange for the Plunket nurse to call in a few days and you can contact us if you are worried about anything. Now I will carry your daughter to your car and see you safely on your way."

***

Madeline brought her mind back to the present. It didn't take long to hand wash the dishes and leave them on the drainer to dry. She put a load of washing in the machine and added the soap powder.

Today she would clean out Bradin's room. Their son had surprised them about six months previously when he announced that he was off to try his luck in Australia.

"My mates are all over there and joining a roofing gang. The money's good and there's not much work around here at the moment."

Bradin was right. There had been a slump in the housing market lately and many young people were heading across the Tasman to find a job.

"At least it's Australia and not the other side of the world," Steve had consoled her. Apart from a dutiful phone call each week, they heard little from their son but they knew he was in good company and his employer was fair.

"As long as Bradin joins the rugby club he won't go too far wrong." Steve was pleased that his son was keeping up his favourite sport.

Since Bradin's departure the spare bedroom had become a dumping ground for all manner of items. Tennis racquets and an old guitar stood in the corner, along with an unused knitting machine and a pile of magazines.

The corner cupboard would be her mission today. It was ages since she had looked inside and she had almost forgotten what was stored there. Photograph albums, old road maps, framed pictures and a box of Christmas decorations were soon taking up all the space on the bed.

She paused to hang a load of washing on the clothes line then set about the task with renewed energy. Soon the cupboard was almost empty and she reached up to pull down an old tin box from the very top shelf.

Oh boy! She had almost forgotten about this box which had lain in the cupboard for more than 20 years. She pulled it down and carried it into the living room. This called for another cup of tea.

Just at that moment there was a tap on the glass door and Flo, her neighbour, walked in. She wore a loose cardigan over her floral dress and bedroom slippers. "Any chance of a cuppa?" she asked and sat down at the end of the table. "I'm having a bad day. The vacuum cleaner refuses to suck and I put Stan's woollen jersey in the washing machine by mistake. I think it will fit a 10-year-old now."

"Never mind Flo. Just sit yourself down and join me. I've managed to trash the spare room, but look what I've found."

"Well, I never. Have you discovered where you hid the family jewels or that bundle of cash you didn't want the tax man to know about?"

"I wish. No, I remember putting this box away just after Joanne was born, but I don't really remember what is inside it."

Flo and Stan O'Connor had moved onto the subdivision shortly after the Bennetts and the two couples had been friends ever since. With their families growing up side by side there weren't too many secrets between them.

"Come on then. Open it up and let's see what's inside." Flo was inclined to be a little outspoken but had a heart of gold.

Madeline poured the tea and sat down. She tried to take the lid of the box but it was stuck fast.

"Here, let me have a go." Flo took the box and ran a sharp knife around the rim of the rusted lid. She levered the lid off the box and it fell onto the floor with a loud clang.

Madeline looked inside the box. First she brought out a tiny leather shoe, then a little box that contained a lock of hair. "That was from Bradin's first hair cut," she recalled. Next came two Plunket record books and a baby rattle.

A cutting from an old newspaper was unfolded to reveal the news of President Kennedy's assassination. November 23, 1963. "That was the day Joanne was born, but we didn't know about her until a few days later."

At the very bottom of the box lay a large brown envelope. Madeline drew it out and opened it carefully. There was the sheet of paper that the woman had handed to Steve all those years ago. The baby's date of birth, weight and where she had been born.

"Parkhaven Nursing Home. That was a pretty flash place back then. I believe it's an old people's home now days." Flo peered at the words on the paper. "That place had quite a reputation for a while. It was where rich men's daughters went to have their babies. Very discreet. No questions asked."

"I'd never heard of it until we went to pick up little Joanne, but I remember it being very grand."
Madeline stared at the sheet of paper in her hand. So little information for the beginning of a life. She would show Joanne the paper that night. Although their daughter knew she was adopted she had rarely shown any curiosity about the circumstances of her birth.

"I'd better get on and repack the cupboard, but I'll keep the box out and show it to Joanne and Steve."

Flo took the hint and returned next door to sort out her own housekeeping dramas, but the thought that Joanne was born in such an exclusive place stayed on her mind. November 23 1963. What an auspicious date to come into the world.

***

Joanne's day had not begun well. First she missed her usual bus and had to wait 10 minutes for the next one. She arrived at the college just in time for her first lecture and searched through the books in her bag. Oh no. The text book she needed was missing and she broke the lead of her pencil when she tried to write.

She looked across at her friend Tracey who was already taking notes and shrugged. She would have to catch up with the work later. The lecture dragged on. Sometimes the philosophy of learning was so boring. Joanne just wanted to get into a classroom and start teaching.

Her attention wandered until the lecturer asked the question: "What do you think is the most important? Nature or nurture?"

This led to quite an animated discussion over whether genetic makeup was more important than upbringing in shaping a personality. "For example, quite often when an adopted child meets his or her birth mother for the first time, there is a real connection. There are many similarities between them, even though the child has been brought up in an entirely different family."

Now Joanne was really interested. While her childhood had been a happy one, she sometimes thought that she belonged in a different place and time. Although she had idolised her big brother as they grew up, she had often played in her own little world, speaking to an imaginary friend.

As a small child she would wake up and reach out her hand, but no-one was there. Then she would pick up the floppy toy rabbit and hold it tightly. So tightly in fact that the stuffing eventually fell out and one ear came off.

"Come on Joanne. Time for a coffee." She shook herself out of the day dream to find Tracey standing beside her, ready to head for the cafeteria and a welcome break.

"Okay, I need a muffin. My mother was right. I should have eaten more breakfast."

The pair joined the crowd as they trooped along the corridors leading to the large cafeteria where they helped themselves at the coffee machine and waited in line for a muffin.

The end of term was close and there was lots of excitement about the summer break. There were still the final exams to get through and then the wait to be assigned to a school for the first teaching year.

Tracey had found herself a holiday job at a bookstore where she would be busy selling Christmas decorations and gifts of every description. She had worked there every year since leaving school so had been elevated to supervisor and was right at home in the familiar surroundings.

"Don't forget, we've promised ourselves a week's holiday before the school term starts. We'll have to work out where we want to go."

Joanne had put her name down at several stores but had not yet secured a definite placement. She would call at the coffee lounges around the city over the weekend and try her luck. With long shiny brown hair and regular features she was an attractive girl, but preferred casual clothes and rarely wore make up.

"We'd better get back to the next lecture. It should be quite interesting as we are going to make some equipment I believe. I'm not sure about my wood working skills but it should be fun trying."

Tracey usually led the way and Joanne followed. She didn't want to stand out as a Tall Poppy and liked to be just part of the crowd. Tracey often teased her about this. "Come on Joanne. You could be gorgeous if you styled your hair and accentuated those beautiful eyes."

It was almost dinner time when Joanne arrived at her destination and walked the short distance to her home. The gardens were colourful with summer flowers which brightened the plain wooden and brick houses which had been built during an earlier housing boom.

With low deposits and mortgage rates it had made first home ownership easy and created many suburbs where young families were raised. Over the years the Bennetts had made a few improvements to their property, adding a large wooden deck and barbecue area where they spent many long summer evenings.

Madeline had prepared potatoes ready for baking and a tasty salad. Steve poured everyone a cool drink and fired up the barbecue ready for the steaks. They sat on the canvas chairs eager to share the news of the day.

"It's just as well we got the contract for that shopping mall or I'd be joining Bradin in Australia." Steve was hot and tired from the day's work, but grateful that he still had a well-paid job.

"We tried to make a jigsaw puzzle but my fretsaw skills leave a lot to be desired. I'm afraid I don't have your talents," Joanne added.

"I tidied our Bradin's room today and look what I found." Madeline produced the tin box and placed it on the barbecue table. "It's more than 20 years since I put that box in the cupboard and it's never seen the light of day until now."

Steve was curious. "I remember that old box," he said. "When I was a kid I used to keep my Scout badges in it. What's in it now?"

"Just a few reminders of our babies. Bless them." Madeline handed the box to Steve who took out the small items.

His large hands clumsily grasped the small shoe and the baby rattle which he shook vigourously. "This sure takes me back. You learnt to grasp this rattle when you were only a few weeks old." He handed the small toy to Joanne who looked on in amusement. She couldn't imagine why someone would want to keep such simple items for so many years.

Her parents compared the Plunket books. "Look at this Joanne. You were just six and a half pounds on the first page, but you grew steadily and soon caught up with the average line."

"Bradin was a much bigger baby. Almost nine pounds at birth. His line goes right off the chart." Steve had forgotten what a solid child Bradin had been.

When they came to the brown envelope Steve handed it to Joanne. "You open this. It probably concerns you."

Joanne's mind flashed back to that morning's lecture. Would there be a clue inside about her birth parents? She unfolded the page and scanned the contents. "Not much I didn't already know. Where was this Parkhaven Nursing Home and what was it like?"

"It's a home for the elderly now, I hear. Flo seemed to know something about it. Very flash she said, so your birth family was well connected I would say." Madeline looked around their dated home. Joanne probably could have lived in much grander surroundings.

"All their money didn't bring them happiness by the look of things. It must have been a sad day when they gave up a child." Steve gave Joanne a quick hug. They had no reason to feel ashamed of their circumstances.

Joanne picked up the newspaper cutting and read it with astonishment. "I didn't know I was born the same day as the Kennedy assassination. We learned about it in school but I had forgotten the date. It would be interesting to talk to someone who worked at the nursing home. They might remember what they were doing the day John F Kennedy died."

Although Madeline knew she would encourage their daughter to learn about her birth family, the idea of it actually happening filled her with apprehension. What if Joanne found her mother and the meeting was not a success? Maybe there were secrets that were better left unanswered.

Steve refilled their wine glasses and poured himself a beer. He turned his attention to the potatoes and the steaks. A pot of mushrooms was cooking on the side of the barbecue and Madeline brought out the salad and the jug of home-made dressing.

Joanne washed her hands and arranged the cutlery on the outdoor table. This was the first barbecue of the season and the first one without Bradin. She would have to help make it a happy occasion.

Chapter 2

The next few weeks were busy ones for Joanne. She passed her final exams, but her marks were unexceptional. Tracey had come out top of the class but Joanne was satisfied to have completed the course and the chance to move on.

She had found a holiday job working in a garden centre and would start next week. The work would be physically challenging but she would enjoy working in the outdoors and she could wear her favourite jeans and t-shirts.

"Don't forget to keep the last week of January free. I have borrowed a tent and some camping gear and we can head off to the beach." Tracey was enthusiastic about the upcoming holiday and her parents had bought her a small car as a reward for her good exam results.

They had submitted a number of requests for a school placement but had heard nothing back. Tracey was aiming high, targeting some of the popular Auckland schools while Joanne had chosen three smaller schools in the outer suburbs.

"I'd rather teach regular kids who come from homes like mine. I'm not interested in the spoilt children of indulgent parents." Tracey just shrugged. She knew Joanne well and appreciated all her good qualities, but she intended to go to the top of her career.

"Okay, so are you coming to the dance to celebrate that we are now full-blown teachers?" Tracey was keen to catch up with her friends. They often went along to the country club on a Saturday night when a popular band was playing.

"Sure. Mum and Dad will probably be going and they can sign us in. Most of the regulars are sure to be there." Joanne had been out with a number of guys over the years, usually friends of her brother.

"There could be some new talent. That could be interesting." Tracey swung her long pony tail and tucked in her ruffled blouse.

"I'll see you at the club then. We'll be there around eight." Joanne would have to look through her wardrobe and find something new to wear. Most of the kids should be back from university so it promised to be an interesting night.

A she opened the gate and checked the mail box Joanne heard Flo's voice from over the fence. Flo was pulling weeds from the garden and wore a large sunhat and green rubber gloves.

"Joanne, my love, only a few more days to go and the holidays will be here. The boys are already home and driving me mad, wanting food at all hours of the day. But, bless them, they'll be off to work next week and out of my hair."

"It's a few months since I caught up with Jason and Geoffrey, but I guess we will get together soon." Joanne looked forward to seeing Flo's sons again.

They had gone through school together and now the boys had been at university in Wellington.

"And another thing Joanne. I've been thinking a lot about the place where you were born. It closed about 10 years ago and I recall there was a bit of a scandal involving doctors and illegal operations if you know what I mean."

Joanne waited for Flo to explain.

"Anyway, it's now a respectable rest home for the elderly and I know someone who lives there." Flo leaned over the fence in a conspiratorial way. "Would you like to go and visit my aunt and see the place for yourself ?"

"I'm not sure about that. I haven't really given much thought to where I was born and it would surely have altered a lot over the years."

"That may be so, but the character of the building won't have changed. I believe it is still as grand as ever." Flo could sense a mystery and wanted to solve it. "It's a while since I visited Aunt Grace so would you like to come with me if I can arrange a time?"

Joanne hesitated. She wasn't keen on digging up the past but she didn't want to upset her mother's friend. She found herself reluctantly agreeing to a visit to the rest home on Sunday afternoon.

She unlocked the door and let herself into the house. Her mother wouldn't be back from work for two more hours and Joanne had promised to take out the minced beef and prepare a shepherd's pie. A fat black and white cat came out to greet her. He rubbed himself against her legs and purred loudly.

"Hullo Whisky, old friend. I suppose you want a saucer of milk." She poured the milk and helped herself to a glass of juice and an apple, then switched on the radio. Her father had been listening to talk back, so Joanne quickly switched to another station to hear the latest tunes.

Now would be a good time to choose something to wear to the dance tomorrow night. Short skirts over coloured tights were in vogue or patterned jeans with an off the shoulder top. Joanne sighed. Her wardrobe really did need a makeover.

She brought out a silky red shift dress and teamed it with a pair of black tights. A chunky necklace and dangly ear rings would complete the picture. She unfastened her pony tail and let her hair fall over her shoulders. She could use the blow dryer and tease it up into the latest 'big hair' style. A little eye shadow would enhance her grey/green eyes.

She pulled out the box of makeup. Eye liner, mascara, foundation, face powder, lip gloss. It was all there and would transform her. Tracey would be most impressed. Maybe she should try a bit harder to make the most of her looks.

****

Sunday morning was a good time to catch up on sleep and Joanne opened her eyes lazily around nine o'clock. The dance the night before had brought a few surprises. Everyone commented on her new look and Jason had been most impressed.

In the past few months he had grown from gangly youth to a seriously handsome young man and at first Joanne had hardly recognized him. The cheeky smile was still there, however, and it was great to spend time with him and catch up with all the news.

Tracey had been swept off her feet by a medical student who was spending the weekend with some cousins who lived close by. The pair disappeared early and Joanne was waiting for the phone call that she knew would come.

She remembered her promise to visit the Parkhaven Rest Home this afternoon. That was the last thing she really wanted to do but she couldn't let Flo down. It would give her an excuse to meet up with Jason again and she felt a surge of excitement at the thought.

The morning passed quickly and after a leisurely brunch, Joanne was ready to leave for the rest home. She dressed casually in a short navy skirt and red tights and pulled her hair back in the usual pony tail.

Madeline had just returned from church and this afternoon Steve had promised to take her for a drive in the country. They often headed off in the weekend following the back roads which led to the river or one of the numerous beaches along the coast or harbour's edge.

Jason was reading the Sunday paper when Joanne appeared. He opened the door for her and called out to his mother to let her know that Joanne had arrived. "It was good catching up last night. We should do it again some time." He seemed a little nervous.

"Yea, that sounds great. We could check out the new bar down town or have a coffee." Joanne wanted to reassure him. "Not much has changed since you were last home."

"I don't know about that. You sure have changed." Geoffrey heaved his frame off the couch. He had grown even taller and lankier than his brother. "Are you sure you want to go out with Jason? I could show you a much better time."

Flo had come into the room and laughed. "Cut it out Geoffrey. Don't try to compete with your brother. Take no notice of him Joanne. It's just his hormones talking."

Joanne smiled at the two brothers and followed Flo out to the car. "I think you've got your work cut out keeping those two in order."

"You're right. One moment they are shy teenagers and the next I have two rampant males to contend with, and that's not counting Stan."

The Parkhaven Rest Home was in a leafy suburb close to the city, and Flo turned off the motorway and headed in the general direction. "Could you look at the road map? I thought I knew the way but they've changed the layout since I was last here."

Sure enough, a new interchange had been added which was not marked on the map and Flo drove slowly, unsure of which direction to take. "I recognise that shopping centre. It can't be too far away."

A few moments later Joanne saw a sign. Parkhaven Rest Home with an arrow pointing up a side street. "Turn up here Flo and we should find it."

Flo turned into the narrow street and then onto a driveway which led to a large brick building set in a manicured garden. She pulled up in the parking lot and looked around.

"It's a while since I was last here. I know I should visit my aunt more often." Flo was carrying a bunch of flowers and a tin of biscuits. "We do talk on the phone and I always send her a birthday card."

Joanne got out of the car and straightened her skirt. So this was where she was born. How had her birth mother felt when she came up this path, knowing she wouldn't be taking a baby home?

They walked past a rose covered gazebo and past a smooth lawn where two old gentlemen sat on a park bench enjoying the sunshine. They stared at Joanne as she walked by. A ramp led up to the front of the building where a glass door opened silently as they approached.

The entry foyer was bright with pictures and posters as well as a large notice board featuring all the activities for the week. A pleasant looking woman sat behind a desk and looked at them enquiringly. "Can I help you?" she asked.

Flo explained that they were here to see Grace Adams and that she was expecting them.

"You're right. Dear Grace has been most excited at the prospect of a visit. I will let her know that you are here. She was soon on the intercom, calling out Grace's name and a few moments later an elderly woman with blue/grey hair walked briskly into the foyer.

"Flo my dear. How good to see you, and this must be Joanne. Welcome to Parkhaven. I hope you don't find it all too depressing."

"I'm sure it won't be." Joanne smiled at the woman. "It actually looks a very pleasant place."

"It's fine if you don't mind doddery old people. But, come with me and we'll find a comfortable place to sit." Grace led them into a small lounge with landscape windows looking over the rose gardens. She rang a bell and a young Indian girl came in wearing a white apron over her dark blue uniform.

"We'd like to order tea, thank you Sarah. And could we have some of your nice chocolate cake?" Sarah smiled and went from the room to order the tea and cake.

"I see you haven't changed a bit Grace. Still the same bossy school teacher that you always were." Flo loved to tease her aunt who obviously still liked to be in charge.

"We will have tea and then I will show you my room. I have managed to keep a few of my favourite treasures." Grace had travelled widely since she retired from teaching and she had collected many precious momentoes of her travels.

Joanne sat quietly listening to the women talk. Her eyes kept straying around the room and out onto the lawn and garden. Had her mother looked at these same walls when she was here?

A pot of tea and a plate of buttered crackers with thin slices of tomato, as well as three pieces of chocolate cake were placed on a small round table and Flo took over the job of pouring the tea into flowered china cups. A milk jug and sugar bowl matched the cups and plates.

"How nice. English china." Flo was most impressed. Grace held her tea cup daintily, her small finger raised. Joanne nursed the cup and saucer awkwardly on her lap. She was used to a coffee mug.

No-one had mentioned the true purpose of Joanne's visit and she was beginning to think the whole afternoon would prove to be a waste of time, however pleasant the company.

It wasn't until they were sitting outside in the garden that Flo brought up the subject of Joanne's birth in this building when it was a nursing home.

"Oh my dear, how interesting," Grace looked at Joanne thoughtfully. "I did quite a bit of research on this place before I came here and learned many interesting facts, some of which you probably wouldn't want to know about."

"It was obviously a very expensive place to have a child. Most women would have gone to the women's hospital which isn't too far from here." Flo remembered the birth of her own two sons in a small cottage hospital but knew that if there were any problems, the big hospital was where you would have to go."

Grace was still thinking hard. "You know, there is a woman here who worked at the hospital all those years ago. She's away with the fairies half the time but can recall past events surprisingly well."

Joanne's heart thudded. Did she really want to find out more about her birth mother? Once in a while she had thought about asking Madeline for more details, but for some reason she had always wanted to stay in her secure little world.

"There would have been so many babies born during that time. I'm sure she wouldn't remember any details." Joanne was still reluctant to delve any deeper into her past.

"How exciting. I know there would have been many babies but if we tell her what date you were born it might jog her memory. Most people remember what they were doing the day John Kennedy was shot." Flo wasn't going to let the opportunity slip. She wanted to find out more even if Joanne sounded hesitant.

"You wait here in this nice shady spot and I will go and find Marie. She's a lovely woman but was having problems caring for herself. I'm sure she will enjoy talking to you."

Grace walked purposefully back to the building and Joanne and Flo sat in silence wondering what secrets would be revealed. Flo was bubbling with anticipation but Joanne was anxious. She clasped her hands in her lap and played nervously with the rings on her fingers.

Several minutes went by before Grace came back into view accompanied by a short plumpish woman with springy grey hair. Flo judged her to be about 70 years of age but it was hard to tell as her skin was smooth but her posture was stooped.

She studied Joanne for a moment then sat down on the wooden bench and gazed back towards the building. "I'd like you to meet Marie. She has so many interesting stories to tell." Grace waited for Marie to speak but there was a long silence.

Flo grew impatient. "Nice to meet you Marie. Grace tells us you worked here when it was a nursing home. You must have helped deliver many babies in your time."

Marie turned to face them, a faraway look in her eyes. "I could tell you many a sad tale but they told us not to say a word. I'll lose my job if I share any secrets." Marie stood and paced up and down a few times.

Grace was afraid that the woman might get agitated and she stood and took her by the arm. "It's quite alright my dear. That was many years ago and no-one can hurt you now."

Marie sat back down and looked again at Joanne. "I remember the good times and the bad. Young girls giving birth and never seeing their baby, while other families were given a precious child."

Joanne's eyes filled with tears at the thought. This woman must have so many sad memories. "I was one of the babies given to new parents. I have been very happy with the only mother and father I know."

Marie didn't answer. She was staring into space, her hands gripping the front of the seat. "You were one of the lucky ones. Some of the babies were given to wealthy people who thought they wanted a child but paid little attention to it once the novelty wore off. Boarding schools are full of such children."

Flo could see that they were getting nowhere. "There must have been some births that stood out more than others. Do you remember the day John F Kennedy was shot? Were you working here on November 23, 1963?"

Marie's face turned pale. She sat for a moment and then began to talk slowly. "I remember the day well. The news came over the radio when we were having a tea break. There had been no births that day but there were a number of mothers and babies to care for.

"Several of the women cried when they heard the news. They felt so sorry for poor Jackie." She stopped, recalling the day clearly.

"So you don't remember a baby being born that day?" Joanne asked, anxious now to hear the truth.

"There was a young lass who had been brought in. Barely 16 years of age if I recall and no-one with her to share her ordeal. Just dropped off at the door like a sack of potatoes."

There was another long silence as everyone looked at Marie in anticipation.

"We delivered a baby girl, strong and healthy, and everything seemed normal." Marie stopped again. "But when the other one came, we couldn't do anything to stop the bleeding. The poor girl died right in front of us, the same day as Mr Kennedy."

"The other one? You mean there was another baby?" Joanne stood up and turned to Marie, her face pale and her eyes huge and anxious.

"Yes, a poor little scrap of a thing. She went off in an incubator to the big hospital. I never found out what became of her."

Flo put her arms around Joanne as she tried to catch her breath. Marie had drifted off into a daydream and sat rocking to and fro on the bench. Grace looked at them all with concern in her eyes.

"This has been rather a shock to us all but I'm sure Marie is right. Once she recalls something it is usually correct. I think you would remember someone dying in front of you the day the president was killed."

Joanne tried to pull herself together. The mother she never knew had died just after she was born. She might have a twin sister alive and living somewhere nearby. It was all too much to take in.

Chapter 3

It was four o'clock on a Friday afternoon and the editor was calling out for the last minute stories. "Come on Rachel. It's already past deadline and I'm still waiting for that front page lead."

Bill Osborne put his head around the cubicle where Rachel was frantically typing. "Hold on to your hat Bill. I know you just want to get to the pub and catch up with your cronies."

Rachel tossed her pony tail over her shoulder and concentrated on the job in hand. It had been a slow news week and it wasn't until the last minute that a potential front page story had surfaced.

The council had just signed off on a new road which would bypass a busy section of the town. Rachel had been working on the story earlier but had to wait until the final decision had been made before she could complete the article.

"Half the town is going to be pleased about this but the business owners in King's Road are going to be far from happy." She read her work through and took the page off the typewriter. It would go straight to the editor for approval and then down to the back of the building where the typesetters were waiting.

"One of these days those new-fangled computers will be doing all this work for us. In the meantime we battle on." Bill accepted Rachel's article and read it through quickly. "Right, that will do nicely." He added a headline 'New bypass needs council okay' and Rachel took the article and handed it to the head of production who proceeded to retype the story ready to be pasted onto the page.

"When do you think we'll have computers here?" Rachel asked. "It always seems so much extra work for the same story to be typed a number of times." She had recently attended a workshop introducing the IBM personal computer and although it appeared to be complicated to use she knew that the days of cut and paste would soon be over in the newspaper industry.

Carol scowled. "The day we get computers, half of us will be out of a job. You journalists will be laying out the pages and we will only be making up advertisements."

"I hope not, but I'm off now. Hope you're not here too much longer." Rachel gave the girls a wave as she gathered up her bag from the cloakroom locker and set off to catch the bus which would take her the short distance to the flat she shared with a fellow journalist.

She would have the place to herself this weekend as Julie was off to her parents' home for the weekend.

Rachel enjoyed the buzz of living in the city. She had grown up on a sheep farm in an isolated part of New Zealand and after graduating from the journalism course she was lucky to get a job on a weekly newspaper.

Her secondary school days had been spent at a boarding school many miles from her parents' home and although she had been shy and lonely at first, she eventually made friends with some of the other girls.

Tonight she would stay in and have a long soak in the bath. She could have joined the others at the corner tavern, but after a busy week, a glass of wine and a frozen meal in front of the television set was all she needed. She had promised to go to a 21st birthday party tomorrow night so a quiet evening would suit her fine.

Rachel took off her jacket and laid it on the bed. She untied her pony tail and shook out the light brown hair which curled softly to her shoulders. Her unusual grey/green eyes were her best feature and she had learned how to enhance them with skilful eye makeup.

She preened herself in front of the mirror studying her face from every angle. Just last week a fellow journalist had told her she should try out for television. "The cameras would love you," he had said. "Mind you, they'd probably insist that you became a blond."

Rachel squirmed at the thought. Female presenters were not taken seriously. They had to look pretty, talk with an affected accent and dress correctly. She didn't think she would fit the bill.

She ran the bath and lowered herself into the warm water. She would phone her parents before she ate and catch up on the latest news. Being away from the farm so much had made it difficult for her to stay close to them. Marjorie and James Saunders were older than most of her friends' parents and expected a lot from their only child

Although she knew she was loved, they had found it difficult to show affection towards her during her childhood. They had paid for speech lessons, music tuition and all her sporting fees but she felt herself becoming more distant from them as time went on.

Her mother answered the phone. "Rachel my dear. How nice to hear from you. Yes, we are all well although your father is complaining about his arthritis which is slowing him down considerably, I'm afraid. It's probably time for us to think about moving into town and letting a manager take over the farm."

"Dad would hate to leave the farm. It's his life blood and he would be bored if he had to live in town." Rachel was horrified at the thought.

"I know dear, but one has to accept that we are not getting any younger. I would actually quite like to live closer to a shopping centre. It's always such a drag to shop once a fortnight and hardly see anyone from one day to the next."

Rachel let her mother carry on and when she stopped for a breath she was able to talk about her week, although there was really very little to tell apart from work, going to the gym and sharing a meal with Julie.

"I think you could do better than working for that little gossip rag, Rachel. After all, you are well educated and have had every opportunity to succeed. I would like to see you working for one of the dailies or how about radio? You have a lovely speaking voice and we know you are a very good journalist."

"I'm happy where I am at present but big changes are coming with all this talk about computers. My job could change drastically."

"Perhaps you need to take some computer lessons so you are prepared for the change." Rachel's mother was really on a roll tonight.

"Actually, one of my friends suggested television. How would you like to see me reading the evening news?"

"Rachel, that would be wonderful. Is there any chance of that? You know you can look quite beautiful when you try. But I'd better be off. Your father and I are about to have our meal and you know he hates to eat late."

Rachel returned the phone to its cradle and took a deep breath. Ever since she was a small child her mother had encouraged her to try new things. Even living out in the country there had been dancing lessons, as well as speech and piano. When she showed a talent for athletics she had been coached and encouraged to win.

Maybe if there had been other children there would not have been so much pressure on her to succeed. But her mother meant well and had certainly given her everything she had ever needed, everything but kisses and cuddles, Rachel thought wistfully.

****

The party was in full swing by the time Rachel's bus got her there. A small hall had been hired for the occasion and she was greeted by the host, Nigel, the moment she walked in the door. He had been in her journalism course and was employed by another small newspaper as sports reporter.

"Good to see you. Come and join the others. Most of our classmates have been invited and hopefully a few of them will turn up."

He led Rachel to a table where half a dozen young people were already gathered.

"Rachel. You're looking good. We weren't sure whether you would make it." Claire, a tall blonde wearing a silver sheath dress pulled her into the group and handed her a glass.

"They have a good fruit punch with quite a bite to it or white wine and beer. Some of the boys have brought something stronger though if you are interested."

"Thanks, I'll start with the punch and see how I go. You are looking very hot tonight."

"Yes, it's my new image. No more tights and leg warmers for me. I'm working for a fashion magazine, did you know?"

Rachel was amazed as Claire had not been at all interested in fashion the last time they met and she hadn't really been a very good writer, at times struggling during the course.

"Well, it's a matter of who you know. I'm getting good at writing short, snappy captions to go with the photographs so it doesn't take too much skill." Claire swung back her long hair and poured herself a drink from the flask she carried in her handbag.

Rachel was soon in the middle of the group, catching up with what everyone was doing. Her job at the weekly paper seemed a little dull compared with where some of the others were working.

At that moment Nigel came over to introduce a friend. "Everybody, this is Dirk who works with me at the paper. He wants to meet my old partners in crime."

Dirk was very tall, with longish fair hair that fell over his forehead. When he spoke he had a distinct accent and Rachel couldn't make out whether he was Dutch or South African. "It's good to meet you all. Nigel tells me about the great times you had when you were together. As for me, my training was a very long way from here."

"Dirk's family left Zimbabwe and recently settled in New Zealand." Nigel explained. Once again he was called away to welcome some more guests and Rachel found herself standing beside the newcomer.

"You were lucky to get a position so quickly on a daily paper," she said. "Those jobs are very sought after."

"I guess it was my lucky day. I'm looking after the travel pages and they wanted someone who had lived in other places." Dirk had an engaging smile. "Why don't we sit down and you can tell me about yourself?"

Rachel filled her glass from the bottle of white wine on the table and they found two seats together. "There's not much to tell. My job at a small paper can be a bit boring at times. The excitement of my week has been a road works story."

Dirk laughed. "I'm sure there is always some scandal hidden away just below the surface. Maybe the contractors are working for the local gangs or the Mafia. Or perhaps they will dig up some old bones that need to be identified."

Rachel looked up at him, her eyes sparkling with amusement. "Something like that would really make my day. Council news and advertorials are usually my lot."

Most of the guests were dancing by now and Rachel and Dirk were dragged up to join them, moving to the disco beat. Conversation was impossible and after a time they sat down, exhausted from their efforts.

Rachel looked at her watch. "I don't want to stay too late. I have to get home. It's been nice meeting you."

"I've liked it too. Can I call you some time?"

"Sure." Rachel searched in the bag for her card and scribbled her home number on the back. She went in search of Nigel to say 'good night' and made her way out of the hall. A few party goers were smoking, and drinking from beer bottles outside the hall but she ignored them and headed for the bus stop. The party had gone better than she expected. She felt a tingle of pleasure at the possibility of seeing Dirk again. It would be good to meet him for a drink or a meal. He seemed to be a really nice guy.

Rachel sometimes wished she could get involved with someone. She always had plenty of acquaintances but few close friends. Perhaps if she had had a brother or sister it might be different. She had often talked to an imaginary friend when she was young but her mother had disapproved of it and she kept the thoughts to herself.

She really should try to get back to the farm some time soon. It would be good to see first-hand how her father was faring. Looking back they had always seemed old, her mother being around 40 when Rachel was born.

"My miracle child," Marjorie said to her friends as she showed off the little girl with her pretty dresses and curly hair. "Where did she get those glorious eyes?" they would ask but Rachel never recalled an answer.

Arriving home she took the elevator up to the fourth floor apartment. It was just large enough for two and the best thing about it was the view from the small balcony which looked out over the city with a glimpse of the harbour in the background.

Sharing with Julie suited them both as they had similar jobs and interests, and they gave each other all the space they needed. Julie often stayed over with her boy friend and Rachel liked to have the flat to herself.

She thought about the people she had met tonight. All from the same journalism course but all doing different things. Yes, her job at the weekly newspaper was rather dull. Perhaps it was time she tried to get into something more exciting. Yes, she would start looking around next week.

Chapter 4

Joanne was quiet as Flo drove carefully back to their suburb. She would never meet her birth mother now. She had been so young when she died, around sixteen years old. She must have had a family, one that could afford to pay for the expensive nursing home. Or maybe it was the father of the babies who had paid the fees. For the first time in her life Joanne wanted to know the truth.

"How could I find out who my parents were? Is there a chance of tracing the other baby?" She wanted answers and knew she would not rest until she found them.

"You poor dear. What a lot to learn in one day. We will talk it over with Madeline and Steve who have been wonderful parents as you know. They will be devastated to learn that there was a second child and they were never told about her."

"You are right. They may have adopted both babies if they had been given the opportunity. But there is a chance that the baby didn't make it. She was very small, according to Marie."

"There must be some record of the births and death of the young woman. Marie may have forgotten about another birth that day. Perhaps you were born later that night." Flo's mind was reeling with the possibilities.

"You're right. Marie may not have known of another birth. Her mind was certainly quite unclear. I had better not get too excited about the idea of having a twin sister. It would be very difficult to find her if she did exist." Joanne's rational mind was beginning to take over. The poor woman named Marie was obviously demented and the facts were most unreliable.

"Bring your folks over for a drink and we'll tell them about our visit. As you say, we won't get too excited until we make some more enquiries. Poor Marie may be quite deranged." Flo would love to believe the woman's intriguing story but they really needed more information.

She hurried inside to tell Stan of their interesting visit. The boys were watching television and Jason couldn't help overhearing the conversation. He knew that Joanne had been adopted but it was something they had seldom discussed. As a law student, he would love to get to the truth.

"What's this about Joanne's birth? Do you think that woman can be trusted?" Jason couldn't help interrupting the conversation. There were so many unanswered questions.

"I really don't know, Jason. Marie seemed really clear about what happened on that particular day but her mind was quite confused in other ways. She wouldn't make a very reliable witness if that's what you are thinking."

Jason laughed. "I'm not about to put her on the witness stand, Mother. I'm just wondering if there could be any truth in her story." He went to the refrigerator and took out two cans of beer.

"Here you go," He handed a can to Geoff who was watching the cricket game. "We can drown our sorrows if Auckland loses. I think Wellington is going to beat them again." They settled down once more to watch the last few overs of the cricket game.

****

Over the next few days Joanne had little time to think about Marie's story. She was kept busy at the garden centre, serving customers and planting out the small seedlings into larger pots. The work was varied and interesting but the long hours on her feet took a bit of getting used to.

She had received word of her appointment to a school close to where she lived with a good bus service. "That's a bonus," she said to Tracey. "It would have been difficult to save enough for a car." Joanne would be teaching a small class of seven and eight-year-olds under the supervision of a senior staff member.

Tracey was thrilled that she had been appointed to a popular school in a trendy neighbourhood. "I will be needing my car. There isn't a direct bus link from where I live and anyway, I hate catching buses."

Joanne had shared her story about the visit to Parkhaven and Tracey was intrigued at the news.

"Wow, imagine if you have a twin sister. I wonder if she looks like you. Is there any way to find out more about what happened the day you were born?"

"Jason said he would help me locate the birth and death records. He has taken a real interest in the story." Joanne blushed. She was enjoying Jason's company and knew the feeling was mutual. In a short time, however, the holidays would be over and he would return to Wellington where he was working towards his law degree.

"Wow. I think you fancy him. You used to say he was just like a big brother." Tracey laughed at Joanne's discomfort. She was dating the student doctor since they had met at the country club dance, but like Joanne she knew he would be returning to university soon.

In the meantime, Jason couldn't stop thinking about Joanne's story. His job at the gas station left him plenty of time to go over the possibilities. There must be some way of getting hold of the death and birth certificates.

He filled the gas tank for an elderly woman and replaced the petrol cap. "Thank you, young man. I refuse to fill my own tank. It's something I've never done and never likely to do." She bustled into the shop to pay her bill while Jason washed the front window of her car.

He and Joanne were going to try out a tavern in the city tonight. Geoffrey was coming along as well and they planned to take a bus and share a taxi home. The tavern was a new addition to city life and promised live music in a smart environment.

Joanne knew she was in good hands with two solid males for company. Geoffrey was hoping to meet some mates there but Jason was content with Joanne's company. He took her hand as they walked along the footpath toward the bus stop and it wasn't long before they were clambouring aboard.

They found seats towards the back and watched the streets go by as the bus meandered through the suburbs. Several of the town centres displayed colourful Eastern clothing and the people on the streets were of a wide variety of ethnic origin.

"These towns sure have changed. You could be anywhere in the world right now." Jason was surprised. He thought Wellington was a diverse city but Auckland seemed to be close behind.

The tavern had been styled on an old English pub with sturdy wooden tables and chunky seats. Colourful beer tankards hung from shelves and a three piece jazz band was warming up on the small stage.

They squeezed into a corner booth and Geoffrey made his way to the bar to order drinks. Jason took the opportunity to put his arm around Joanne's shoulders. "You look great tonight. I can't believe my little sister is all grown up."

"You're not too bad yourself, but enough of this little sister stuff." Joanne snuggled closer to Jason and only pulled away when Geoffrey appeared with the drinks. The small tavern was beginning to fill up fast and Geoffrey called some friends over to share their space.

"Wow, Geoff. It's getting kind of cosy in here." Jason tried to object. The keyboard, bass and saxophone combination was loud and Joanne was beginning to feel hot and uncomfortable. Several of the group got up and began swaying with the music including Geoffrey who had picked up one of the newcomers.

"Trust my brother to be quick off the mark. But he missed out on the best one." Jason smiled at Joanne. "I think we could try somewhere quieter. What do you think?"

"Sure, but we need to let Geoff know. We can't just abandon him."

"We'll go and get something to eat and come back later. Geoff won't mind." Jason steered Joanne towards the door, waving to his brother as they went.

They pushed their way through the crowd and were close to the exit when Joanne bumped into a young woman coming the other way. She turned to apologise and stopped in amazement. It was like looking in a mirror.

Two pairs of grey/green eyes looked curiously at each other and Joanne's heart almost stopped beating. The stranger moved quickly away and Joanne found herself being propelled out onto the footpath.

"Did you see that girl? She looked exactly like me."

Jason had been walking ahead and had not seen the incident. "It's probably your imagination. Now you've heard about a twin you will be looking for her everywhere." Jason took Joanne's arm and steered her towards a small restaurant just a few hundred metres away.

"Her hair was longer and lighter, but she had my eyes. I had the weirdest feeling when we looked at each other." Joanne shuddered and sat on the chair that was being offered to her. "You're probably right. I'll be seeing my likeness wherever I go."

The waiter came over and offered them a menu. Joanne was still flustered but she didn't want to spoil their evening. She studied the selection but couldn't make up her mind.

"The specials are on the board, madam. They are very much recommended." The young waiter had a strong accent and Joanne tried to make out whether he was from Germany or Eastern Europe.

Jason made a drink selection and they decided on the chicken pasta with herbed vegetables. "This is more my style," he said. "You can at least have a conversation in a place like this."

Joanne relaxed and smiled. The encounter with her look-alike had unsettled her but she focused on what Jason was saying. By the time the waiter brought their bottle of wine they were deep in conversation. The restaurant was filling up but was less crowded than the tavern.

Their food was set down with a flourish and proved to be delicious. By the time they returned to the tavern, there was barely room to move. Geoffrey was sitting very close to a cute blonde with a very short skirt and shiny tights. Her hair had been teased into a high style which was held back by a silver head band

"This is Chloe. We're having an awesome time." They finished their drinks and were soon back on the dance floor rocking to the beat.

Jason and Joanne set off in a more sedate manner but were soon twisting until they were exhausted. "I've eaten too much to do the twist. It is so crazy." She laughed as Jason whirled her around and they made their way back to an empty seat.

"Let's get out of here. I'll see whether Geoff is ready to come home." Jason fought his way through the crowd until he came to his brother who was still obviously besotted with Chloe. He shook his head and said he'd find his own way back.

As they were leaving, Joanne thought she saw her look-alike on the other side of the room. She couldn't be sure and it probably meant nothing. She was having too good a time to worry about it now.

Chapter 5

Rachel was having a very weird evening. Firstly she had to cover a prize-giving event at a sports club, then after taking a couple of photos she hurried home to get ready for a night out. Dirk said he could meet her at the new tavern which was close to the apartment but he wasn't sure what time he would be there.

Tracey was away at her boyfriend's house and there was a note on the door to say there was a parcel to collect at the post office. Oh damn! That would be from her mother and she would need to get it tomorrow as it probably contained farm fresh food.

She took her time changing into a silky shirt and jeans and then set out to walk to the tavern. A shower of rain came across and she was forced to shelter in a doorway. A few unsavoury-looking characters were hanging around so she set off quickly in the direction of the tavern.

There were road works on the corner and she had to take a detour, so by the time Rachel reached her destination she was feeling far from happy, and then some-one bumped into her. The shock came when she stared at the other girl. She felt as though she was looking in a mirror. The same eyes, the same face, but darker hair. It was uncanny.

She turned to look again but the girl had gone. That was seriously weird. Rachel went straight to the bar and ordered a brandy. She needed to calm herself down. There was no sign of Dirk and she headed for a corner seat where she could hide until he arrived.

The place was crowded but there was no-one there she knew. This was a really bad idea.
The jazz band was warming up and more people were coming through the door. Where was Dirk? He had promised to be here. She finished her drink and was about to leave when Dirk came into view. He looked anxiously around and when he saw Rachel he smiled that great smile that would melt your heart.

"Hi gorgeous. Sorry I'm late. The travel agency is promoting trips to the islands and wanted to impress me. I was lucky to escape when I did." He bought a handle of beer and came over to where Rachel was cowering in the corner.

Rachel was still feeling unhinged after her encounter with her look-alike, but she smiled at Dirk and began to relax in his presence. They talked about their week and ordered some nachos and French fries and refilled their drinks. Rachel was beginning to feel much better. She didn't tell Dirk about her experience but it wasn't every day that you saw someone who could easily be your twin.

They sat back and listened to the music. Dirk was a big jazz fan and explained the variations to the tunes as each musician improvised and played their solos. After a busy week Rachel was feeling weary and in a dreamy state. It was good to have an interesting companion and she was feeling very relaxed.

"Would you like me to walk you home? Then it's a bus ride for me back to the suburbs." Dirk was ready to leave and Rachel agreed. She looked across the room and saw the other girl return with a tall companion. She watched as they danced for a while then sat down laughing. Perhaps she should talk to her and find out who she was. But next thing she had disappeared into the night and the opportunity was lost.

It didn't take Rachel and Dirk long to walk the few blocks back to the apartment. The showers had cleared and a new moon was struggling into view from behind a cloud.

Rachel unlocked the door and led Dirk inside. It was the first time he had been in her apartment and he strolled around looking at everything with interest. "This is a bit nicer than my flat. Tidier too."

He sat down on the comfortable couch while Rachel nervously poured them a glass of red wine. She had resisted the temptation to be alone with Dirk who was seriously good looking and she wasn't sure where the evening would lead.

She was still puzzled about the girl who looked so much like herself and sat beside Dirk in silence for a moment. Then she decided to tell him about the encounter. "It was so strange seeing my double. Her hair was different but her face was so familiar and as for those grey/green eyes…"

Dirk looked at her. "I'm sure no-one has eyes like yours. That's the second thing I noticed about you."

Rachel looked puzzled. "What was the first thing you noticed?"

Dirk put his glass down on the small table and turned to face her. "Everything. I noticed everything about you." Rachel reached out to put her glass beside Dirk's. Her eyes never left his face and next thing she was in his arms.

The kisses were tender at first and then more passionate. They untangled themselves and Rachel led the way to the bedroom where the Queen size bed was waiting. There was no way that Dirk was going to leave just yet.

****

Jason O'Connor had been thinking about Joanne's story all day as he filled petrol tanks and washed car windows. Seeing a girl who looked so much like her had really unsettled Joanne and although she tried to cover up her feelings, Jason knew that she had been shaken by the encounter.

The best thing he could do was use his contacts to search for birth and death information around the time Joanne was born. It sounded as though the old Parkhaven Nursing Home may have a few stories to tell but he wouldn't say anything until he had found out the truth.

Someone must have paid for the baby to be born there. Was it the young girl's parents or the family of the baby's father? Would the names of the mother or father be somewhere in the birth records?

If that had been the only birth at the nursing home on the day President Kennedy was shot, other people would probably remember it. The tragedy would have been all over the news, with households sitting around their television sets, their dinner trays in front of them.

It was time to pack up for the day as the evening shift was arriving. Jason cleaned his hands in the washroom and said goodbye to his boss. His cycle was leaning against the back wall of the garage and he was soon riding the short distance to his home. It would be great to own a car but that was out of the question until his university days were over.

A can of cool beer and his mother's cooking would be welcome when he got home and then he would call over and see his lawyer friend and get his advice about tracking birth and death records. He knew you could apply through the usual channels but there was no guarantee you had the right person until the certificate arrived. He'd heard of many people paying out precious dollars and receiving the record of a complete stranger.

His friend William was surprised to see him when he knocked on his door that evening. Jason knew he should have phoned but William and his wife Jamie were pleased to see him. "It's been a long time between drinks. I have a fine bottle of red wine to sample and this is a good excuse."

William uncorked a bottle and poured three glasses and soon they were sitting on a sheltered patio which overlooked a colourful garden. "Jamie is the gardener, not me," William admitted. "I don't know when she finds the time with little Samuel to care for and all the committees she is on."

Jamie smiled. "It's all in a day's work. You've just missed our pride and joy. I think he's asleep already." She took a sip of the wine and placed her glass on a low table where a photograph of the family took pride of place.

"Samuel at six months. Now he's nearly a year old and into everything." William looked proudly at the photograph.

Jason hadn't really come to admire baby photos so he hurriedly changed the subject. He was soon telling his friends about Joanne's discovery at the nursing home. "Do you know where we could find out what happened there? Surely there would be records somewhere."

William thought for a while. "It's about 20 years since the nursing home changed into a rest home. There are probably old filing cabinets full of information, unless the papers have been destroyed."

"Is that likely? I would have thought that medical records would need to be retained somewhere." Jason's curiosity was aroused.

"I'll try to find out who the previous owners were and then we would have more chance of finding the documents. In the meantime I can look up the birth and death files at the office."

William was refilling their glasses and they went on to talk of other things. It had been a while since Jason had visited his friends and the rest of the evening passed quickly as they caught up on the news.

****

With just two weeks left before the school term was about to start, Tracey was urging Joanne to start packing for their camping holiday. The tent and sleeping bags would fit in the boot of the car along with foam mattresses and pillows. They would stay in a camp ground where they could use the facilities and as long as the weather was fine it would be a perfect way to end the holidays.

Although Joanne was looking forward to the break she had never camped before and was unsure about the whole arrangement. The idea of sleeping out under the stars was a romantic one, but a small tent wouldn't provide much security.

Jason laughed at her when she told him of her concerns. "Come on, Joanne. You'll be fine as long as you stay near other people. Nothing will go wrong. Unless it rains and the tent leaks and you get drenched in the middle of the night."

"Now you've really put me off. Maybe you should come along and keep us safe." The words were out before Joanne realized what she was saying. She reddened. "Just joking of course," she added hastily.

"I could get away for a few days. What about Tracey's new friend? Do you think he would consider going along?"

"That would be fun if we all went together. You'd have to borrow another tent or two. I'll see what Tracey thinks of the idea." Joanne would be much happier if Jason was there to keep an eye on them, and besides, she would miss him if she went away alone.

The next time she saw Tracey she couldn't wait to make the suggestion.

"Funny you should say that. I had been thinking the same thing. In fact, Mike and I talked about it last night and he would be happy to come along if that's what you want."

They laughed and talked over their plans long into the night. Tracey was sleeping over and they tried out new make up and hair styles just as they had when they were children until Madeline had to bang on the wall to quieten them down.

****

The boys weren't due back at university for another few weeks so they could afford to take some time off. It was decided that Mike would drive his car and he was able to borrow two small tents and some sleeping gear.

The girls would leave a couple of days earlier and set up their camp and Jason and Mike would join them at the weekend. Joanne couldn't remember when she had felt so content. She had hardly given a thought to her visit to the nursing home and the surprising facts she had learned. She was surprised that Jason hadn't mentioned it again as he had seemed so interested.

Madeline had not brought up the subject either, as she was not convinced that Marie's story was true. The poor woman sounded most unreliable. It was best to leave the past alone and get on with living in the present.

On the other hand, Flo was still intrigued about what they had learned at the nursing home. If Joanne had a twin sister it would be so special if the two could meet. It would be like something out of a romantic novel and Flo's imagination was running wild.

"Mother, leave it alone." Jason tried to discourage Flo. "There needs to be some solid proof before we claim a twin sister for Joanne. I don't want her upset with wild speculation." He was as anxious as his mother to learn the truth but didn't want to raise Joanne's hopes.

"Who would have thought that one day you would be courting our Joanne? You played together as children and now what a lovely couple you would make." Flo was in a romantic mood.

"I don't think you could say we are courting. Just enjoying each other's company until I go back to Wellington and she starts her teaching job. Most of the time I still think of Joanne as my little sister."

Jason did not want to give his mother any false hopes. He was very fond of Joanne but it would be some time before he was in a position to think about a long-term relationship.

He was still waiting for news from his friend William. He said he would find out who owned the nursing home back in those days and they would go from there. "When we know who was involved we have more chance of finding the information," he said.

When Geoffrey heard about the camping trip he thought it would be a good idea to bring Chloe along, but Jason was not so keen on the idea. "This is supposed to be a quiet few days for the girls before school starts. I don't see Chloe as the outdoor type."

"Don't be so stuffy. Chloe would love to share a tent with me." Geoffrey wanted to take advantage of the situation.

"Behave yourself Geoffrey. Don't spoil your brother's holiday plans." Flo was used to sorting out the family arguments.

****

The summer days were long and the weather had finally settled when the time came for Joanne and Tracey to set off on the two-hour journey to the Coromandel peninsula where they had booked into a small holiday park.

By the time the tent and bedding were packed, the boot of Tracey's small car was full and their back packs took up most of the rear seat. Madeline insisted on adding some canned food and coffee. Tracey's mother sent along a container of biscuits and a carton of eggs and the girls had packed a chilly bin with wine.

The highway was busy with holiday traffic but once they crossed over the steep ranges the ocean could be seen, sparkling in the sunlight. The rich green forests opened out to white sandy beaches and they stopped the car at the rest stop to get out and admire the view.

"Wow. You forget how beautiful it is outside the city. It is so quiet and peaceful." Joanne looked around in delight. Tracey smiled. She had made this journey many times as a child but driving her own car was a new experience.

"I won't be sorry to leave these windy roads. We will be down on the farmland soon." Sure enough, the forest gave way to fertile grassland as they got closer to their destination. Soon they came to a turn off which led to the coast.

"We're nearly there. Just around the next corner." Tracey drove expertly along the narrow road and over a one-way bridge before turning into a rustic gateway.

A flat grassed area with shady trees was dotted with around 20 tents and caravans. A concrete block building housed a basic kitchen and toilet facilities. "There's usually someone here each day to supervise. Otherwise you just choose a site and make yourself at home."

A group of children were playing cricket at the far end of the field and several adults were sitting on deck chairs outside their caravans. Tracey drove slowly until she came to a site right beside a wooden picnic table.

"Great. We will be able to make use of this. There's nothing worse than trying to eat a meal while you're sitting in a small tent."

They backed the car up to the camp site and opened the back door. Soon most of their luggage was piled on the table as they pulled the tent out from underneath. "I hope I can remember how this goes up. It's ages since it was last used." Tracey puzzled out the flaps and ropes and soon the job was done. Although you couldn't stand upright, Joanne was surprised how much space there was inside the tent.

The two mattresses and sleeping bags easily fitted inside and there was room for their bags as well. "This is so cosy." Joanne was delighted.

Next they parked the car beside their tent to save the space for Jason and Mike who were arriving in two days, then they went to check out the facilities. "This is where we find out what we haven't got." Tracey laughed.

The kitchen was clean and tidy with gas cookers and even a refrigerator in the corner. When Joanne opened it she found food and drink bottles all labeled with people's names. "That is so cool. It's great to know that people can still be trusted."

They weren't sure that they wanted to put their wine in at this stage. They could cool it in the freezer just before they were ready to drink it, but they would pack away some butter, eggs and a packet of sausages.

"OK. Time to check out the beach." Tracey couldn't wait to change into her bikini and work on her tan. It was awkward undressing in the tent but it wasn't long before Joanne had changed into her two-piece bathing togs and found a large beach towel. They locked the car, put on their sun glasses and headed for the sand.

Tussock grass grew along the edge of the sand which sloped down to the water's edge and several children were playing in the gentle waves, riding on their boogie boards or splashing about in the shallow water

Soon the girls had applied sunscreen and were stretched out on their towels, relaxing in the warm sun.

Chapter 6

Jason didn't have long to wait before his friend left him a message on his mobile phone. "Call me tonight. I have some interesting news about the nursing home." He and Mike were leaving next morning and he was looking forward to the break away from the busy garage.

Geoffrey was still annoyed that he had not been included in the camping trip but Jason knew that he would soon get over it. Their disagreements never lasted very long.

As soon as he got home that evening he put his cycle in the garage and found his back pack. He would only need some shorts, t-shirts, bathing trunks and a towel. "You'd better take your jeans and a jacket. You never know what the weather will do," his mother called out.

After dinner he found the time to call William. What had he discovered that was so interesting?

William took the call in his office as he was working late. He had talked to one of his older colleagues who had been working at the law office for several years and was surprised at some of the information he received.

"It seems that there were several big names involved at Parkhaven when it was a nursing home. I can't tell you who they were right now. It was all a bit confidential when the hospital had to close."

"What do you mean, it had to close?" Jason was mystified.

"They were being investigated for malpractice when the case was suddenly pulled. It looks as though someone was paid off to keep everything quiet. My colleague hinted that there are people around who would be very nervous if anyone started asking questions."

"So you can't give me any names." Jason asked.

"Not at this stage but I'm sure I will be able to find out more. I think we are dealing with some very powerful people. I'll see what else I can find out but I think we will have to be careful."

Jason came off the phone more mystified than ever. So there was some sort of cover up when the nursing home closed. Powerful people were involved. He would have to be patient until William got back to him. In the meantime there was packing to be done.

****

At the law firm of Barlow and Reid, William put down the phone and sat for a moment at his desk. The older lawyer Ted Baker had left for the evening and he still had some paperwork to complete before he could go home.

He picked up the photograph of his wife and child. He hated having to work late. He would much rather be home with his family, but his career was important to him and he had a difficult case to defend.

His mind went back to the conversation with Ted Baker. He was sure that Ted knew more than he was letting on about the closure of the nursing home. Maybe he had been involved at the time.

Ted kept talking about retirement but could never quite bring himself to make the break. He had dealt with the same clients for many years and they trusted him to do a good job. He wasn't likely to want to rock the boat at this stage of his long career.

William could no longer concentrate on the case in hand so he packed up his brief case and headed for the door. Jamie would be pleased to see him but Samuel would already be in bed by the time he got home. He would like a romantic evening with no distractions, but Jamie was usually tired and she always had an ear out for any sound from the nursery.

The alleged rape case with which he was involved was due to be heard by the judge in a week's time. There were few witnesses and it was really mostly a matter of who to believe. The young defendant said the sex act was mutual and the woman declared that she had been molested.

As is turned out, Jamie was already in bed when William drove into the garage. His dinner was on the bench ready to go in the microwave and a scribbled note read: "Gone to bed early. Don't wake me. Love you, Jamie."

William turned the television on with the volume down low and opened a can of beer. He undid his shoes and his tie and left them on the floor. He knew it was going to be another quiet night.

****

It was just after 10 o'clock on Saturday morning when Mike pulled up outside Jason's house. The tents and sleeping gear was piled on the back seat and a box of beer took up most of the space in the boot. There was just room for the two back packs and a bag of groceries that Flo had packed.

"Nothing that will perish," she said. "Just some bread and a few cans of beans and beef stew. You wouldn't want to go hungry."

"Thanks Mum. As long as we have a few beers we'll be fine," Jason joked. The day promised to be warm and sunny and Mike drove as Jason read out the directions that Tracey had prepared for them. As they passed through the last town, they stopped at a hot bread shop and bought fresh rolls and donuts as well as a bag of crispy apples.

"That will be lunch. I'm not sure what the girls have with them. We didn't really talk about it before they left." Mike drove on, not really too bothered about where their next meal would come from. The thought of all that sunshine and cool water was all he cared about right now.

They almost drove past the side road which led to the camping ground but Jason noticed the turn off just in time. Soon they were bouncing along the gravel track until they came to the driveway into the camp.

Joanne was sitting at the picnic table and waved when she saw the car. She called out to Tracey who was tidying the tent. "Here they are. They didn't get lost after all." She met Jason as he unwound himself from the seat of the car and gave him a hug.

"Tracey can move her car and your tents can go up next to our's. This is such a great place. We've already had a swim today but the water is a bit too cool for me."

Mike backed his car up to the camp site and began to unload the gear.

"What's the rush. We have all day for that." Tracey caught Mike in a bear hug. "It's great to see you. You will love it here. There's nothing to do but lie in the sun or cool off in the sea."

Joanne noticed the bag of food and carried the bread rolls to the fridge along with a bottle of wine. She raised her eye brows at the box of beer. Typical males, she thought. That could be cooled later.

Mike was in no hurry to put up the tents. "Come on. Let's check out the surf." He pulled off his shirt and raced down the grassy strip towards the sea. Jason followed more slowly. Soon the two of them were swimming strongly a few yards off shore.

Joanne and Tracey sat on the sand and watched them frolic in the water. They looked at each other and laughed. "They'll be ready for lunch when they come out. Those donuts looked really good." The sea air was giving Tracey an appetite.

It wasn't long before the boys were back, dripping water everywhere. "We'll change in the toilet block and then have lunch," Mike decided. Tracey and Joanne soon had the rolls buttered and added some hard boiled eggs. Luckily Madeline had thought to pack some plastic plates, cutlery and paper napkins. The donuts and apples were placed on the table by the time the boys came back.

"Quite a feast. Flo thought we would go hungry but I don't think that's going to happen." Mike opened the wine bottle with a flourish and filled the plastic glasses and there was a contented silence as they sat back and enjoyed the impromptu meal.

Joanne was bubbling with excitement. She was so pleased to see Jason even though he still treated her like a little sister. She would have to work on that.

****

As the moon came up that evening, Jason drew Joanne aside. The tents had been erected and all the equipment stowed away. They had eaten a meal of canned stew and tomatoes and washed it down with a quantity of beer and wine. She was ready for bed but Tracey had disappeared into Mike's tent and she and Jason were left sitting at the picnic table.

"Would you like to see what is around those rocks at the end of the beach? I think Tracey and Mike want to be alone."

Joanne felt a little embarrassed that Tracey was being so obvious but she pulled on her jacket and was soon walking hand in hand with Jason towards the far end of the bay. Jason had brought a flashlight along, though the moonlight made it easy to find their way. "I want you to know that I think the world of you," he was saying. "I wouldn't want to cheapen our friendship with a one-night stand."

Although Joanne would have liked nothing better than to share a tent with Jason, she found herself agreeing. He was right. It would be so easy to sleep together tonight but they might regret it in the morning.

They walked to the far end of the beach and sat on a rock, watching the silver spray ebbing and flowing. Jason took her in his arms and his kiss was far from brotherly. She responded, but he pushed her gently aside and led her back to the camp site in silence.

Joanne let herself into the lonely tent, unsure whether Tracey would be joining her. She undressed and settled into her sleeping bag and hardly woke when her friend slipped silently into the tent in the early hours of the morning.

****

The next few days passed by quickly. One of the campers loaned the boys a small dinghy and a fishing line and they proudly returned a few hours later with enough snapper for a really good meal. Luckily they

65

were given a lesson on filleting the fish and that evening it was pan fried and tasted delicious.

Nothing was said about Tracey and Mike sharing a tent and most nights she was back just as Joanne was falling asleep. Joanne had to make do with long walks with Jason each evening but was always disappointed when he kissed her tenderly and disappeared into his tent.

On the last evening they were invited to a barbecue. Several of the campers had got together and pooled the rest of their food and luckily there was a small amount of wine and beer left as well. Canned stew over barbecued sausages was a winner and someone had baked potatoes in their jackets over the fire.

A large bonfire had been built by the children who were roasting marshmallows in the embers. One of the campers was playing a guitar and Joanne leant back in Jason's arms relaxed and happy. Tomorrow they were heading home and the holiday would be over.

Joanne wasn't surprised when Tracey disappeared into Mike's tent. She lay in her sleeping bag looking back over the past few days and recalling all the highlights. There was a sound outside the tent and she thought it was Tracey returning.

A moment later she realized that it wasn't Tracey, but Jason who was undoing the tent. She lay quietly, unsure how to react. Without a word, Jason lay beside her and took her in his arms. His kisses were tender and she felt herself responding. Somehow she was out of the sleeping bag and lying on top of the covers, wearing nothing but a thin nightdress.

"Are you sure about this?" he whispered but she didn't answer. Her body was doing the talking. Their love-making was passionate until Jason stopped long enough to pull on a condom, then they were working in harmony until they reached a glorious, simultaneous climax.

Chapter 7

Every day Rachel was becoming increasingly dissatisfied with her job. There must be more important things to write about than social events and council meetings. The problem with the new bypass had escalated and whatever angle Rachel took she knew she would offend someone.

"It would be so good to cut so much time off the trip into the city, but I do feel sorry for the small shopkeepers whose living will be compromised," she said, as Bill Osborne was standing over her waiting for her copy.

"You can't please everyone, we can only report the facts. Don't concern yourself about it." Bill just wanted to get away from the office to share a pint with his friends at the club.

Rachel covered her typewriter and prepared to leave the office. She had promised to meet Dirk for a drink on the way home. Her flat mate Julie would be home already and was probably waiting to share a meal. She had recently broken up with her boyfriend Nick and was looking for another job in a new town.

The bar was a short walk from the office and Rachel arrived just as Dirk was finishing his first drink. They kissed and settled down to share the details of their day.

Dirk could hardly contain his excitement. "That travel company I was telling you about wants me to do a story on the Pacific islands. They will pay my fare over and accommodation and all I have to do is write nice things about them."

"All right for some. When do they want you to go?" Rachel was envious. Her job offered little excitement. Imagine travelling to a beautiful resort and getting paid to be there.

"The best part about it is that I can take a friend along. Would you be interested in coming with me?" Dirk's eyes were shining with anticipation. This was the break he had been waiting for.

"Would I what? That sounds very exciting. I've always wanted to go to the islands. When do they want you to go?" Rachel was almost breathless. This was exactly the sort of holiday she needed.

"It would be quite soon, probably within a month. The weather will be great by then and the swimming should be amazing." Dirk couldn't believe his good luck. Rachel would be the perfect person to travel with. In fact, she could probably help him write the article and she'd look great in the photographs.

Rachel's mind was racing as she ordered a drink from the bar. She had plenty of holidays owing and it would give her a chance to think about her career.

"I'd need to let the newspaper know that I'm taking time off. But that shouldn't be a problem." She made herself comfortable on the bar stool and stirred her drink. "Just think, soon we could be sipping martinis in a grass hut surrounded by coconut palms."

"Or lying in a hammock on a white sandy beach watching a dancing girl swaying sensually beside the sun-drenched sea." Dirk was letting his imagination run riot.

"You've been reading too many of those travel brochures. I don't think it's like that at all." Rachel tried to look serious. She played with her gin and tonic, squeezing the slice of lime. "I wonder which island they will choose?"

They talked about the possibilities as Rachel finished her drink and got up to go. Julie would be annoyed if she was late for their meal and Rachel knew her friend needed the company.

"I'll come and see you tomorrow night and we can talk about it some more." Dirk could see a group of his work mates sitting in a corner and wasted no time in joining them. He had made several new friends since joining the staff of the daily paper and often shared a drink with them.

It only took Rachel a short time to walk back to her apartment where Julie had a casserole cooking in the oven. She was onto her third glass of wine, however, and sounded despondent.

"I know Nick wasn't right for me, but it's so hard to be on my own after all those months. I don't feel like going out and most of my friends are in relationships."

"Come with me next time and meet some new people. You don't have to sit here feeling sorry for yourself." Rachel didn't like to see her friend so unhappy.

She dished the meal onto two plates and turned on the television. A local talent show was in progress and they were soon watching as all the young hopefuls appeared on the screen. Some were mediocre but once in a while one of the acts stood out from the rest.

"I know we should vote for our favourite after the show but I can't choose between the young country singer and that amazing magician." Julie was caught up in the atmosphere. Her troubles were forgotten for the moment.

Rachel was relieved. She didn't want to relive every moment of Julie's break up with Nick all over again. She flicked through a travel brochure that Dirk had given her. Would it be Tahiti or Rarotonga, Fiji or Samoa? They all looked enchanting. The thought of 10 days on a sun-drenched island sounded too good to be true.

****

Although Jason's friend William was busy working on his client's trial, he found himself becoming curious about the former Parkhaven Nursing Home. He sensed that Ted Baker was holding back information and there must be records somewhere in the office that would tell him why the nursing home had closed.

The back room was full of old files which hadn't been touched for years but it would be difficult to know where to start searching. There must be some sort of cataloging system and the only one who would know about that was Beryl Griffin, an elderly clerk who had been with the firm for many years.

William suspected that the only reason she hadn't left was that she was fond of old Ted and would stay there until he retired. She always kept her desk in immaculate condition. Typewriter covered. Pens neatly placed in a round container. No photographs or personal belongings crowded the desk.

Yes, old Beryl would know every secret that was locked away in those filing cabinets.

In the meantime he had better get some work done. He had received statements from the young man's parents and workmates, all vouching for his good character. On the other hand, the complainant was known for her flashy appearance and loose morals. It should be easy to convince the judge that the woman was at fault.

But William knew that nothing was that simple. It was his client's word against hers and the judge's sympathy was often with the alleged victim. He gathered his papers together and placed them in his brief case. That was all he could do for now and Ted Baker had promised to look over his work next morning and offer advice.

****

The last day of their camping holiday came around far too soon. Jason had returned to his own tent in the early hours of the morning leaving Joanne to sleep on alone. She woke early and dressed quickly, disappointed that Jason was not beside her.

She emerged from the tent and walked down to the water's edge. Jason was already sitting on the sand dune gazing out over the glittering bay. He pulled her down beside him and put his arm around her shoulders. "Last night was very special. I hope you don't regret it."

Joanne gave him a hug. "It was inevitable. I'll miss you when you go back to varsity, that's for sure."

"Me too, but I don't leave for another two weeks and then I'll be back for the Easter holidays before you know it." They sat in contented silence until Tracey and Mike wandered down to join them.

"I guess we need to cook breakfast and start packing up." Tracey sounded reluctant but the girls dragged themselves away to check on the remaining food supplies. A can of peaches, half a loaf of bread, a container of eggs were soon gathered up and once the eggs were fried the meal was set out on the picnic table.

The friends sat around in silence, no-one wanting the holiday to be over.

"We'll have to do this again. I could easily stay for another week," Tracey declared. They reluctantly rinsed off their dishes and set to work. The tents were soon dismantled and packed away and there was time for a last walk to the far end of the beach.

"We don't need to drive straight home. We can take the back road along the Firth of Thames and stop for fish and chips for lunch on the way." Tracey knew they would enjoy the scenic drive and the fish and chips shop was world famous.

With the cars finally packed they were soon on their way, winding over the steep ridge and then along the straight roads that cut through drained swamps which had been turned into fertile farmland. They took the turn off that led along the water's edge until they arrived at the small village where the fish and chip shop was a local landmark.

Fresh fish straight from the sea cooked in delicious batter with crunchy fries came wrapped in a huge parcel and they were soon tucking in, enjoying the holiday atmosphere before returning to the city.

"That was a good break before we are faced with a classroom full of kids." Joanne sighed at the thought. She knew that there would be plenty to do to prepare for the start of term. As university didn't start for another two weeks the boys were returning to their holiday jobs "Back to the petrol pump," Jason laughed. "But at least the day goes by quickly."

Mike was working in a hardware store which was also busy. He'd be back to his studies before he knew it.

No-one was in a great hurry to leave but they had another hour's drive ahead of them so they reluctantly returned to their cars. Joanne was quiet. She would miss the close contact with Jason but knew he would be right next door for a short time.

She didn't regret sleeping with him but it changed the easy relationship they had shared in the past. He wasn't her big brother any more. Her feelings for him ran much deeper than that. It was all very confusing.

Chapter 8

While he said little to Joanne, Jason was also uncertain about his feelings. As a student, there was no way he could afford a full-time relationship yet every time he thought about her he knew that he didn't want to lose her friendship.

It would mean so much to her to learn the truth about her birth and he had tried to search the records around the time she was born, but it was virtually impossible when the names were unknown. The only evidence would be filed away in an office somewhere, and he was hoping that his friend William would be able to help him find them.

They didn't even know which law office had been handling the affairs of the nursing home 20 years ago. It would be like looking for a needle in a hay stack.

Joanne had been busy setting up her classroom ready for the start of term, but they had met each evening to go for a walk or watch television in each other's homes. It had become a comfortable pattern.

On Saturday night they planned to meet up with Tracey and Mike for a meal and drinks at the new tavern in town and this time Mike had offered to drive out to meet them. When the time came, Joanne took extra care over her hair and makeup and Jason looked at her appreciatively as she opened the door. "Come in and wait. Mike should be here any time."

Madeline and Steve Bennett were preparing to leave for a night at their local club and greeted Jason warmly. They had noticed the developing friendship between their daughter and the boy next door and whole heartedly approved.

Jason and Geoffrey were like sons to them, especially now that Bradin was living in Australia. Madeline was thrilled that Joanne was paying more attention to her appearance. She had always encouraged her to make the most of her looks and tonight Joanne was sparkling.

"You look gorgeous tonight Joanne," she commented. "You have done something different with your hair and it really suits you."

Joanne blushed. She hated attention being drawn to her appearance. It was much easier just to tie her hair back and wear a touch of lip gloss.

Jason agreed. "Your hair looks amazing and your eyes are more beautiful than ever." He took Joanne's arm and they went out to join Mike and Tracey who had pulled into the driveway.

The tavern was already crowded when they arrived but Mike managed to find a table near the back with room for the four of them. He beckoned the others over and they squeezed through the narrow gap beside the dance floor.

"Hi Rachel. Long time no see." Joanne felt an arm around her shoulder and turned to face a complete stranger who was smiling at her.

She pulled back in astonishment and the bearded young man stepped away. "Sorry. I thought you were someone else. I didn't know Rachel had a twin."

"I don't know any Rachel and my name is Joanne. Maybe you need new glasses."   The young man continued to stare as Joanne made her way to the table. She was still startled by the encounter. Jason was buying drinks at the bar so he had not heard the conversation but Tracey had been close by.

"What was that all about? Do you know that guy?"

"I've never seen him in my life, but he thought my name was Rachel."

Tracey laughed. "He's either trying to pick you up or there is a Rachel who looks just like you. I wonder who she is."

Joanne was shaken. So her look alike was named Rachel. She had tried to put the thought of a twin sister out of her mind but once in a while something came up that reminded her of the visit to the rest home and the story she had been told by the demented woman named Marie.

Jason returned with the drinks and they settled down to enjoy a bowl of nachos which had been placed on their table. It was the first time they had all been together since the camping trip and Tracey had brought along a packet of photographs which had been developed.

They were soon admiring the scenic shots and laughing at many of the images. "Good one, Tracey. I didn't see that one coming." Mike had been caught with a bottle of beer in one hand and a fat sausage dripping with sauce in the other.

Joanne shrunk at the sight of herself, crawling out of the tent still in her sleeping bag.

"I'd like to be back there right now," Jason whispered in Joanne's ear. "We haven't had a chance to be together like that since we got back home. I'll have to borrow my folks' car and we can go somewhere quiet and romantic."

Joanne cuddled up closer. She wanted to be alone with Jason more than anything, but the closer they got, the more difficult it would be to say goodbye when he returned to university. They could write and see each other in the holidays but there would be so many lonely weeks in between.

Mike and Tracey had moved onto the dance floor and Joanne urged Jason to join them. There was so little space they could hardly move but soon they were jiving to the beat. After a time Joanne was pleased to sit and enjoy another drink while Tracey and Mike continued holding each other close and swaying to the music.

"Let's take the bus home and leave those love birds to it. We can have a coffee back at my house." Jason took Joanne's hand and led her to the exit. They caught Mike's eye and waved to him on the way out.

Joanne looked around and could see the bearded stranger who had spoken to her earlier. He was still staring at her in a puzzled way which she found unnerving. Maybe he was a stalker and would try to follow them, but he stayed where he was and carried on talking to the group he was with.

The night was chilly as they waited at the bus stop and Joanne wished she had brought a warmer jacket. Jason wrapped his arms around her to keep her warm and luckily they didn't have to wait too long before the bus pulled up at the stop.

It was surprising how many people were still wandering the streets so late at night and Jason pointed out the street girls who stood on the corners waiting for clients. She shuddered at the risk they were taking. Many of them looked younger than she was yet were willing to sell their bodies for cash. She realized what a sheltered life she was living.

****

The first chance she got, Rachel approached Bill Osborne to ask for time off to go to the islands with Dirk in three weeks time.

"You're not giving me much notice," he blustered. "Don't forget we have the local body elections coming up soon and I want you to interview the candidates. There's one fellow standing for council who sounds interesting. About 40 years old, owns a big company and has a society wife much younger than himself. You'd better get on with that one straight away."

Rachel looked at the name on the sheet of paper. Greg Alexander Forman. Age 38. Married with one son. A business card was attached with a cell phone number and a small photo of Mr Forman.

"Good looking guy. I wonder what sort of business he owns. Vitex Industries. That doesn't mean anything to me."

"It's some sort of agricultural chemical company. They have a factory down in the Waikato and mostly export their products. There were a few protests from neighbours when they first set up but they seem to have kept themselves out of trouble as far as I know."

Rachel knew the procedure. Each mayoral candidate would take out an advertisement in the newspaper and receive one free promotional story. It would be a difficult task unseating some of the current councilors, but there were sure to be a number of people willing to try their luck.

She phoned the number on the card and set up a meeting with Greg Forman for two days time. That would give her the chance to do her research and try to get some background information.

First stop was the library where she spent some time browsing through the trade magazines. The librarian was helpful and it wasn't long before they came across several references to Vitex Industries. "Very soon you will be able to do all that work on the computer," she said. "Millions of records will be stored and it will be just a matter of typing in a name and searching the results."

"That will make my job a whole lot easier. Imagine having all that information at the touch of a button." Rachel was impressed.

"We are starting to use the computers which have just been installed, but we are all a little nervous about it."

Just as she was about to leave, the librarian came over carrying a magazine. "I remembered there was a story written about Greg Forman a few months ago when he received a business award. I can make you a copy of the article which will give you most of the information you need."

"Thank you so much. You have been a great help." Rachel paid for the photo copies and stuffed them in her bag. She returned to the office and was soon engrossed in reading the notes.

Greg Forman came from a well to do family and was brought up in an affluent neighbourhood. He attended private schools and went on to university, coming out with a science degree.

His interest lay in agricultural products to improve animal health and he had successfully developed a number of additives containing minerals and salts which could be safely given to dairy cows. Most of the products were exported to countries with low mineral content in their pastures and the factory in a small Waikato township employed around 50 people.

Rachel wondered how such a busy person would find the time to be on the city council and that would be one of the questions she would ask him. There was very little personal information in the articles apart from the fact that Greg Forman had been married twice and had a son, who was still at school, from his first marriage.

With several stories to complete before deadline, Rachel was kept busy over the next two days. Using the work car she drove to downtown Auckland where the offices for Vitex Industries were located in a high-rise building overlooking the waterfront.

Luckily there was parking available and she took the elevator up to the eighth floor where she stepped out into a spacious foyer furnished in a modern simplistic style. As she approached the reception desk, an attractive woman emerged from an office. Her blonde hair was pulled back in a fashionable French plait and her face was perfectly made up to emphasise the high cheek bones and vivid blue eyes.

The receptionist greeted her and handed her a number of carry bags from the city's top boutiques. "Is there anything else I can do for you Mrs Forman? I hope you enjoy the rest of the day."

Rachel couldn't help staring at the woman as she stepped into the elevator. So that was Greg Forman's wife. She looked about 25 years old and dressed like a fashion model.

"Can I help you?" The receptionist attracted Rachel's attention. She nodded when Rachel gave her name and picked up the phone to alert Greg Forman that she was there.

He came to the door almost immediately and beckoned Rachel to follow him into his office. When she sat in the seat opposite him, he stared at her for a long moment, his face turning a little pale.

He quickly pulled himself together and his face lit up in a charming smile. "I'm sorry about that, Rachel. You reminded me of someone I knew a very long time ago. Now what is it you want to know?"

Rachel was soon down to business, laying out the information she already had on Greg Forman and asking a number of questions. Greg was every bit as handsome as his photograph had promised. His hair was light brown and wavy and his face was tanned.

He answered her questions carefully, not giving too much away. He was married in his early 20s to a family friend and their son Martin was born two years later. "Unfortunately the marriage didn't last. I guess I was too busy making money and didn't give enough time to my wife and son." Greg looked sad for a moment. "I was lucky enough to meet my new wife Gaynor on a business trip and we have been happily married for almost a year. She will be a great asset if I am successful in my bid to become a councilor."

Now Rachel had to ask the tricky questions. "What do you hope to achieve if you are elected?" she asked.

Greg sat back in his chair and folded his hands together. "I have made you a list of my ideas to improve this city. I want to make it a better place for everyone, no matter what their circumstances." He pulled a sheet of paper from a folder. "I have efficient managers who handle most of my business affairs and now I feel that I have the time to give something back to the community."

Rachel smiled. "That sounds like a good way to start, but there must be certain areas where you hope to see change. Is there anything in particular that you will be promoting?"

Greg sat for a moment and thought about it. His eyes returned to Rachel's face and he smiled. "A young girl who looked a lot like you died from lack of proper medical care a few years ago. I would like to think that conditions have improved and there would be suitable care for someone like her in this day and age."

Rachel gathered up he notes and thanked him. Greg smiled as he posed for a photograph and then accompanied Rachel to the door.

"It has been a pleasure talking to you Rachel. I hope we will meet again while I'm out on the campaign trail." Greg turned back and as soon as he was alone he took out a small packet that was hidden at the back of a filing cabinet. He carefully took out a faded photograph and a young woman was smiling up at him. A young woman with light brown hair and spectacular grey/green eyes.

Chapter 9

When Rachel met Dirk that night, the date had been confirmed for the trip to the islands.

They had decided to meet for a pizza and Dirk was in a teasing mood. "Which island are we going to?" Rachel's eyes shone with excitement.

"That would be telling. I think I'll keep it as a surprise." It had been decided that the travel company would pay the air fares then Rachel would repay her share later. The accommodation on the island would be for two people.

It wasn't long, however, before Dirk gave in and showed Rachel the information he had picked up from the travel agent. "Okay. We're off to Rarotonga in the Cook Islands and we leave two weeks from tomorrow."

"Awesome. I've heard that Rarotonga is a beautiful place to visit. I'll have to finish off my election stories before we go and then we will be out of here."

The pizza, golden and delicious, was set in front of them, along with a glass of beer for Dirk and a red wine for Rachel. "Are we really going to eat all that?" They both spoke at once and laughed.

"Two more weeks and then we will be sitting on a sandy beach. I'll even buy a new bikini." It was a long time since Rachel had been so excited. She must remember to phone her parents and let them know what was going on.

Dirk had spent most of the morning interviewing a couple who had just returned from a river cruise. Luckily their photographs were of a high standard and he could weave their experiences into an interesting story. Arranging the Rarotongan trip had occupied most of the afternoon.

"Lucky you. I have to try and find something fascinating to write about the election candidates. I did meet an interesting guy today." Rachel described her visit to Greg Forman's office. "It was a bit strange at times though. When he first met me he looked as though he had seen a ghost. He was quite shaken, but soon recovered his smooth manner."

"I wonder what that was all about. Did he explain it?"

"Yes. He said I reminded him of someone he knew a long time ago. Apparently the young woman died in some way that could have been avoided. He wants to try to improve the medical system that failed her."

"That sounds interesting." Dirk was intrigued. "Did you learn much about him?"

"Most of the information was in the business magazines, but I felt he was being very careful about his private life." Rachel was finding it difficult to forget Greg Forman. There was something about him that intrigued her, but she couldn't afford to spend too much time thinking about it as she had several more interviews to complete.

They finished their pizza and chatted for a while. Rachel was ready for an early night so they agreed to meet again the next evening at her apartment where they could finalise the arrangements for their island adventure.

****

Joanne was looking forward to the start of the school term with a mixture of excitement and nervousness. It was all very well studying and learning about teaching, but to face a roomful of youngsters for the first time was a bit daunting. She knew that new teachers were usually given a relatively easy class, but to keep all those young minds occupied day after day would be a challenge.

The classroom looked bright and cheerful with pictures and charts already displayed. There was a comfortable couch in the library corner as well as large colourful cushions if the children chose to sit on the floor.

Joanne had arranged the small wooden desks in groups of six and made sure there was plenty of paper and card as well as crayons and felt pens that worked. It would take a few days to organize the stationary supplies so scrap paper would come in handy in the meantime. Enough library books had already been delivered and work sheets had been printed off.

There had been a staff meeting and morning tea the previous week and everybody had been very friendly and supportive. "If you need anything, just ask," they had said. Now it was time for the buzzer to sound for

88

the start of the day and all the students assembled outside on the playground.

As the names of her new pupils were called, Joanne saw that several looked just as nervous as she was feeling. They were wondering which class they would be in and who their teacher would be. She gave the children a warm smile as they joined the group and soon they were following her into the classroom.

"You can just sit anywhere for now. I will sort you into groups later." Joanne soon had all the children sitting silently at their desks and eyeing her in anticipation. So far, so good. The first day had begun.

By the time the buzzer sounded for morning recess, Joanne was feeling more relaxed. She had asked the children to write their names on a sheet of paper and then make up a sentence about the holidays. "You can draw the best thing that happened to you over the Christmas break. Then we will share our stories."

As she poured a cup of coffee, Joanne looked around the staffroom. Everyone seemed to be talking at once and she wondered where she should sit. There were several new teachers who all looked equally unsure until they were welcomed by the older staff members and made to feel at home.

"Just find a seat where you can. We don't stand on ceremony around here."

Joanne found herself seated between a pleasant young woman with short blond hair and a tall man with graying hair and horn rimmed glasses and they all looked up as the principal banged a spoon on the table to get attention.

"A big welcome to you all to another great year at our school and a special welcome to the new staff members. We are all here to help each other and we want you to enjoy being part of our team."

Everybody was asked to introduce themselves and before Joanne knew it, it was time to return to the classroom. Being such a beautiful warm day she decided to risk taking her pupils out into the grounds where a shady tree beckoned. A sturdy wooden seat had been conveniently placed beside the tree and she was able to sit and face the group as they sprawled on the grass. Joanne had brought a nature book along and soon she was reading about all manner of bugs and small creatures which could be hiding all around them.

"I'll give you a few minutes to search around in the dirt and under the leaves to see if you can find anything interesting. We won't pick anything up. Just observe what they do when they are disturbed."

Joanne strolled around watching the children hard at work. Most of them had picked up small sticks and were scraping around in the earth. Suddenly there was a shriek and one of the girls jumped up in fright. A small boy with sandy coloured hair was waving a fat worm close to her face.

"Hey, that's not very nice. I think you need to put the poor worm back in the soil and apologise to

Amelia." Joanne had to hold back a grin as she saw the mischievous look on the boy's face.

"It's okay, Amelia. I think the worm is much more frightened than you are." Joanne decided it was time for the children to return to the classroom away from the temptation of scary worms and slugs. The rest of the day went by without incident and Joanne was grateful when the buzzer sounded for the end of school. She felt exhausted but pleased with the way her first day had gone.

****

When the weekend came, Rachel was relieved that she had almost completed the candidates' stories. Some were more interesting than others but she would try to give them all equal promotion. The photographs had been developed and the profiles typed out and placed in the tray on the editor's desk.

With two free days she would start sorting out her clothes to pack for Rarotonga and phone her mother to keep her up to date with the news. To Rachel's relief, Julie was going to spend the weekend at the parents' house. It would be good to have the apartment to herself, and there was always the chance that Dirk would like to stay over.

She dialed her mother's number and waited. "Hullo. Marjorie Saunders speaking."

"Hi Mum, it's only me." Rachel was soon filling her mother in on all the events of the week. She told her about meeting the electoral candidates and the strange reaction from Greg Forman. "It was weird. He said I reminded him of someone he used to know. Someone who looked just like me."

There was a moment's silence on the other end of the phone. "Did he give you any more details?" Rachel's mother sounded anxious. "Did he tell you who she was?"

"No. Just that she died and he wants to make conditions better so that sort of thing won't happen again. I'm bound to see him again at some of the council promotions. Perhaps I will have the chance to ask him more about it."

Rachel saved the best piece of news to last. "Guess what? I'm going to Rarotonga next week to help with a travel article. My friend Dirk is writing the article and has asked me to go with him."

"Really Rachel. Who is this Dirk person? Are you sure you know him well enough to go off to a strange island with him?"

"It's all right mother. He is a very nice young man and we have become good friends. I am so looking forward to lying in the sun and swimming in the warm sea."

"Well just be careful Rachel. I would hate to see you get hurt. You are very precious to us you know."

Rachel was quite taken aback. Her mother didn't usually speak like that. She had certainly acted strangely about the young woman who looked just like her.

"Well, I must go now mother. Give my love to dad and I'll come and visit you as soon as I can get away."

When Marjorie put down the telephone she stood for a moment and stared into space. Her husband was in the next room and called out to ask how Rachel was.

"She seems fine, except she's off to Rarotonga with a young man she hardly knows. I'm not sure what that city life is doing to our daughter."

"Never fear. Rachel has her head screwed on right. She has always been an exceptional child."

"I was just thinking about that. It only seems the other day that we brought that dear wee soul into our home. But James, I'm feeling very nervous about something she said to me."

Marjorie told her husband about Rachel's experience with Greg Forman. "I hope there is no connection with this man and the circumstances of her birth. I feel so guilty that we have never told her the truth and now it seems almost too late."

"We have always thought of Rachel as our natural daughter and there seemed no point in upsetting her." James spoke quietly and took his wife by the hand.

"I know. She was just a tiny thing when we first saw her and then she grew into such a pretty baby. I'm afraid my vanity got the better of me and I couldn't ever admit that she was not my child."

At the time the Saunders had recently moved to the area and knew no-one. Everybody just assumed that they were the natural parents of the beautiful little girl and neither Marjorie nor James had corrected them.

"I'm sure it will all be fine. Now let's go for a walk and forget all about it." James liked a peaceful life and tried to avoid any confrontation.

Marjorie agreed, but in her heart she knew that she must broach the subject with Rachel at the first opportunity.

Chapter 10

Although Joanne had been too busy to think much about the mystery of her birth, Jason had been quietly gathering information. He had urged his friend William to help him and the two met at William's house early one evening to discuss the situation. Jamie had little Samuel all ready for bed and Jason dutifully admired him.

William smiled broadly as he showed off his precious son. "Wait until you have a child of your own. You have no idea how exciting it is."

"He is very handsome, but I don't think that is likely for quite some time." Jason was keen to get on with the business in hand and produced a folder with a few of the facts that he had gathered together.

He had found the time to visit the library and search through directories and lists of medical facilities. Twenty years ago, Parkhaven had been owned by a group of investors but the maternity wing had closed suddenly a short time later. He had a list of names but they meant nothing to him.

"Let me take a look. I might know something about these people." William ran his eyes down the list, then looked up at Jason in amazement. "This is practically a who's who of all the top businessmen at the time. Many of them are still clients of Barlow and Reid."

"Then there must be some records filed away. Babies can't be born and women die without some sort of accountability." Jason felt a tingle of excitement. Perhaps they would be able to learn something about the mysterious nursing home.

"I'll do my best to try and find out something about these people and their involvement in Parkhaven. Do they still have shares in the new rest home? That would be interesting to know." William drained his glass and poured the last of the red wine. "You seem to be rather interested in this girl's story. You should bring Joanne around to meet us some time."

"Yes, she's a great girl and we have grown up together. She is like the little sister I never had."

"Oh yes? I think there is more to it than that." William laughed. "Jamie is looking forward to meeting her as well so how about we make a time to come here for dinner."

It was agreed that they would get together on the following Saturday night as long as that suited Joanne. Perhaps William would have more news for them by then as well.

****

It was two days later that William got the chance he was waiting for. Ted Baker had not come in to work that day and the secretary, Beryl Griffin, had left early to visit an old friend who was in hospital.

With the office to himself, William decided to make the most of the opportunity. He had never been told not to look through the filing cabinets but Beryl had always given him a stern look if he ventured too close.

But where to start? He opened the first of the long row of cabinets and saw that the files in the drawer were listed on the first card he pulled out. That should make his search easier. He consulted the list of names that Jason had given him. He would look for any information about these people first and keep his eye out for any information about Parkhaven nursing or rest home.

Although he knew he was doing nothing wrong, William felt guilty. The phone went at one stage and he jumped with fright. He picked up the receiver and wrote down a message for Ted Baker.

It wasn't until William got to the third filing cabinet that the first name from the list came up. He quickly ran his eyes over the files but there was no mention of Parkhaven. He sighed and continued his search. The next name that came up was Terence Forman. There was a thick file of notes on Mr Forman who must have died as many of the more recent letters referred to his will and beneficiaries.

William closed the drawer and took the files over to his desk and sat down. This could take some time. Mr Forman had been a client for at least 30 years and had been involved in many business dealings.

As he sifted through the information William was startled by the sound of a door opening. Who could be coming into the office at this hour? He quickly slipped the folder of notes into his brief case and went out into the foyer. It was Beryl Griffin returning from her hospital visit.

"Hullo Beryl. I wasn't expecting you back. I was just finishing up and I'll be out of here."

"I needed to type some notes for Mr Baker. They couldn't wait until morning." Miss Griffin bustled up to her desk and William realized with dismay that he wouldn't be able to replace the folder without being seen. He would take the files home and read them. They wouldn't be missed in that short time.

He picked up his brief case as though it contained a bomb and set off to the car park. He would find an opportunity to return the files in the morning.

Jamie had dinner ready when William got home and for the next hour or so he was kept busy entertaining his small son and eating their meal. Once Samuel was put to bed he finally had time to take the file from his brief case.

Terence Forman had been an influential man. He had set up a manufacturing business and sat on a number of boards for which he received a very good income. William sorted through the documents to find any reference to Parkhaven Hospital or rest home.

Sure enough, the hospital was mentioned several times. During the 1960s the directors were paid very well. The balance sheets were healthy with a large amount of money earned in fees and donations. William scanned the pages to try to discover where the money came from and where it was spent.

Hospital equipment, wages and pharmaceuticals as well as expenses on the building were high, but a staggering amount of money seemed to have come in, all under broad headings such as consultants' fees and hospital admissions. There was nothing specific about the type of care the patients were receiving.

In 1964, all records ceased. It was as though the hospital no longer existed. What had taken place to shut down such a lucrative business? He was not going to find the answers in this file. He would have to search for more information about the closing of the hospital.

Wearily he packed away the papers and turned on the television. Jamie was already in bed and he would join her soon. He just had to relax his mind before there was any chance of sleep.

****

Joanne's first week at school had been an enjoyable one. The rest of the staff members were very friendly and they arranged to meet at the local pub for a drink after work on the Friday evening. She had become friendly with one of the other first-time teachers and they shared experiences as they waited for the others to arrive.

Fiona had been given an infant class and was busy coming to terms with finding the right reading books and providing suitable activities for children with a short concentration span.

"I'm glad my kids are a bit older. At least they can work for quite long periods." Joanne was pleased she had opted for the next level. She was looking forward to the weekend even though she knew she had the next week's programme to plan. She had received the invitation to have dinner at William and Jamie's house and agreed to go along.

Jason would borrow his father's car for the drive to William's house. "I didn't think you would fit on the back of my bike," he laughingly told Joanne. "I'll pick you up around six o'clock."

Rain was falling as they drove the short distance and parked in the driveway. It was a short sprint to the house where William was waiting to welcome them in. "I've heard a lot about you Joanne. It is good to meet you at last." He welcomed them into his home and took the umbrella which Joanne was clutching.

They were ushered into the lounge where Jamie was waiting with little Samuel in her arms. By the time Joanne had admired the baby, William poured a cool drink. "We normally eat out on the patio, but the rain has changed all that. Make yourselves comfortable in the lounge while Jamie settles the baby."

Joanne looked around the cosy room with a large open fireplace and upholstered couches. There was no need for a fire tonight as the temperature was warm in spite of the rain.

She could see a formal dining table in one corner of the room with a modern kitchen behind. As soon as they were settled William filled Jason in on the results of his search for details about Parkhaven. "Not too much right now but it looks promising. I managed to return the files I borrowed and I'm sure I will be able to find more about the closure of the nursing home."

He gave Jason a copy of the notes about Terence Forman. "This man had a substantial interest in the venture but we need to find out exactly what they were up to and why it suddenly closed down."

Joanne was intrigued to think that Jason should be making all these enquiries on her behalf. She wandered into the kitchen to join Jamie. "Lawyers tend to take their job rather seriously. You just have to get used to it," Jamie said. "He does seem genuinely concerned for you."

"I like him a lot but we are just starting out on our careers. We can't afford to get too involved at this stage." Joanne blushed. "The thing is, I couldn't help overhearing their conversation about this man called Terence Forman. The name sounded familiar and then I realized that I have heard that name before. Mr Forman was often mentioned in the papers for his good work. There was quite a write-up about him recently when he died."

"The funny thing is that I was reading about one of the new local body candidates and his name is Forman. I wondered whether there is any connection."

Jamie walked over to a small rack where a few newspapers were stacked. She found the page and gave it to Joanne. "Mr Greg Forman is hoping to be elected as a council member. He's very cute and sounds like a nice guy."

Joanne looked at the page in front of her. Mr Forman was certainly very good looking and his profile sounded too good to be true. "He wants to make the city a safer place for young women like someone he knew many years ago. That sounds rather vague. This person could have been mugged or hurt in a motor accident. Who wrote the article?"

"The name is in small print. She works for the paper. I'm sure you'll find it." Jamie went back to dishing up the meal.

Joanne scrolled the page and at the very end was the name, Rachel Saunders. Rachel? Surely not. That would be too great a coincidence. She was getting paranoid about her invisible twin, that was for sure.

She moved back to the living room and sat beside Jason. William refilled her glass and soon they were sharing a delicious meal

Chapter 11

With just a few days left before the Rarotongan holiday, Rachel was working long hours to finish all her stories. Her friend Julie hadn't returned from her parents' house and Rachel had a feeling she may not be back at all.

As it turned out, Dirk stayed over several times. He had bought himself a car and they made good use of it when they weren't working. They read through the literature about the Cook Islands and learned a great deal of the early history of the island. "I don't want to write the same stories as everybody else. We need to find a different angle and tell people about more unusual aspects of the place." The glossy brochures and travel articles mostly concentrated on the famous island culture experience, the boat ride to the lagoon and dining at the luxurious resorts.

"I want to see you climbing a coconut palm or para sailing on a tropical beach." Rachel agreed. Between them they would find some exotic experiences to whet the readers' appetites.

The last week came to an end and Rachel had one more assignment before she could pack her desk and hand her typewritten notes to her editor. A reception was being held in the town hall to introduce all the candidates and give the public a chance to question them about their policies.

She dressed carefully in a dark green trouser suit and arranged her hair in a becoming style, pulled back from her face with a few wisps falling over her forehead. She took extra care with her make up, emphasising her eyes with mascara and subtle green eye shadow. You never could tell who might be there.

Although Dirk wouldn't be on journalism duty, Rachel knew that he would be at the function. Hopefully they would be able to leave after the formal session and go back to the apartment to get ready for their morning flight to the island.

When she arrived, the hall was half full and the candidates were beginning to take their seats on the stage. Rachel had met them all by now and written their profiles for her newspaper. The big city newspapers had also published articles. Some candidates were more experienced than others at creating photo opportunities.

Greg Forman was last to arrive. He caught Rachel's eye and nodded in her direction. His wife Gaynor had accompanied him and she sat prominently in the front row of the hall, elegantly dressed, her long legs encased in sheer dark stockings.

The chairman asked the group to stand together for a formal photograph and then Rachel and the other journalists were free to sit and take notes of the proceedings.

Each speaker addressed the crowd, then the meeting was opened up for question time. As a new candidate, Greg received more than his share of questions. Many people had the same reservations as Rachel. "How would Mr Forman have time to attend council meetings when he had a major business to run?" "What sort of improvements would he strive for if he was elected?"

Greg Forman answered each question with care. Rachel had to admit he had a winning smile, but he was careful not to make any false promises. Towards the end of the session, she noticed Dirk sitting near the back of the hall. She felt a surge of excitement. Tomorrow they would be winging their way to Rarotonga and all this would be far behind them.

As the meeting concluded, the candidates were surrounded by potential voters and Rachel found herself close to Greg's wife who looked at her for a moment and smiled. "Hi, I'm Gaynor Forman. You did a nice job on my husband's story. Thank you."

Rachel felt flattered. "We try to give everyone equal coverage. Mr Forman's story was more interesting than some of the others."

"Yes, he has been very successful and we have a pleasant lifestyle. I am still getting used to having a teenage son, however. Martin lives with his mother most of the time and is a nice boy but I didn't have any brothers, so I have no experience with growing lads."

Rachel was sympathetic. "I'm an only child myself and was at boarding school when I was growing up so I know nothing about teen-aged boys."

Just at that moment Greg Forman came into view. "Hullo Rachel. Thanks for the story. The photo wasn't bad either. I see you've met my wife Gaynor. She is new to these parts and doesn't know too many people yet." He was interrupted by a large man with a very loud voice who was determined to have his say.

"I'm not sure about supporting a candidate who owns a chemical company. How do we know what goes into the atmosphere from your products?"

Greg turned his back on the assailant and took his wife's arm. "Come my dear, afternoon tea has been served they tell me." Rachel was startled when he turned to her. "Please be my guest. I feel the need for some pleasant company." Soon she was being shepherded to a room at the back of the hall where food and refreshments were waiting.

"Excuse me. I have a friend waiting. Can he come in as well?"

"Sure. The more the merrier. Bring your friend in and we'll have a welcome drink together." Soon Rachel and Dirk had joined the invited guests and were offered a glass of wine. Gaynor looked on in amusement as her husband gathered a large group around him.

Rachel introduced Dirk and soon he and Gaynor were in deep conversation. The subject of Dirk's age had never really come up but he was probably a few years older than Rachel, possible 24 or 25, which put him close to Gaynor Forman's age.

"Just as well I'm not a jealous type," Rachel said to herself. A moment later she was standing beside Greg and the way he was looking at Dirk and Gaynor, perhaps the same thought was going through his head.

"Rachel, tell me about this interesting young man. How long have you known him?" Greg gave her a crooked smile. Rachel thought for a moment. She was growing fond of Dirk but wasn't sure that he was the only one for her at this stage.

"We met recently and are having a good time together. Nothing too serious." Greg was giving her his intense look which was a little un-nerving to say the least.

"You are a beautiful girl and have a great future in journalism, but I think you are wasted at a small newspaper. I could get you an interview with my friend at the television studio if you were interested." Greg spoke with sincerity. Every time he saw Rachel it brought back memories of poor Jenny, but this was not the time for such thoughts.

Soon they were enjoying another round of drinks and sampling the delicious savouries and sandwiches that had been prepared for them. He caught up with Gaynor and drew her into the conversation.

"I think we could slip away now, my dear. I hope this event hasn't been too much of a trial for you."

"On the contrary Greg. I've had some interesting conversations with these young people and hope to see them again. I've taken the liberty to invite Rachel and Dirk to our home for a meal." Gaynor took Greg's arm as they said their farewells and left the hall. Greg looked at his wife in surprise. It wasn't often that she took the lead when it came to making new friends, but he was pleased that he would have the chance to get to know the young reporter better.

****

It was almost a week before William had another chance to search through the office files. Ted Baker was on court duty and Beryl Griffin had come down with a bad cold and decided to stay home.

William had files of his own to return to the file room so he did have a legitimate excuse to be there, but he was nervous about the Parkhaven information. For some reason it had made Ted Baker uneasy when he first mentioned it. It had been confirmed that Greg was Terence Forman's son. There was also an older daughter named Susan who was living in Australia.

William's assault case had gone well with the young man being acquitted of all charges. The woman concerned had been most unhappy with the verdict and had become quite abusive when the result was announced. She was last seen mouthing obscenities in William's direction.

As soon as he was alone with the files, William discarded the idea of finding information on the directors and went straight for anything directly relating to the running of the hospital. He knew it was a long shot but was worth a try.

He went straight to the fourth filing cabinet and read through the list. Nothing there. No luck with the next two cabinets either. William was just about to give up the hunt when his eyes fell on the heading 'hospital closure'. It didn't specify which hospital, but he searched through the files until at the very back he came to a large manilla envelope with 'sensitive information' written on the front.

Now he did feel rather nervous. What could this envelope contain? He closed the drawer and took the envelope back to his desk. William poured himself a glass of water from the cooler and sat and carefully opened the envelope. The first few pages appeared to be a sale agreement for a hospital. The name Parkhaven didn't appear.

It could be any hospital, as there was no street address and it was in corporate ownership. The date was interesting, however. March 1964. Not too many months after the date they were researching.

Maybe an unexpected death did occur there and the hospital closed soon afterwards. William made copies of the pages and was about to put them back in the envelope when he noticed a thin sheet of paper which had remained in the envelope.

He reached inside and carefully pulled it out. His face turned pale when he realized what he was looking at. It seemed to be an agreement signed by Terence Forman as chairman of the advisory board.

The paper was thin and the typing faint. He smoothed the document out and placed it in the photo copier. He could get a clearer copy that way.

As soon as this was done, William placed the page and the sale document back in the envelope and carried it to the file cabinet. He knew he had stumbled on something very confidential that he would not be able to share, even with his best friend Jason.

He stared at the words on the paper for several minutes silently digesting the information.

It was dated December 5, 1963 and read: 'We, the trustees of the hospital known as Parkhaven, agree to close the existing maternity unit following the death of a young woman due to lack of suitable equipment. Sixteen-year-old Jennifer Blake died from a hemorrhage a short time after giving birth to twin girls on November 23, 1963. The theatre lacked the equipment needed to carry out a blood transfusion and it has since transpired that the patient should have been sent to a major hospital for the complicated birth which was outside the scope of the staff on duty.

'The maternity unit will close immediately and the hospital will be sold. We recommend that a suitable amount should be paid to the parents of the deceased in the hope that the whole matter shall remain confidential. Signed: Terence Forman, Trust Board chairman.'

"Whew." William let out a sigh. He would keep most of the information to himself, but now he had the name of the poor young girl he should be able to find the death certificate.

Obviously the parents of Jennifer Blake had been paid off. Somebody must have provided the fees for the expensive nursing home and who was the father of the babies? There was obviously much more information somewhere in the filing cabinets that would give him the answers.

He packed the photo copies in his brief case. They would be safer at home where he would have to conceal them. He felt more like a detective than a lawyer right now. If he could find the death records, Joanne could be told the name of her mother. The girl's parents' names would be on the document. There may also be a record of the twins' birth, although the girl may have used a different name.

Although he couldn't share all the information it might lead to something so his efforts hadn't been totally wasted.

Chapter 12

After their evening at William's house, Jason was in no hurry to drive straight home. It was a beautiful summer night and it wasn't often that he had the use of his father's car.

"Let's drive along the waterfront and find a nice little coffee shop. I don't want to go home just yet."

"Sure." Joanne agreed. She was happy to be with Jason but they were seldom alone together. "Did William have any more information about the nursing home? He seems certain that he will find something in the files at his office."

"Yes, it's a very old law office and there is sure to be a great amount of information hidden in all those files, but the senior lawyer seems reluctant to tell him anything."

Joanne decided to change the subject. "By the way. How's your brother getting on with Chloe? Are they still going out together?"

"No way. She threw him over when she found he didn't own a fancy car. His latest girl friend is named Samantha I believe."

Joanne laughed. "Where does he find them? He's obviously just having a fling before he goes back to varsity."

"You're right. Our Geoffrey is not ready to settle down by any means." Jason was quiet for a moment as they pulled into a parking space beside a small café. "He doesn't realise that the best girl lives right next door."

"Yeah, right. Come on. Let's see what the coffee's like." Joanne didn't want any serious talk and led them into the café. "This looks okay. We can probably sit outside on a night like this."

They ordered coffee and found a table in a small courtyard behind the shop. It had an Italian look about it with red candles set in old wine bottles and lanterns hanging from the rafters. A grape vine grew along a fence and white roses were flourishing in round wooden tubs.

The waitress who brought their drink was definitely not Italian, however. She was blond and had a distinct Yorkshire accent. "Can I get you anything else?" she asked as she put the coffee on the table.

"No, We're fine at the moment. Thanks. Quite the place you've got here." Jason smiled in her direction.

"Just trying to introduce a bit of Europe into Auckland. Not sure about the lanterns though." The girl moved on to clear the next table.

"I guess it is a bit over the top, but makes a change from 'olde English' taverns." Joanne looked around appreciatively. "It's sure good to get into the city once in a while."

They finished their coffees and walked across the road to the beachfront. The city lights shone brightly all around them and the shape of the harbour bridge stood out against the night sky.

"We'd better get back I suppose. It's been a nice evening." Jason put his arms around Joanne and held her close. "I'm sure going to miss you when I'm back in Wellington."

"Me too. That's why we should just be friends for now. It would be too difficult if we got any closer."

"I know you are right, but I'm very tempted to make love to you right here on the beach." Jason held her tightly for a moment, then reluctantly let her go.

They drove home in silence. Joanne knew she was right about keeping things on a platonic level, but regretted her decision all the same. However, making love in the back seat of a car did not seem like a very good idea right now.

****

Armed with the name of the girl who had died at the nursing home, William called at the local library and asked to use the microfiche system to look up the death records. He wasn't sure how up to date they would be but it might be worth a try. The librarian showed him how to scan the files but they were indistinct and quite difficult to read.

"It would probably be easier just to send away for a death certificate, if you know the name and date of death. I can find the right form for you." It didn't take long to fill in the information, write a cheque to cover the fee and post it off, then William was on his way back to the office.

As he walked into the foyer he noticed that Beryl Griffin was not at her usual desk. It was not like her to miss a day of work and Ted Baker was looking very hot and bothered as he tried to find some papers on his desk.

"What a day. Beryl has been called away to take care of her mother who has had a fall. She may not be back for some time. I don't know what I will do without her as she is the only one who knows where to find anything."

William felt sympathetic for his boss but a little annoyed as well. It was time that a younger person was trained to carry out the clerical duties. It was quite irresponsible to have all that information in the hands of one person.

"I'm sorry to hear that. We will need to call an agency and bring in a temporary office clerk. Would you like me to arrange it?"

"Very well. I suppose that is for the best. But some of the files here are quite sensitive. I wouldn't want just anyone having access to them." Ted Baker's hands were shaking. He appeared to be very nervous indeed.

William returned to his desk and found the name of an agency in the directory. He would insist on a woman with experience in dealing with confidential documents. He had several jobs lined up for today, mainly finalizing wills and property agreements. He should be able to find the papers that he would need.

He had hoped for an early finish so he and Jamie could spend some time together. They had enjoyed their dinner party with Jason and Joanne but it would be good to have a night out together sometime. Perhaps Jamie's mother would be willing to baby sit.

"I know I can work the coffee machine. I'll make us a drink and we can see what needs to be done today." William smiled at his boss and tried to make light of the problem.

"Unfortunately, Beryl's mother lives way down country. About two hours' drive, so she can't even come in to help us out. I do hope they send a reliable person as there is a great deal of typing to be done." Ted could only look on the gloomy side. He was totally lost without Beryl Griffin.

****

The day had finally come for the long awaited trip to Rarotonga. Dirk drove his new car to the airport and they left it with a company which took them in a mini van to the terminal. It didn't take long to find their check-in counter and have their luggage weighed. Rachel held her breath as her bag went on the scales. It felt heavy but fortunately was well within the limit.

With their passports and travel documents in hand they took the escalator to the next floor and were soon through customs. "Now I really feel as if we are on our way. We have more than an hour to fill in so let's find a drink and somewhere to sit."

This was a new experience for Rachel who had been no further than Sydney and as she sat and watched the people walk by her excitement mounted. Many different languages could be heard as the crowds mingled together in colourful waves.

Rachel was happy to sit for a while but once she finished her drink she was anxious to find their gate in plenty of time. "There's no hurry. We'll be sitting on the plane for about four hours. Are you sure you don't want another drink?" Dirk was content to stay a little longer.

"Come on. Our gate might be miles away." Rachel checked the flight monitor and found the gate number and they were soon striding along the corridors until they reached their waiting area. The room was almost full and they just managed to find two seats together. There was a happy mix of island families returning home and a few holidaymakers, mostly from Britain or America, wanting to escape their winter weather.

It seemed to take forever until their seat numbers were called and they made their way through the gate and onto the plane. Rachel found herself in the window seat and Dirk in the middle. A young island woman had the aisle seat.

Luckily the flight was a smooth one with time to watch a movie, eat a light meal and enjoy a glass of wine, before the air hostess brought around a container of sweets and instructed them to prepare for landing. Rachel held Dirk's hand tightly as the plane descended and landed with a slight bump in the middle of the tarmac.

"We get to walk from here by the looks of things," Dirk said. Rachel could see the runway and a grass field fringed by tree-covered hills. It was early evening and as they stepped off the plane, the warm balmy air greeted them.

The sound of guitars playing island music serenaded them as they walked into the terminal where colourfully dressed island women placed floral garlands around their necks.

A young man in a bright shirt was holding a sign with the name of their resort and as a group gathered around him he shook their hands and welcomed them to Rarotonga. It wasn't long before the bags were unloaded and packed into a trailer behind a minibus and they were on their way.

It was hard to distinguish much in the semi darkness but Rachel was aware that they were passing a small settlement, then scattered houses surrounded by coconut trees. The minibus stopped at two resorts where guests disembarked and finally arrived at their destination where the last passengers were pleased to climb down from the vehicle and stretch their legs.

The guests were checked in by two attractive island girls and Rachel and Dirk were soon following a sturdy young man who carried their bags with ease along the paths which wound through colourful gardens. "You have a beautiful beachfront room. I'm sure you will be happy here."

Rachel looked around the room in delight. A king size bed with a tasteful arrangement of hibiscus flowers took up most of the space. There was also a single bed on one side of the room and two armchairs as well as a small dining table and two chairs. A shelf was set up with a fridge and microwave and a cupboard held an assortment of china and cutlery.

"Just in case we want to dine it, but I don't think so." Rachel bounced on the bed and opened the door to check out the bathroom. "Oh look Dirk. There's an outdoor shower. How cool." Sure enough a door led out to a walled in shower with the moonlit sky above.

Although they were tired, neither Rachel nor Dirk was ready for bed. They wandered out onto the verandah and down the steps towards the swimming pool and patio. A little further away was the restaurant where a few couples were still sitting around.

A wide strip of sand could be seen and the ocean beyond, sparkling silver in the moonlight, the breakers cascading over the reef. Everywhere they looked were coconut palms silhouetted against the night sky.

Dirk smiled and took Rachel in his arms. "What do you think? Can you handle this for the next 10 days?"

"It looks like magic. I'm dying to see it all in the day light." They returned to their room and opened their bags to take out their toiletries. They would have a good sleep and unpack in the morning.

Chapter 13

The thought of Jason returning to university was a depressing one. Joanne was getting used to him being right next door and she knew she would miss him greatly when he returned to Wellington. They would write of course and maybe phone once in a while, but that was expensive. It had been such a happy summer being with him and catching up with Tracy and Mike most weekends.

She sighed as she looked at the work in front of her. A pile of exercise books to be marked and the next day's worksheets to be printed off. She wouldn't be home until five o'clock at the rate she was going.

Her mother had been full of excitement that morning because Bradin was coming home. The job in Australia had finished and he and his friends were heading back to try to find work in New Zealand.

"It will be good to have our boy home, even though the grocery bill is sure to be higher. Luckily Joanne is paying board these days so we should be able to manage." Madeline was a little worried about their finances but Stan looked up from the newspaper and smiled. "We've done it before, we'll do it again," he promised.

Joanne was about to pack her belongings into her bag when she heard someone come through the corridor outside the classroom. Probably the cleaners. She was surprised to see Jason standing at the door.

"Hi. I thought I would take you for a drink on the way home." Jason was still wearing his service station uniform but they would just be calling at the local tavern.

"Sure. Good idea. I've finished here. I'll just give my mother a call to let her know I'll be late. She tends to worry if she doesn't hear from me." Joanne went to the telephone on the wall of the foyer and dialed the number. "I should get one of those new mobile phones but I can't quite get my head around it."

Jason laughed. He hadn't been tempted into a mobile phone either, but knew the day would come when everyone would be using one.

They bought their drinks and settled into their usual seat in the corner of the lounge. Jason looked a little troubled. "I wanted to show you something Joanne. I thought it would be better to give you this somewhere private. It may come as a bit of a shock."

Joanne took the envelope from Jason and looked at him enquiringly. "What is it? What have you found out?"

"I'm almost certain that this is your mother's death certificate. It would be too much of a coincidence for it to be anyone else."

Joanne's hand trembled as she drew the paper from the envelope. She held her breath as she scanned the information inside. Could this really be her mother? There it was in black and white.

Joanne's face was pale, but an excitement surged through her. Jason had gone to the bar to refill their glasses and it gave her time to pull herself together. An overwhelming feeling of sadness swept through her when she read about the cause of death, followed by elation as she studied the details of her mother's family.

That small piece of paper provided so much information. Her grandparents were from Scotland and had probably lived in Hamilton. They may still be alive. Jason was relieved when he returned to the table to see the excitement in Joanne's eyes.

"I guess you have already read this. It is most exciting news. Thank William so much for finding the information. How did he know my mother's name?" There was so much that Joanne wanted to ask but Jason didn't know all the answers.

"I think William knows a bit more that he's letting on, but once he had the name it was easy to get the death certificate through his law office."

"I didn't know I had Scottish blood. No wonder I like the sound of bagpipes." Joanne felt unreal. All this information on top of two glasses of vodka was making her head whirl.

"I think we'd better get some food. I don't want to take you home like this. I'm sure your mother won't mind you missing dinner when we tell her the news." Jason went back to the bar to order a pizza while Joanne continued to stare at the piece of paper. It seemed a bit strange that Jennifer hadn't been checked by her doctor for almost a month. Surely the nursing home would have been more careful, especially if such a young girl was expecting twins.

Maybe this was why the maternity services had suddenly closed down. Jennifer Rose Blake, such a pretty name. What had she looked like? There was so much that Joanne wanted to know.

She put the envelope in her bag as Jason returned. There was so little time left to enjoy his company. She didn't want to spoil their last few days together.

****

When Rachel woke next morning, she sat up with a start. She looked around the strange room and remembered where she was. Dirk was already up and she could hear him in the outdoor shower. She pulled on a wrap and opened the curtains. The view was even better than she had anticipated with the colourful garden merging with the smooth raked sand

and the vivid blue of the ocean just a short distance away.

She chose a light t-shirt and shorts as she knew it would be very hot outside. March was still a little early for most New Zealand tourists who preferred to come a few months later when the weather was cooler. It didn't worry the Brits and Americans though. They loved to come 'down under' to escape their cold winters.

Dirk appeared wearing nothing but a towel and he pulled some clothing from his bag. "We need to call at the travel office first thing. I've got to show my face and they will have several places lined up for me to visit, no doubt. There should be a car booked for me or we can hire motor bikes if you prefer."

It didn't take Rachel long to try out the shower. It felt really exotic to be standing naked outdoors, knowing that she couldn't be seen unless someone was sitting up in the tree. Dirk poked his head around the door and she turned her back to him and continued to soap herself under the warm spray.

Breakfast was set out in the restaurant with its sand floor and palm fronds creating just the right atmosphere. Island music played from the speakers and a welcome breeze came in through the open shutters.

It seemed that a car had been organized by the travel company, so Dirk thought they could hire a motorbike for a day later in the week to try out the experience. The car was very small, very old and likely to be very hot.

"We would probably be cooler using motor bikes but for today we'll take the car into town. It seems that I have to get a driver's licence at the police station so we can do that while we are there." Dirk was learning how things were done in Rarotonga.

The trip to town was an interesting one. The narrow road was busy with dozens of motor bikes and small cars carrying residents and tourists alike. Rachel loved the island women wearing large white hats as they drove towards the village. Occasionally a small truck rumbled by with several young men standing on the deck, usually accompanied by several large brown dogs.

Several of the small concrete houses had a grave yard in the front yard, with white cement headstones and vases of bright flowers. Rachel looked at them and shuddered. It would be strange having your relatives buried in the front yard.

Dirk had been told about the church services on the island where visitors were made welcome. Several denominations were represented including the island's own Cook Islands Christian Church and the white-washed stone buildings were impressive.

They called first at the police station to pick up a driver's licence then headed for the travel office a few doors along the street. The young woman in charge sat them down in her office and proceeded to bring out a selection of brochures, but Dirk shook his head. "Everyone seems to do the same things when they come to the islands. I want to try something different. I'd like to get closer to the people who live here and experience something of their lives."

The woman smiled. "I get the message. No sugar-coated tourist traps for you. You want to sample the real Rarotonga. I think I can sort something out. Take the day to explore the island and come back here tomorrow. I know just the right person to help you."

"Let's look around the shopping centre while we are here. I'd love one of those colourful wraps that everyone is wearing and you definitely need to buy an island shirt." Rachel was ready for a shopping spree.

Half an hour later they returned to the car, armed with shopping bags. Rachel had found a bright pink and orange sundress and a vivid piece of hand printed cloth which could be tied in all sorts of ways to wear over a bikini.

"I love that colour," Rachel teased as Dirk held up the bright red shirt adorned with tropical flowers and palm fronds. "Your friends at the tavern should see you now."

They set off in the opposite direction from where they were staying, knowing that the road went right around the island and they would eventually end up back at the resort. The scenery was much the same all the way with houses, coconut palms and an occasional store, with glimpses of water in between.

They were headed for the eastern side where several luxury resorts were set on a fabulous lagoon.

A side road took them down to the water's edge where they could park the car and walk along the powdery white sand. Several kite boarders were testing their skills and Dirk decided that this was one of the things he would like to try. Rachel thought that lounging on the beach in a bikini was more her style.

They wandered along the beach until they came to a cool-looking bar and restaurant and they decided to enjoy a drink and maybe something to eat. Several young people were already sitting around the tables out on the deck, trying out the exotic cocktails that the bar was famous for. The women looked at Dirk curiously. Rachel realized that he was very attractive with his tall physique and long blond hair.

"What is that you are drinking?" he asked a young woman who caught his eye. "It looks quite exotic."

"I don't know, but it sure tastes good. I suggest you try it." The woman definitely had a strong US accent.

"Why not?" Dirk ordered two coconut sunrises and they watched the bar tender pour in the ingredients and give the container a good shake. They found a table and sat looking out over the beach. Children splashed happily in the warm water and several sailing boats could be seen out on the lagoon close to the small islands just inside the reef.

"We must have a swim when we get back to our resort. The water is so clear and they say you can see

hundreds of little fish swimming around your feet."
Rachel was entranced.

The cocktail was delicious but they decided to leave
before they were tempted to have another. They had a
car to drive and a long afternoon ahead of them.
They followed the road around the coastline and
stopped when they saw a sign for a beach hut and bar
a few minutes later.

"Let's check this out for lunch. We must almost be
back at the resort but this looks interesting." Dirk
was attracted by the sight of a hammock swaying in
the breeze between two coconut palms. They drove
slowly along the gravel driveway and parked in a
space behind a small hut that appeared to be perched
up on stilts. A wooden deck jutted out towards the
beach and several tables and chairs were scattered
around a grassy area.

"Castaway Shack. Sounds authentic. Let's see what
they have to offer." Dirk led the way up the steps to
the deck where a long wooden table and stools was
set up with place settings and menus.

The seafood chowder sounded like the perfect lunch
with a glass of island-brewed beer to wash it down.
They took their drinks down onto the grassed area
where they sat under a shady umbrella and relaxed in
the warm air.

They had a whole afternoon ahead of them in this
peaceful, idyllic piece of paradise.

****

With the news that Bradin was returning home, Madeline was busy emptying all the gear from his room and finding places to store it in the garage. "Why do we keep all this stuff? I should take it all down to the opportunity shop, but you never know when it might come in useful."

She struggled with an old airing rack and a shabby suitcase that had seen better days. Joanne tried to help but wasn't sure what to keep and what to throw away. "I don't think you'll use this again," she laughed, as she came across a dressmaker's dummy left over from when Madeline sewed her own dresses.

"Okay. I'll get your father to take that to the dump along with the knitting machine. That stack of magazines can go too." It was time to get ruthless.

Joanne had arrived home too late the night before to share the new information she had been given about her birth mother. This didn't seem like the right time either, so it would have to wait a bit longer.

Bradin was due to arrive in two days' time and there was to be a welcome home barbecue for him on Saturday night. Flo and Stan O'Connor had been invited as well as Jason and Geoffrey. Joanne was curious about Geoff's new girlfriend. Would he invite Samantha along? Steve would cook sausages, steaks and lamb chops and Madeline decided to buy containers of cole slaw and potato salad which was produced locally.

Flo promised to bring desserts and Joanne would contribute fresh bread rolls from the bakery. "Bradin won't have had a real Kiwi barbecue for a while. He'll feel right at home, that's for sure." Steve would help by making sure there was a good supply of cold beer.

Joanne was looking forward to her brother's return. She hoped he wouldn't have trouble finding a job as there was still a downturn in the building trade, but Bradin was always willing to try his hand at anything. It would be good to show him around and introduce him to the new night life, especially as Jason would be back in Wellington in just over a week.

"Bradin will have to be my new partner once Jason goes away," she said as she helped Madeline pack away the last of the clothing that had found its way into Bradin's dresser. "I'm sure he'll be keen to check out the night life as soon as possible."

"He won't have any money to be throwing around. Not until he gets a job anyway." Madeline looked grim. Your father and I won't be paying out for Bradin to socialize.'

"I'm sure he won't expect you to. If we've finished here I'll make us a cup of tea. I've got something I want to share with you."

Madeline had made up the bed with clean sheets and bought a bright new duvet cover. She looked at the tidy room, knowing it would look like a disaster area once her son was back. It would be good to see him safely home though. She smiled and took the last load of clothing into the laundry. She would sort it out and see what could go to the opportunity shop.

Joanne had set out the cups and found a container of biscuits. She wondered how her mother would react to the information on the death certificate. Luckily she was distracted by Bradin's home-coming at the moment.

When Joanne produced the envelope and handed it to her mother, Madeline took a deep breath. "Is this what I think it is?" She looked sharply at Joanne then took out the slip of paper. "Oh my goodness. That poor, poor girl. It looks as though the woman at the nursing home was right." The implication took a moment to sink in. "If she was right about that, then it is probably true that there were two babies."

"Jason's friend William was able to get this information, but it would be more difficult to find out what happened to the other baby. We wouldn't be certain of the name that was used. If I think about it too much I imagine that I see my twin everywhere."

"It would be wonderful to find your twin sister though she might not have survived. But now we know your mother's name we could probably start searching for her parents. After all, Hamilton isn't very far from here. Fancy them being Scottish. Who would have thought it?"

Joanne knew that Madeline would waste no time in sharing the information with her friend Flo. No doubt between them they would come up with a plan to find the Blake family in Hamilton.

Chapter 14

Madeline had forgotten how crowded their house had been before Bradin had left for Australia. Now he was back, his dirty clothes were piled on the laundry floor and his belongings spread around the bedroom. She looked around in dismay. "I didn't do a very good job of training our son, but never mind. Even though he's untidy, it's great to have him home."

Steve laughed. "The good news is that he and his mates have already been promised work. The builder they were working for across the ditch has got the roofing contract for the new university just north of the city. That job should take at least three months."

"I heard Bradin talking about a job. I didn't quite catch what it was. That is very good news." Madeline was relieved. At least Bradin would be earning a living and helping out financially. They always seemed to be down to their last dollar.

The barbecue was planned for that evening. With Jason and Geoffrey leaving next week it would be the last chance for them all to be together for a quite some time.

Flo had been intrigued when she read the information on the death certificate. "I thought at the time that Aunt Grace's friend was telling the truth, even though she didn't know what day it was. We could find out whether the poor girl's family is still living in Hamilton, although it seems as though they left her to fend for herself at the nursing home when she needed them most."

"We don't know what the circumstances were. Obviously someone paid for her care, although it apparently wasn't adequate. Luckily our Joanne came out of it unscathed." Even though she had suggested it, Madeline was nervous about contacting the dead girl's family. It was sometimes better to let sleeping dogs lie.

Bradin had taken the news in his usual nonchalant fashion. "Good grief, little sister. Imagine another one like you. That would be too much."

Jason had filled him in with the information they had collected so far. "I'm sure William will let us know if he comes up with anything new. I'll get him to contact you while I am away."

By five o'clock, Joanne's father had marinated the meat, and the salads and rolls were set out on dishes in the refrigerator. "Leave some space for the beer," he said, as he took the top off a bottle and sat outside to wait for their neighbours.

Flo and Stan arrived together carrying the desserts and a bottle of wine. "The boys are on their way. Geoffrey decided not to bring his new girl friend. He plans to meet her later in the evening as far as I know."

Soon everyone had gathered and the drinks were flowing. Steve fired up the barbecue and Bradin was filling them in on his time on the Gold Coast. "The girls are all blond and gorgeous. You guys don't know what you're missing."

Steve looked around at his family and their friends. "This calls for a toast. Here's to the safe return of Bradin, and best wishes to Jason and Geoff for another great year in Wellington."

They all raised their glasses. Joanne swallowed a lump in her throat. Jason would be leaving on Monday and she wouldn't see him for several weeks. She squeezed his hand and sipped her wine. This was not the moment to be melancholy. Tonight was a time for celebration.

****

After their first relaxing day on the island, Dirk was ready to get into action. They were expected back at the travel office at 10 o'clock and when thy arrived they were greeted by a burly islander with a wide smile. "Kia orana. I'm Tobias and I've been asked to look after you. Come with me and I'll drive you to your first stop."

Rachel wasn't sure what to expect as she and Dirk followed Tobias out to the car park where a dust-covered utility was parked. They soon left the main road and were driven up a steep unsealed road through vegetable plots and exotic plantings of mangoes and bananas. Giant taro grew right to the edge of the narrow track which led to the rocky outcrops at the highest point of the island.

The utility bounced and bumped over the uneven ground and Rachel hung on tightly as they negotiated the tight bends. Suddenly they stopped in a clearing beside a large water tank. "Okay. This is the best view on the island. From here you can see everything. I thought it would be a good place to start."

Tobias got out of the vehicle and proceeded to roll himself a cigarette. "Just climb up on that ridge and take some photos of the beautiful lady." He sat down on a fallen log and waited as Dirk and Rachel did as he suggested. Tobias was right. The turquoise waters, enclosed by sparkling white surf crashing over the reef, stood out in vivid contrast to the dark blue of the ocean.

Rachel laughingly posed on the top of the ridge, her arms outstretched and the breeze blowing through her hair. Dirk aimed the camera in her direction and took several shots. "Mmm. Great scenery. I'm glad I brought you along." Although he had work to do, Dirk was in a light-hearted mood. "I wonder what else Tobias has in store for us."

They clamboured back into the ute and were soon careering down the track and back towards civilization. They came to a halt, this time in a roughly grassed driveway which led to a corrugated iron shack.

"Come. You will be surprised what you will see inside." Not knowing what to expect, Dirk followed

Tobias into the shed with Rachel hanging back a little.

Once inside the building it took a moment for their eyes to grow accustomed to the darkness. Tobias pulled aside a torn curtain and the light streamed in, lighting up a number of amazing carved statues, some made from stone and others created from gleaming wood.

"This is where our master carver carries out his work and passes on his skills to the young ones. From this humble dwelling, great works of art emerge." Tobias sounded quite eloquent. "You will see many of these statues around the village, especially outside our major buildings."

Once again, Dirk photographed the images and scribbled a few words in his notebook. He realized that tourists wouldn't normally see where these treasures were created.

Back on the main road they recognized the area from the day before. The beautiful white sandy beach inside the lagoon was close by. What was next on the programme? It didn't take long to find out. As they rounded the bend, Rachel could see a strange object lying on the sand.

"Okay. Time for some action. I hope you are wearing a bathing suit." Dirk peeled off his jeans and exposed his board shorts. He had a feeling that he would be getting wet really soon. After a short explanation he found himself out on the water ready

to try his luck at kite boarding, while Rachel got
ready to photograph the action.

The breeze picked up the kite and suddenly he was
being pulled through the clear water. Then he landed
with a splash. Rachel laughed while Tobias lay back
on the warm sand and closed his eyes. He had seen it
all before.

After taking a few photos, Rachel decided to strip
down to her bikini and cool off. Leaving Tobias to
watch her belongings, she waded into the shallow
water. A few yards out it was deep enough to swim
and she wallowed in the warm sea, fascinated with
the brightly coloured fish which darted to and fro.

Dirk was having more luck on the kite board and
was heading out across the bay. She hoped he could
make his way back, then shrugged and lay on the
sand in the shade of a palm tree. Tobias would know
what to do if anything went wrong. She may as well
relax and enjoy the moment.

Rachel realized she had dozed off for a moment
because Dirk was suddenly beside her on the beach
elated from his experience. "That was choice. I hope
you got some good photos." He picked up a towel
and dried his dripping hair then headed for the toilets
to change his clothes. Rachel decided she was dry
enough and pulled on her shorts and singlet. Her
damp hair hung around her shoulders and she
toweled it dry.

"That is probably enough for today. I'll drop you
back in town and you can see me again in the

morning. I'll pick you up at your resort about nine o'clock. We'll be out all day so bring a drink and some sunscreen as well as a warm jacket."

Rachel was mystified. Why would you need a jacket in this warm climate? She was sure they would find out soon enough.

****

Tobias was in the parking lot a little after 10 next morning and Rachel had packed their jackets and drinks. Once again they were wearing their swimming gear under their clothing just in case.

Soon they were heading towards the main village and onto the wharf where several fishing boats and yachts were moored. Tobias had stopped to pick up some packed lunches so it wasn't hard to guess that they were to spend the day out on the water.

Joanne looked longingly at the sleek motor launches but Tobias led them further along the jetty until they came to an old cruising yacht which had seen better days. "My friend Thomas will take you out on his boat today. You will learn to sail and should catch yourselves a fish for lunch with any luck."

Thomas proved to be slim and dark with a trim beard and wore the inevitable flowered shirt. He took their bundles and placed them in the hold, then helped Rachel down into the boat.

The only boating experience she had had was trout fishing on a lake whereas it turned out that Dirk had once belonged to a sailing club back in Capetown. They settled onto a narrow wooden seat and put on life jackets while Thomas started up the motor. It hesitated for a moment and then roared into life.

Rachel hung on to the side of the boat as they motored away from the shore and out towards a gap in the reef from where they could access the open sea. It was all very well for Dirk to crave adventure but she wasn't sure that she really wanted to be part of it.

As they got close, the spray surged over the reef but once they were in the open sea, it was remarkably calm. Thomas prepared the sails for hoisting and turned off the motor. Rachel was amazed that Dirk seemed to know exactly what to do. She realized she knew very little about him. Soon they were powering through the water with just the wind in the sails. Without the motor it was very peaceful and Rachel began to enjoy herself.

"Okay. You can take a turn at the rudder. It's really easy, but don't turn too quickly or we might end up in the sea." Dirk changed places so that Rachel was in the stern of the boat holding the stout wooden handle.

As Dirk said, it wasn't difficult to steer the small craft and soon they were far enough from the shore to stop at what Thomas informed them was a great fishing spot. "If you don't catch something here, I'll swim back to shore," he joked.

Soon the anchor was thrown overboard, three fishing rods were baited and they all sat waiting for the first bite. There was a strong tug on Rachel's line. "I think I've got one," she gasped.

"Keep the line tight. Wind it in slowly. Good. That's the way." A few minutes later a medium sized snapper was scooped up in a net and landed in the boat. Rachel looked away as the fish was stunned and placed in the ice chest.

"It's not snapper we want. We need to go out a bit further." Thomas pulled up the anchor, started the engine and the boat slowly nosed its way through the water. A school of fish could be seen darting past the boat.

Thomas slowed the engine and put down the anchor. Soon they were trying their luck once again. Thomas was reeling in a good sized gurnard when Dirk felt a strong pull on his line. He let out his line and reeled it back in, playing with his catch. Thomas readied the net and five minutes later a yellow nosed tuna was brought aboard.

"Make sure you get this one on film." Dirk stood and held up his prize. It gleamed in the sunlight and Rachel made sure she captured the moment. Thomas decided that there was enough fish for a barbecue and pulled out a battered pan which he set on the grill which was attached to a gas bottle.

The filleted fish took a few minutes to cook and Rachel brought out the sandwiches that Tobias had supplied. There was a cool beer each to wash it all down. "This is the life," Dirk decided. "Warm sun, a calm sea and a fresh fish sandwich. What more could you ask for?"

"On the way back you can snorkel inside the reef if you wish." Thomas had brought along all the gear. Once again, Dirk was all for more action, but Rachel declined. She would try snorkeling in the shallow water near the resort.

The sun was setting as they motored up to the wharf where Tobias was waiting with the utility to take them back to the resort. As they had no way of cooking it, Dirk divided the tuna between the two men. "I wouldn't mind a sample next time we see you," he said as they were delivered safely back to their accommodation.

"I think you need a day to yourselves tomorrow. We will meet again the next day. You will probably know by then what else you would like to do."

Chapter 15

"Mike and Tracey want us to go on a picnic tomorrow," Joanne said as she sat close to Jason in the warm evening air. "Mike leaves on Monday as well so it would be good to all spend our last day together."

"Sure. Suits me. I just need to pack and that won't take me long." Jason looked around at his family and friends and knew he would miss these family gatherings when he returned to Wellington. Geoffrey was less sentimental and had gone off earlier to find his friend Samantha.

No-one was ready for the evening to end but eventually Madeline made a move and they began the job of clearing away the left-over food and dirty dishes. Steve placed the empty bottles in a container to go to the recycling depot and Stan helped stack the plastic chairs behind the garden shed.

"I guess I'll see you tomorrow." Jason was reluctant to let Joanne go, but at least they would have another day together. They kissed and drew apart.

"See you in the morning. I'm not sure where Mike is planning to take us, but be sure to bring swim gear along. We'll make the most of the time we have left." Joanne disappeared into the house before she broke down in tears. She went straight to her room and lay down on her bed.

She knew she loved Jason but she had to give him some space. He needed to be free to make new friends over the next few months, but there would be some long lonely nights to come.

Mike's car drew up early next morning. In fact, Joanne had scarcely got out of bed when the horn sounded and Tracey was waving out the window. "Come on, lazy bones. It's a gorgeous day and we want to make the most of it."

Mike went next door to find Jason while Joanne picked up the bag which she had packed the night before. Swim suit, sun block, towel, sunglasses. She added a water bottle and grabbed a buttered muffin from the bench. "Hey, that was my breakfast," her brother protested. He came to the door and noticed Tracey sitting in the car.

"You'll have to introduce me to the babe."

"She's taken for now, but you will meet her soon. You're going to be our escort for a while, big brother."

Soon they were in the car and heading for the surf beach a few kilometres along the coast. "We can hire boards when we get there. It's an awesome place." Mike was familiar with the wild, west coast.

The girls looked at each other. Surfing was not exactly their scene, but it would be a good chance to work on their tan. They drove out of the city and through fertile countryside where orchards and vineyards flourished. Half an hour later they had arrived. The black sand stretched out towards the churning ocean, the white-topped breakers crashing onto the shore. They spread their blankets on the grassy slope just above the water line.

Jason and Mike went across to the surf club where they hired two boards while Joanne and Tracey settled down in the sun. "It's been a great summer. I don't know how I feel about Mike going away. There's no commitment between us, but I'm going to miss him so much."

Joanne looked up at the white clouds above. "I feel the same way. I know I love Jason but we're not ready to settle down. He needs to go out with other girls while he's in Wellington. I wouldn't want to stand in his way."

"It's easier said than done. It's been so good to have someone to party with but I'm sure we'll be dating again soon." Tracey sat and watched the two guys paddling their boards out through the waves.

"Luckily my brother Bradin will be around to take us places for a while. He's got plenty of friends but I'm not sure whether they are your type." She thought about Bradin's building mates but wasn't sure that they would be a good match for Tracey.

"It feels a bit like the movie 'Grease'. I keep singing 'Summer Love' all around the house. Tracey laughed. "Let's not get morbid. Today is going to be great." They lay for a while and soaked up the sun's rays, then decided to cool off in the shallows.

Joanne ran down towards the waves but the water was cool and she ran back again. An extra high wave caught her by surprise and she was drenched. She splashed around, letting the water carry her in and out.

Tracey had headed further out where the surf was strong. Joanne caught sight of her once in a while and she could see Jason and Mike even further out waiting for the right wave to bring them in.

Not being much of a water person, Joanne returned to the grassed area and picked up her towel. She wished that Tracey would come back in. It made her uneasy to see her friend so far out in the surf. Luckily, the life guards were sitting on their stand, keeping an eye out for any trouble.

Joanne was just about to settle back down on the rug when the life guards jumped down and hauled their rubber boat into the water. She caught a glimpse of an arm raised in the air, a sign that someone was in trouble. She ran down to the water's edge to see what was going on.

Mike was close by on his surf board and he had seen the incident as well. He lay on the board and paddled frantically with his arms but made little headway. The small craft motored towards the stricken swimmer Could it be Tracey? Joanne was filled with dread. This lovely day out could turn into a disaster.

She could see someone being pulled into the rubber boat and next thing it was heading back to the shore. Mike had managed to control his board and arrived back at the same time.

The life guards helped Tracey from the boat and sat her on the sand. She was cold and exhausted but otherwise none the worse for her mishap. Joanne wrapped her in the blanket as the life guard checked her out.

"It's lucky you stayed inside the flags or we may not have noticed you. We'll take you back to the club house and get your details then we can offer you a warm drink if you would like it."

Joanne could see that Tracey was already feeling much better and was enjoying the attention from the handsome young life guard. A four wheel drive vehicle pulled up and Tracey and Mike hoisted themselves aboard. By this time Jason had caught a wave back to the beach and joined the group.

"We'll get the gear and meet you at the club house."

"Sure. The car keys are in my bag. We'll see you there."

Joanne was so relieved she put her arms around Jason and held him close. "Ugh. You're dripping wet." She released him and they laughed, releasing the tension. Jason found the keys and soon the car was packed with their belongings. They headed for the club rooms a short distance away.

"You return the surf boards and I'll take Tracey some clothes. She is probably feeling a bit under dressed by now." Joanne had already pulled a shirt over her bikini.

Half a dozen bronzed young surfers were lounging around in the large room which overlooked the beach and two guards were on duty on the wooden deck that ran along the front of the building. Joanne was still wrapped in the blanket and Mike was feeling a little foolish in his wet board shorts. He took his bag and disappeared into the changing room.

Once they were dried and dressed, everyone felt much better. Hot coffee was being served and Jason thanked the life guards profusely. "You guys do a great job. Everything happened so fast but you were right on to it."

"All in a day's work. But we do get angry when people deliberately swim in unpatrolled areas of the beach. There are so many holes and dangerous rips out there and the situation changes all the time." The senior life guard had taken down the details and entered them in the log book. "But all is well this time."

There was silence as Mike drove the car back up the hill and onto the main road. They were all a little shocked at what had happened to Tracey. She was sure she would have nightmares about being dragged out of her depth in the swirling current. It would be safe harbour beaches for her from now on.

"I know a quiet place where we can go and relax. We'll stop at a store and buy ourselves some food and then I'll take you there." Mike wanted to make up for the morning's incident.

They bought filled rolls and meat pies and a bottle of drink and were soon heading for a quiet little bay on the harbour side of the city. The tide was out and wading birds were foraging in the mud flats, but the sand was white and inviting. They settled under a Pohutakawa tree and shared out the food. Luckily one of the blankets was still dry and Joanne hung the wet gear over a tree branch.

"This is like being on our holiday again. I would love to go back there some time." They all agreed. The Coromandel holiday had been perfect. They would all remember the happy times over the months ahead.

****

Rachel was ready for a quiet time lying on a deck chair and snorkeling in the shallow water in front of the resort. She and Dirk had slept in that morning and made love as the sun shone through the curtains. They laughed as they shared the outdoor shower and soaped each other and made love again.

The breakfast was served in the beach-side restaurant and today they had time for bacon and eggs as well as the delicious fresh fruit that was readily available. Pineapple, melon, and papaya as well as bananas and the strange looking star shaped fruit.

A new group of tourists had arrived the night before and were excitedly planning their day's activities. Dirk thought this would be a perfect time to hire scooters from the shop beside the resort and Rachel agreed. They would lounge around all morning and head off in the afternoon.

Dirk needed some time to assemble his notes. He was also keen to get the films developed to see which photographs they would be able to use with the story. He knew he already had almost enough information but he would like to get together with a group of locals to experience some music or dance. He was sure that Tobias would be able to arrange something.

After a leisurely morning, Dirk led the way to the office across the parking lot where the rental vehicles were kept. The paper work seemed endless but after a time, he and Rachel both had a bright red motor scooter to use for the afternoon.

"We'll go through the village and leave our films to be developed then head for the back road. There are apparently some interesting gardens and plantations along there."

The town was busy with visitors wandering about in the heat and locals sitting around in the shade. Rachel had never ridden a scooter but after a short time, she felt confident. It was good to feel the breeze in her hair as she followed Dirk along the narrow road.

Sure enough, the luscious vegetation stretched up towards the mountainous interior of the island, with bananas, taro and citrus mingled with brightly coloured flowering bushes. The houses were partly hidden by the thick foliage. Most were small and built from concrete or sheets of iron with open porches around three sides.

Several homes had not been replaced following a recent tropical storm, leaving a deserted shell with no roof or windows which would soon be overgrown with invasive plants.

They passed schools where children played in the spacious grounds, neat and tidy in their uniforms. Rugby and soccer appeared to be favourite sports. Back on the main road, they were soon back at the lagoon beach where Dirk had kite boarded a short time before.

They left their bikes in the car park and walked down to the water's edge. Their attention was caught by a group of dancers, resplendent in native costume, swaying to the music from a guitar and drum. "Oh look, they're making a film," Rachel said.

Dirk pulled out his camera to capture the moment. It wasn't every day you met a group of gorgeous dancers on the beach. They watched for a while as the dancers stopped and started their routine at the cameraman's request. Rachel found herself swaying to the beat, until she sat beneath a tree fanning herself with a leafy frond.

"Come on. Let's cool off." Dirk pulled off his shorts and raced for the water in his boxers. Rachel stripped down to her bikini and followed suit. They lay in the clear water for a time, then dried off in the sun on the almost deserted beach. The dancing group had left and there was no-one in sight.

"We could do it right here on the sand." Dirk was on fire. He pulled Rachel into his arms. "Why not?"

Rachel heard herself saying and next thing they were holding each other closer. His hands were on her breasts and she pulled her bikini off in one movement. He entered her and thrust strongly. At the last minute Rachel realized Dirk hadn't used protection, but she was past caring, caught up in the heat of the moment.

They rolled over and stayed in each other's arms. They were still alone with just the sound of the waves and the sun warming their naked bodies. Rachel was the first to move. She hastily pulled on her bikini and sat up reluctantly.

"I think we should go back to the resort. I feel like making love all afternoon."

Dirk gathered himself together. "I'm sorry. I don't know what came over me. We'll go back and return the bikes and let the rest of the day take care of itself."

The resort was a short ride away and Rachel realized that she was hungry. They settled for seafood and salad with crispy bread rolls which they ate with relish. Rachel ordered another exotic looking cocktail and Dirk chose a local beer. With the sound of the surf lulling their senses, they relaxed on the lounges and soon fell asleep under the palms.

****

Once they had eaten their lunch, Jason and Joanne were content to lie close together on the blanket. It wasn't long before they realized that they were alone. Mike and Tracey had wandered off and Joanne had a feeling that it would be some time before they reappeared. The events of the morning had shaken her. Life was so precious and every moment should be appreciated.

She cuddled closer to Jason and felt his body stiffening against her. Why had she resisted him? She wanted him now and knew he felt the same way. He kissed her deeply and pulled her towards him.

"I am going to miss you so much." His voice was husky. His hand found her breasts and she pulled her bikini aside. Next thing he was astride her and she was more than willing. He stopped long enough to use a condom and then his hands were all over her body and she was responding. They had waited too long for this moment.

They climaxed together and Joanne pulled the blanket over their naked bodies. She would be so embarrassed if their friends came back and found them like this.

Chapter 16

With her sons back in Wellington, Flo O'Connor was feeling restless. She felt sorry for Joanne who had seemed despondent as she said her final goodbyes to Jason. For good or bad, that friendship had developed into something really special and Flo knew that Joanne was in for some lonely times.

She couldn't forget the names on the death certificate and was itching to try to locate the parents of the poor dead Jennifer. She decided to take action and called at the local post office where she knew she could find a Waikato phone book. How long would it take to locate Donald and Jean Blake?

Flo felt a surge of excitement as she read through the listings. There were several Blake families living in and around Hamilton. She found two D Blakes but no mention of a Jean. She noted down the addresses and phone numbers. She didn't want to contact them directly but would persuade Stan to drive her to Hamilton so she could check out the addresses.

It took some persuading but the following weekend they were heading along the highway that led to Hamilton. "I hope you know what you are doing, my dear. I feel we might raise issues that have been long forgotten."

"I'll be careful Stan. There's no way I want to upset anyone." Flo was determined to find out what she could. They drove past the first address. The house was probably built around the 1950s and looked a little dilapidated. The garden was overgrown and newspapers were piling up around the mail box.

"I want to find out who lives here." Before Stan could stop her, Flo was out of the car and walking up the path. She knocked at the door but there was no answer. She tried again but got no response.

She started walking back to the car when a face appeared over the fence. "You won't get any response there. Donald Blake left after his wife Jean died. He's probably staying with his son."

Flo thanked the woman and returned to the car. "We can cross that one off. Maybe we'll have more luck at the next address."

The next house on the list was in a much newer part of town. The houses were well kept and when they pulled up outside the address, there were several children playing in the yard. A little boy stared at Flo as she got out of the car.

This time a young woman opened the door almost immediately. She called out to the children to stay in the yard and looked curiously at Flo. "Can I help you? If it's about the elections we have already voted."

"Sorry to disturb you but I'm looking for an old school friend. His name is Donald Blake and I wonder if he lives at this address." Flo had her story all sorted out.

"We've three Donald Blakes living here. My husband, my son, that's him on the climbing frame, and Donald's father who is staying with us for a while. By the way, I'm Barbara Blake."

"Was Donald married to a Jean Ingram? The person I knew came over from Scotland back in the '50s and had a daughter named Jennifer."

There was a silence for a moment, then Barbara said: "I think you had better come inside. We can talk about it in comfort." She led the way into a hall with toys piled in boxes along the edge. "Don't trip over. With four kids there isn't much space."

The lounge was tidier, and Flo sat on the couch with Barbara beside her. "Dad isn't home just now. He's gone to the senior club for a game of bowls. He's had a hard time since Jean died a few weeks ago."

"That is sad. He's lucky he has you to look after him."

"I don't know how long he will stay. The house is very crowded and the children are too much for him, but we are doing our best."

"When I knew them they only had a daughter. They must have had more children later. The reason I want to talk to him is that we would like to know what happened to Jennifer. We believe she died about 20 years ago. Do you know the circumstances of her death?"

"There were two boys born quite some time after the girl. I've never heard anyone talk about her. Even my husband doesn't seem to know what happened to her. It's almost as if she didn't exist."

"That's a shame. She was such a pretty bright eyed little thing when we knew them. Do you think your father-in-law might be able to tell me more about her? It's really important to someone I know."

"I can't think why anyone would be interested after all this time. But leave your address and I'll talk to Dad about it when he gets in. If he knows any more I can get in touch." Barbara stood and looked out the window to check on the children. "I don't want the little rascals going out on the street," she said.

Flo stood and thanked the younger woman. It looked as though she would learn nothing more today. As she walked out through the hallway, she glanced at the family photos hanging on the wall. Barbara and Donald's wedding, several baby photos and right at the end was an old photograph of two little boys and an older girl. It had possibly been hand coloured and Flo couldn't believe what she was seeing.

The girl in the photo was the image of Joanne, same light brown hair, fine features and enormous grey/green eyes. Flo stared in astonishment, tears coming into her eyes. Barbara noticed her reaction and waited for a moment. "Yes, that's Jennifer when she was just a teenager. The boys were younger as you can see. She was beautiful, wasn't she?"

Flo didn't know what to say. Should she ask for a copy of the photograph? She would dearly love to show it to Joanne. Barbara must have sensed what she was thinking. "If you wait a minute, there is a black and white copy of that photo in an album that Donald's mother gave me just before she died. In fact, there are several photos of Jennifer when I come to think about it."

Flo couldn't believe her luck. She knew that Stan would be getting impatient but she had to look at the photos in the album. Somehow, Joanne would also have to see them.

The album had been placed in a drawer and it only took Barbara a short time to find it. "Here you are. I'll just check on the children while you are looking at the photos. Take your time. They will probably bring back memories of the time you knew Donald and Jean."

Flo felt like a fraud as she had certainly never known Donald Blake or his wife, but she sat down and turned the pages in the small album. The photos were stuck onto black paper with names and dates carefully written beneath.

The first few pages were of a wedding, which Flo guessed would have been Jennifer's parents, then a few baby pictures, with a bonny bright eyed little girl smiling at the camera. A few pages later there were two and then, three little ones and as they grew up their lives were all documented.

Flo felt so sad that Joanne had missed out on knowing her birth family. There must be something she could do. As she turned the last page, a copy of the photograph that she had seen on the wall was loosely attached. It came away in her hand and Flo held it gently. This would mean so much to Joanne.

"Would you like to keep that one?" Barbara had come in quietly and realized that the picture meant something to Flo.

"Yes please. I will treasure it. Please ask Jennifer's father if he has anything he can tell me. Maybe I'll catch him some other time."

"I do hope so. I'll tell him you called. He'll be sorry he missed you. It's a pity that your trip was wasted."

Flo turned and took her hand. "Today has been quite special and I'd really like to see you again." She walked quickly away and burst into tears as she climbed into the car.

"What's this all about, love.? Don't go upsetting yourself. I said we should have left things alone."

"I'm not upset. I'm just happy." She showed her husband the photograph. "I didn't really learn anything, but look what I have for our Joanne."

****

Joanne was glad that her job was keeping her so busy. What with teaching all day and preparation each evening, she had little time to think about Jason. He had sent her a post card from the airport in Wellington, saying he missed her already. She smiled as she taped it to the mirror on her dressing table.

Flo had been giving her some funny looks over the past few days and Joanne wondered what that was all about. She knew that Flo and Stan would be missing their boys so she decided to call over on Friday night before accompanying her parents to their club for fish and chips and a night of Bingo.

Flo had opened a bottle of wine and poured Joanne a glass as soon as she saw her. "Come in, my dear. I had a call from Jason. He's much better at keeping in touch than his brother. They are settling in fine but he misses us all. Anyway, enough about that. I'm glad you called because I've something to show you."

Joanne took the wine and followed Flo into the living room where she sat on the couch. Flo went to the cabinet and came back with something in her hand. "Stan drove me to Hamilton last weekend and we found a Blake family. I wasn't sure whether they were the right ones until I saw this."

She handed the photograph to Joanne who looked at it in amazement. "That girl looks a lot like me and who are the little boys?"

"There's no doubt in my mind that this is your poor dead mother. The little boys are her brothers, which makes them your uncles." Joanne didn't know whether to laugh or cry.

"Did you meet her parents? What did they have to say?"

Flo explained what had happened during the visit and how she came to have the photograph. "Donald Blake is still alive and living with his son at present. He sounds like a sad, lonely old man. I left an address and I'm sure young Barbara will be in touch. I'd love you to see the rest of the photos."

She gave Joanne a hug. "I hope this is not too upsetting for you. To find you have living relatives must be a bit of a shock, and then of course, there are all those other children who are probably your cousins. My, what a lot for you to take in." She refilled Joanne's glass.

"I can't stay too long as we are off to the club. I'll show this to Mum when we get home otherwise it might spoil her concentration for Bingo." Joanne finished her drink and went back to her house. She left the photo on her bed and joined her parents who were almost ready to leave. "Come along Joanne. We need to get to the club early to get a good table."

Joanne hadn't played Bingo before but found it quite entertaining. Unfortunately several people were lighting up cigarettes and the room soon filled with smoke. Her eyes began to smart but Madeline and Steve didn't seem to notice. They were still trying to win a game.

"I'll just go and get some air." Joanne pushed her way through the crowd and found a seat in the foyer. Several people acknowledged her as they walked by. They all knew Steve and Madeline's daughter.

It was times like this that she was going to miss Jason the most. Bradin had gone out with his workmates to celebrate their first week on the job and Tracey had phoned to say she was going to her parents' house for the weekend.

She wandered back and Madeline caught her eye. "One last chance and we're off," she said. The numbers were called and the prize was claimed. No luck for the Bennett family tonight.

Steve drove home carefully and Madeline put the jug on to make a cup of tea. She looked tired after a busy week so Joanne decided to go straight to her room and read for a while. The photograph would keep until tomorrow.

****

With so much going on, their time in Rarotonga flew by. After 10 days of strenuous activities, food and love making, Rachel sat back in her seat on the plane and closed her eyes. Dirk had gathered enough information to write half a dozen travel articles, and they had several packets of photographs to choose from. He had made friends with several of the other guests and was often the centre of attention as he shared his experiences of travelling around the world.

"I feel really boring some times," she complained. "You seem to have done so much with your life, while I just work for a dull little newspaper."

Dirk smoothed the hair back from her face. "You're beautiful and I love you. That's all that matters." He liked to be the centre of attention but knew that Rachel preferred to remain invisible.

"It really has been an incredible few days. It's hard to believe we'll be back home in a few hours." Rachel held Dirk's hand and smiled. "If Julie isn't back soon, I wonder if you would like to be my flat mate? I'll need to get someone in so maybe it could be you."

Dirk put his arm around her shoulders. "That's the best offer I've had in years. I'll have to seriously think about it."

The flight attendant came by and smiled at Dirk. "Can I offer you a drink?" The trolley was laden with an assortment of beverages. "A beer would be nice and a white wine for my girl friend."

She poured the drinks and looked at Dirk again. "Let me know if there's anything else I can do for you."

Rachel almost choked on her first sip. "Let me know if there's anything else I can do for you," she mimicked. "I didn't realise you were such a lady killer, Dirk. You have all the women eating out of your hand."

Dirk blushed and looked innocent. "I don't do anything. I can't help it if they fancy me." They laughed and sipped their drink, but Rachel knew that she would have her hands full keeping up with Dirk.

It was after 10 o'clock that night before they arrived back at Rachel's apartment. There was no sign of Julie so they fell into bed together and slept through the night. They weren't due back at work for two more days so there was no need to get up early.

Rachel had asked her neighbour to collect the mail and she was anxious to check it. There was a letter from her mother and one from Julie to say that she had decided to stay home and work from there for a while. "I'm sorry not to give you any warning but I couldn't bear the thought of living in Auckland without Nick. If I owe you any rent money please let me know."

Rachel picked up an envelope with an embossed seal on the front. "I wonder what this is all about. It looks very official."

"It can't be a parking ticket as you don't own a car. Come on, let's see what it's all about." Dirk was curious. Rachel pulled out an invitation. "We have been invited to a dinner at Mr Greg Forman's home. Look. It says, Rachel Saunders and partner. Would you like to come along?"

"Yes, I can hardly wait to meet the beautiful Mrs Forman again. I think she fancies me." Dirk was teasing.

"I have the same feeling about Greg Forman. He finds me fascinating." Rachel was keen to get her own back.

Rachel opened the letter from her mother. Marjorie Saunders didn't often write, she usually preferred to telephone. It was just a quick note and Rachel turned to Dirk with a sigh. "Oh dear, my mother has decided to pay me a visit. She says she has something important to discuss with me but I'm sure she just wants to check out my living arrangements."

"I can go back to my flat while she is here. I haven't given notice there yet." Dirk didn't want to be living with Rachel when her mother came to stay. He wasn't ready for a parental inspection yet.

Rachel phoned the number on the Formans' invitation to confirm that they would be accepting the dinner offer. Gaynor Forman answered the phone and said she would be pleased to meet them again. "Greg is trying to attract the younger voters. There will be several guests around your age. It won't just be boring old council members."

She came off the phone and turned to Greg. "That was Rachel. You'll be pleased to know that she and her boyfriend are coming to our dinner party."

"Great. I want her to meet Pete from the television channel. It could lead to something, you never know." Greg was sure that Rachel would be perfect as a television journalist. She had the voice and the looks to become a star. Why did she remind him so much of his first love, Jenny, who had disappeared so suddenly.

They had met when her family arrived from Scotland. Her father was to work at the Forman chemical factory as an engineer and they were introduced at a party to welcome the new employees.

At 18, Greg was in his last year of school and was fascinated with this beautiful girl with her long fair hair and perfect Scottish complexion. She agreed to be his partner at the end of year dance and they spent time together, going to movies and hanging out like typical teenagers.

There was lots of kissing and cuddling but Greg was careful not to go too far, except for one special night when they were alone in his parents' house.

They watched a movie on television and he took a bottle of wine from the fridge. It all became a little vague after that. Greg recalled that their love making became very intense and he hadn't been wearing any protection. It was over so quickly, surely nothing would go wrong.

He started at business college the following year and she bid him a tearful farewell. There were a few cards and letters and then silence. He hoped to see her when he returned for the Easter break but the family had moved. Her father no longer worked for the chemical company.

Young love is a painful time and he kept her photograph in his wallet for several months, but she didn't get in touch and he had no idea where she had gone. His father seemed reluctant to talk about the family. He would change the subject quickly if Jennifer was ever mentioned. It was years later, after his father died, that he discovered the tragic truth.

Greg's thoughts were rudely interrupted when his son Martin came into the room. "Gaynor says I must stay in tonight. Why does she treat me like a child? My mother would have let me go out and meet my friends."

Greg sighed. His son was becoming quite a trial. "You know very well that your mother would not let you out at this time of night. Come on. We can watch a game together and tomorrow I'll give you a driving lesson."

"Choice. When can I have a car of my own? All my mates have got one." Martin decided it was best to cooperate with his father. He would be 16 soon and old enough to have a driver's licence.

He had enjoyed the weekends he spent with his father until that woman had come along. Now all Dad wanted to do was please his beloved Gaynor. He hoped they wouldn't make a baby. That would be too gross.

He settled down with a can of coke to watch the cricket. Fifty-over matches weren't too bad and he was hoping to make his college team next season. Spin bowling was his specialty and his coach had high hopes for him.

Gaynor smiled when she looked in and saw Greg and his son watching the match together. She knew that Martin was testing her but she was determined she would not spoil him. She wondered how he would react when they told him the news.

Her pregnancy had been confirmed and the baby was due sometime in August. Even though he was close to 40, Greg had been overjoyed when she told him the news. He had missed out on so much of Martin's childhood after the divorce and was looking forward to being a full-time dad.

Now Gaynor had a dinner party to organise. It was planned for the following Friday and she had arranged for caterers to come in. They would do the work and all she would need to do was be charming to the guests. Greg was certainly taking his election campaign seriously and she hoped he would be successful.

She decided to have an early night and let the boys enjoy their cricket match. She gave Greg a quick kiss on the forehead and said good night. Martin ignored her, but she was getting used to that.

"I'll be up later. I've promised to take Martin for a driving lesson tomorrow, but if there's anything you want to do just say." Greg was eager to keep the peace. He hoped that in time his son would grow to love Gaynor as much as he did. They would need to tell him about the new baby soon.

Chapter 17

With the school term well underway, Joanne was looking forward to the Easter break and hoped that Jason would make it home for the holidays. She received a letter most weeks but he hadn't told her what his plans were.

Bradin had borrowed their father's car and they had driven to the city a couple of times. Tracey came along as well but when Bradin could see that he was getting nowhere he preferred to hang out with his own mates.

The school principal was pleased with her work and congratulated her on the way her classroom was organized. "I hope you will stay on with us next year as well," she said. Today Joanne was preparing some activities at her desk as the class listened to the news of the day. Several children had taken turns and Joanne could see that young Scott was keen to be next.

"Okay. One last chance. You can have a turn Scott. You have been very patient." She carried on with her task, half listening to what Scott had to say.

He held up a page from a newspaper and pointed excitedly to a photograph. "I said to my Mum that this is our teacher and she said, 'Are you sure?' And I said, 'Course it is. But she didn't tell us she had been to Rarotonga'." He stumbled over the word.

Joanne took a closer interest. "My dad said, "If that's your teacher, she can teach me a thing or two anytime."" Scott was in full steam now.

"What's this about me being in Rarotonga? I wish I was so lucky. Show me the newspaper Scott. I think you must have got it wrong." Scott had found a travel article about Rarotonga and Joanne gasped when she saw the photographs. The girl silhouetted against a turquoise sea certainly could have been her, and she was pictured again beside a huge bunch of bananas. She searched for a byline. The writer was Dirk Kloeten and there were photographs of a tall blond-haired guy pulling in a huge fish and carving an oyster shell.

"Can I borrow this for a while? The girl is not me, but we certainly look alike." She would share this with her friend Fiona during the morning break. When Fiona saw the photo, she gasped. "Joanne, are you sure that's not you? If you had a blond rinse you would look exactly like that."

"I know. This girl is starting to haunt me. I think it's time to do something about it." Joanne couldn't live with the uncertainty much longer. She should try to contact Dirk Kloeten and find out who her look-alike was.

She wished that Jason was around to help her. He would know what to do. She still hadn't shown her mother the picture that Flo had brought back from Hamilton. Maybe tonight would be the right time.

Joanne's parents were astonished when they saw the travel article and Madeline looked quite shocked when Joanne showed her the photograph. "That looks just like you did a few years ago. It certainly seems as if you have found your mother."

Joanne gave her a hug. "You'll always be my mother. No-one else could ever take your place, certainly not a young girl who has been dead for 20 years."

"But think about it, Joanne. You may have a grandfather and two brothers living barely an hour away. They probably don't know you exist."

"Perhaps it's better to keep it that way. They may not know what happened to Jennifer and her secret should probably have died with her. They would just be strangers to me. I don't really want to pursue this any further."

"You're probably right. But it would be interesting to meet this girl and hear her story. Surely there is no harm in that."

Joanne felt confused. How could you go up to a complete stranger and suggest she was your twin sister? She would write to Jason tonight and ask his advice.

****

When Rachel and Dirk arrived at the Formans' home the party was in full swing. Greg had brought together a number of people from a variety of organisations and Rachel recognised some that she had interviewed in the past. She was sure that the dark girl had won a debating contest and the tall boy with glasses had been top student of his high school.

She wondered what she and Dirk could contribute to such a gathering. Greg pulled her aside and introduced her to an older man with balding hair and a crooked smile.

"Pete, this is the girl I was telling you about. She's an excellent journalist and the cameras would love her."

Rachel was taken aback. She remembered Greg mentioning a friend who worked in television but didn't expect to see him here.

"Hi Rachel. I'm pleased to meet you. Greg has been hinting that we should try you out on the small screen. I agree. I think you have just the right look for the job."

"I'm not so sure. I thought all presenters had to be beautiful and blond." Rachel laughed in embarrassment.

"I wasn't thinking so much about the presenter in the studio with the perfect hair and makeup. I can see you out in the street interviewing someone, your hair blowing around your face." Pete spoke with enthusiasm. "How about we arrange a screen test to see how you would look."

Dirk had been listening to the conversation. "Go for it Rachel. You know the cameras would love you."

Gaynor had been listening in as well. "I think you would be great, Rachel. By the way, we read the travel piece on Rarotonga. It was very well done." She smiled at Dirk. "It made me want to go there one day that's for sure."

The caterers had been busy and delicious finger food was being handed around along with excellent wine and a fruit punch. It wasn't long before Greg announced that the meal was ready and they could take their seats. Place names had been set out on the long wooden table and Rachel found herself seated between Pete and the debating champion. Dirk was directly opposite between a tall athletic looking girl and a well-known rugby player.

Greg welcomed them and explained that he had invited them because they all showed great skill in their job, or sport or pastime. "You are the type of people we want running this country in the future and the place to start is right here in your own community."

Pete smiled at Rachel. "I think the man is seeking support as well. Younger people often don't bother to vote."

"Fair enough. But I won't be writing about this dinner. Greg has already had his share of publicity in our newspaper." She could see Dirk in conversation with the tall girl and wondered who she was.

"Jo is a champion discus thrower and hopes to make it into the Commonwealth games. Greg has invited some interesting guests tonight."

Rachel turned to make conversation with the girl seated beside her. She seemed rather shy considering she had won a debating contest. "It's a lot easier when you're on the stage with a topic you have learned about. It's a bit scary talking to strangers on a personal level," the young girl confided.

"I know how you feel. Just because I write for a newspaper doesn't make it easy for me in social situations." She glanced at Pete. "Now this man thinks I can stand in front of a camera talking to the nation."

The courses were being served as they chatted, with seafood starters followed by lamb racks and minted vegetables. Dirk caught Rachel's eye and gave her a wink, then turned his attention to the rugby player.

A variety of desserts were set on a long table at the side of the room along with chocolate mints and coffee. Rachel had enjoyed two glasses of red wine with her meal as well as the champagne beforehand.

She caught up with Dirk at the dessert table. "That was so good. Just like being back in Raro again." They moved to an outdoor room to enjoy their dessert. It was a chance to talk with the other guests. Greg took the opportunity to stand beside Rachel. "I hope you will take Pete's offer seriously. I know he thinks you would have a good chance of getting into television. That's where the future lies."

Rachel had already decided to take Pete up on his offer. There was no harm in having the screen test. It could be an interesting experience. "Yes, thanks for arranging it. I will certainly give it a go."

She saw Gaynor approaching and smiled in her direction. "This has been such a lovely evening Gaynor. Thank you so much for inviting us."

"We are so pleased you could come and we want you to visit us again. You would be most welcome at any time. Now, if you'll excuse me, I need to sit and rest for a while.'

"Are you feeling all right my dear. Sit down and I'll bring you a cool drink. You have worked so hard tonight." Greg was full of concern. He didn't want his wife to be overdoing things.

Rachel looked around to see where Dirk had disappeared to. It was probably time they headed home. She didn't want to out stay their welcome. Dirk was having another drink at the bar and deep in conversation with Pete.

"I hope you have decided to try out for television. Just think. You could become a household name." Dirk was enthusiastic about the idea.

"That's the part I wouldn't like. Imagine having no privacy and people wanting your autograph everywhere you went." The idea didn't appeal to Rachel at all, but she found herself agreeing to meet Pete at the studio the following week.

Dirk was reluctant to leave but most of the guests were heading for the door where Greg was instructing them to drive home safely. Rachel waved to Gaynor who was still sitting on the couch. "I hope Gaynor is okay. She looked a bit tired and pale."

Dirk hadn't really noticed. "I'm sure there'll be a team of servants to do the cleaning up. Greg and Gaynor sure know how to lead the good life."

When she got home, Rachel couldn't get the thought of Gaynor out of her head. She had looked so fragile and Greg had been very concerned. She tossed and turned until Dirk held her tight. "What's wrong? You're kind of restless tonight."

Rachel didn't want to share her concerns with Dirk. She just had this feeling that something was wrong. She lay still and eventually fell asleep. The next day was Saturday and she was due to cover a hall opening a short drive out of town. She would need to pick up the work car and return it on Monday.

Dirk was interviewing a couple who had holidayed in the outback of Australia so would be out all morning. "I'll just phone Greg and Gaynor and thank them for the wonderful dinner," she said.

Rachel picked up the phone and dialed the number. It rang for a while then an answering machine kicked in. All she could do was leave a message and hope that someone would return her call.

Armed with her notebook and camera she walked the short distance to the office and unlocked the car which was in the parking lot. It shouldn't take too long to take a few notes, record the cutting of the ribbon and there was sure to be a special cake to photograph.

The organizers were fussing about when she arrived and she was given a seat in the front row. First there was a Maori blessing and then the hall chairman made a speech. Rachel made sure she was in a good position for the ribbon cutting ceremony. So many times the task was done so quickly she would almost miss the moment.

She mingled with the guests and sampled the morning tea. "I thought I saw your photo on the travel pages. The girl looked a lot like you." A woman had been looking at her curiously.

"Yes, I must admit that I have just returned from Rarotonga. It was a gorgeous place to visit."

"It must have been very hot. We normally go later in the year, but you seemed to get a good look around the island. It was an interesting article."

Rachel drove home thinking about the good time they had had. She knew she needed to find another job. There must be something more interesting than attending hall openings.

When she arrived home the first thing she did was check the answering machine. Sure enough, there was a message from Greg Forman. "Thanks for the call. Phone me when you get back."

Dirk was still out working so Rachel dialed Greg's number. He answered almost immediately. "Thanks for calling Rachel. It's very sweet of you. We've had a bit of a fright. This is just between you and me, but Gaynor is about 12 weeks pregnant and wasn't feeling well last night. She's in hospital with a threatened miscarriage. The doctors are hopeful that the baby is still okay. She just needs to rest for a while."

Rachel wasn't sure what to say. "I was so worried about Gaynor. She looked tired last night. I do hope she will be all right and not lose the baby. I certainly won't say anything about it."

"I'm going back to see her soon. I'll pass on the message. Thanks very much for the call. I was supposed to be at a hall opening this morning but I'm sure the event went ahead without me."

"I can tell you that the hall was dutifully opened and everybody seemed happy. A couple of the other candidates were there but you can't be everywhere."

"That's been the problem. Gaynor and I have attended too many functions lately and she is quite worn out. Only a week to go before the votes are counted and I will know my fate."

****

A letter arrived for Joanne and she opened it excitedly and took it up to her room. The good news was that Jason was coming home for the Easter break. He and Geoffrey were able to share a ride back to Auckland with one of the other students. She had told him about the photograph of Jennifer Blake and he said he was looking forward to seeing it.

"We'll visit William and see if he has any more information for us. I'm sure looking forward to seeing you again."

Joanne picked up the photograph of Jennifer and studied it for the umpteenth time. The girl looked up at her with those large vivid eyes. Her shoulder-length hair was held back from her face with a wide band. She wore a knitted cardigan over a white blouse with a collar.

The two little boys looked solemn. They both had longish hair and wore dark grey shirts, probably their school uniform. Joanne knew that one of them was named Donald. What was the other boy's name? Were they really still living as close as Hamilton? Maybe she should write to them. She could enclose a photograph of herself and leave it up to them to get in touch.

Madeline called out to say that dinner was ready so Joanne took Jason's letter down to share the good news. Steve had just arrived in from work and Bradin was working late. "Have you worked out who you are going to vote for?" Madeline had been checking through the voting papers which had arrived by mail a few days before. "They need to be sent in this week."

Steve said he liked the look of a couple of the candidates but would probably stick with the ones he knew. Joanne hadn't really thought about it. She would look through the names tonight and make a decision.

"I'll go over and see Flo after dinner. I wonder if she knows the boys are coming home for Easter. She will be so pleased to see them. I know she and Stan are really missing them."

"We are so blessed to have our family with us." Madeline smiled at her husband. "We're very lucky, aren't we, dear."

"You're right. There aren't many parents as fortunate as we are, but one day it will be just the two of us. As long as you are close enough to visit it will be okay, not half way across the world like so many young ones these days."

As soon as she had finished dinner and helped her mother with the dishes, Joanne picked up the election forms. A short description of each candidate accompanied the voting papers. There were eight positions to be filled and 12 names to choose from.

Two men and a woman were standing for mayor and the others would fill the council seats. She ran her eye down the list. She had read some of their details in the local papers but most of the names meant nothing to her.

Maybe a mixture of old and new would be best, and she definitely wanted at least two women to be voted in. She had soon selected six candidates and hovered over the remainder. Greg Forman sounded interesting but so did four of the others.

"What do you thing, Mum? Do you know anything about this Greg Forman?"

"He owns a big company and has a very beautiful wife. I've read about him in the news. I like his ideas about improving conditions at hospitals, especially for young pregnant women."

A picture of young Jennifer flashed into Joanne's mind. Yes, she would vote for Mr Forman if it helped prevent another tragedy like that one. She completed the form and placed it in the envelope.

"Right, I won't be long. I'll just be over next door."

Madeline smiled. "Our daughter is so happy that young Jason will be home again soon. I do hope he feels the same way she does. I wouldn't like to see her heart broken."

"They're young. There's plenty of time for them to play the field before they settle down. Now come on my dear, the television is waiting."

Chapter 18

A few days before the Easter break Rachel's mother phoned to say that she would be arriving on Good Friday and staying until the following week. She hoped that would be all right.

"It looks as though you might have to move out and stay with your friends, although it doesn't really bother me if my mother sees you here. After all I am old enough to make my own living arrangements." Rachel didn't really want Dirk to leave.

"I know, but the apartment is a bit small for three people. It would be better for you to be with your mother. I'll probably spend most of the time here anyway, and we're bound to take her out and about while she's here."

"Okay, as long as you don't leave me with her too much of the time. I find my mother a little over bearing at times."

Rachel was looking forward to the break. The results of the elections would be out tomorrow and she knew the paper would want interviews with the successful candidates. She had spoken to Greg Forman, and his wife was feeling a lot better. She was resting at home and they would be glad when the election campaign was over.

"You must come around for the victory party. But we will have to make sure Gaynor does nothing but sit around looking decorative." Greg was quietly confident that he would win a council seat.

The appointment at the television studio had been fascinating. Pete and the cameraman had made Rachel feel at ease and had her chatting to Dirk about their trip to Rarotonga. She hardly knew she was being filmed. Next they set up a whiteboard with some short news items written in large letters.

"Now you are reading the latest news, Rachel. Go over it a few times and then we will video it. Hopefully it won't look as though you are reading it." Rachel felt strange at first but soon relaxed and began to enjoy the experience. She had been so nervous but once she started to read she felt more confident.

When it was over, Pete shook her hand. "That was very good Rachel. We'll edit the film then get you to come back and take a look."

Early next morning Rachel was on the phone early. She had to contact her editor to find out the election results and then get hold of the new mayor and councilors for their reaction. Bill Osborne read off the names from the information he had received and Rachel cheered aloud when she found that Greg Forman had been successful. He had polled the third highest number of votes and Rachel could hardly wait to catch up with him to offer her congratulations.

For the first time, a woman had won the mayoral race and that would make an interesting story. Three of the longest serving candidates were back but all the others would be councilors for the first time.

"I've got a busy week ahead of me. Luckily I brought the car home last night. With the Easter holiday, the newspaper has to be finished by Thursday and then of course, my mother arrives on Friday." Rachel said a hasty goodbye to Dirk and rushed out of the apartment.

Dirk knew he would have to tidy away his gear and pack a few things to take to his mates' house. He had moved in with Rachel as soon as they were back from their trip but there was space with his friends if he ever needed to stay there.

He wasn't really looking forward to meeting Rachel's mother. She sounded like a real dragon but he would do his best to charm her. He wanted to make a good impression.

His schedule was not as busy as Rachel's. The travel supplement came out with the daily paper once a month and as long as he organized enough interesting stories to fill it, his boss was happy. He had been pleased with the Rarotongan story and the travel agency had promised to send him to another destination soon.

Rachel was still waiting to hear back from the studio and Dirk really hoped that she would be able to move into television journalism. He had watched her audition and was sure she would receive good news soon.

Dirk knew they were likely to be invited back to Greg Forman's house tonight for a celebratory drink. In the meantime he had work to do.

Rachel's day was going smoothly. She had managed to catch up with three of the successful local body candidates and now she was on her way to the Forman home. When she knocked on the door she was surprised when it was opened by a handsome teenager who showed her into the house.

"Hi Rachel. This is my son Martin. He wanted to share all the excitement today. I hope you and Dirk can come by about five o'clock for a quick drink. I'm sorry you missed Gaynor. She's just gone up for a nap as we will be entertaining a few guests later." Greg gave Rachel a knowing look and she didn't ask any further questions.

"I just need a comment about your success. You did well to gain so many votes. I'm sure you are delighted with the result."

"Yes, as I said before there a few issues I want to work on. I'm worried about the effect the proposed bypass will have on businesses and residents in the affected areas and would like to see more done to improve road safety around schools."

"You mentioned something about safer medical practices for women when I last spoke to you. Have you got anything further to add to those comments?"

"I think I got sidetracked onto that issue when I first met you. As I said, you reminded me of someone I was once very fond of. I doubt that same situation would apply today. I think that pregnant women in this city are now well provided for."

Rachel smiled. "I take it that your wife is well and the situation we discussed before is no longer a problem."

"Okay, off the record, Gaynor will have to be careful for the next few weeks but hopefully everything is back to normal. I trust you not to let the cat out of the bag, Rachel. I know it would make a good story but I only told you about her condition as I knew I could trust you. Even my son hasn't been told the news yet."

"Sure. There's no need for anyone to know at this stage. You will announce the good news when you are ready." Rachel promised to be back at five o'clock and she set off back to the office. There were a lot of notes to type before the end of the day.

****

There had been several changes in the law office since the new clerk had moved in. For a start she was around 50 years old, with dyed blond hair and long finger nails. Ted Baker had looked quite shocked when she first walked in but soon realized that she was a very good worker.

After a few days she had systems in place and William couldn't believe they had made do with Beryl Griffin's old fashioned methods for so long. Betty Long had brought in her own computer and

William was amazed how she could type a letter and make changes so easily.

Ted always looked a little nervous when Betty took papers from the filing cabinets and William couldn't help wondering what deep, dark secrets were stored there. He had received a letter from Jason to say he would be back over Easter. It would be good if he could find some more information about the people running the rest home and hospital but he hadn't really had time to pursue it.

Old Ted was in court today and Betty was busy at her computer. There was no reason why he couldn't take a look through the files while he had the chance. He started at the far end of the room this time and searched through the lists in the front of the cabinets.

Someone would have to sort out these old records one day. There was really no reason to keep most of this information. Property sales and divorce settlements, defamation hearings and industrial disputes. Most of these people were long dead.

Suddenly the word 'adoptions' caught his eye. Surely no-one would keep such personal files in an old office cabinet. He pulled out a thick file and took it to his desk. Betty was busy typing and didn't look up. He opened the pages and couldn't believe his eyes. Someone had been running a very profitable adoption agency. Back in the 1960s, in one month alone, seven babies had passed through the agency's hands. Names of infants, dates, adoptive parents. Large amounts of money had changed hands.

Desperate couples had paid the agency to adopt a child. This information would be dynamite if the newspapers ever got hold of it. He sorted through and pulled out all the pages for the 1960s. The rest were returned to the file and carefully placed back in the cabinet.

William poured himself a glass of water and sat down heavily. Did he really want to be involved in a firm that held so many secrets? No wonder Ted Baker was so nervous about the contents of those filing cabinets. He read through the papers again. He would take them home and study them more closely.

Betty Long glanced up from her work. "Don't work too hard, William. Why don't you take off early and spend some time with that beautiful little boy of yours? I'm about to make tracks myself."

"Sounds like a good plan. I'll lock up after you and see you in the morning."

Jamie was surprised to see him home so early. "I was just going to take Samuel for a walk in the park. Do you want to come?"

"Sure. I'll just get changed and I'll be right there." William pulled out a pair of shorts and a sweat shirt. His track shoes hadn't been worn for months. He really should start going to the gym or at least take a walk each day.

Jamie beamed. "This is nice. Sometimes I think you live at that office. I really wish you didn't have to work so hard."

"I'm sorry love. I know I have neglected you lately but I think I'm ready for a change. After what I found today, old Ted Baker can keep his rotten practice."

"You must have had a bad day. I'm sure you will feel a lot better soon." Jamie bent over to hand Samuel a toy then pushed the stroller rapidly along the pavement. "Daddy's not happy today, Samuel. We'll have to be nice to him."

William caught up and took over the stroller. "Hey, not so fast. I want to be part of this family too." Jamie laughed and put her arm around his waist. Time together was just what they needed.

****

Dirk and Rachel were first to arrive at the Formans' home that evening. Young Martin opened the door for them and escorted them out to the back of the house where a large wooden deck overlooked a swimming pool and gardens, luxuriously planted with palms and grasses.

A long table was laden with champagne, wine, beer and soft drink. Gaynor was seated on a lounger and waved to them to sit down and join her. "Martin will bring you a drink," she said. "He is learning the rules of being a good host."

Greg came out of the house and beamed when he saw them. "I'm pleased that you are early. People have been invited to pop in for a drink, but I guess all the new councilors will be doing the same thing. We may get no-one else at all."

Gaynor laughed. "I think you'll find that there will be lots of people wanting to befriend the new councilors but hopefully they won't want to stay too long."

"Don't forget. You don't have to do a thing. Young Martin is helping tonight."

Martin came over rather reluctantly and took their drink orders. Champagne for Rachel and a beer for Dirk. He was soon back with the glasses which they raised to toast Greg's success.

Rachel sat beside Gaynor and was pleased that she looked so refreshed. She sipped her cool lemonade and asked Rachel about her day. "You must be pleased that all this council fuss is over and done with. I'm certainly glad that things can get back to normal around here."

"It will be good to work on other things, but I'm waiting to hear back from the television studio. I quite enjoyed the audition. It was good of Greg to set it up."

"I have done television work in Australia. It's not all glamour you know. A lot of research goes into a story that only takes about three minutes to air. In some ways it's more satisfying to write something that people will take time to read."

Dirk was gazing longingly at the pool. "You can take a dip if you want. There are plenty of swimsuits and towels in the changing shed." Dirk put his beer on a small table and was off like a shot. "Talk about action man. I sometimes wonder how I keep up with him," Rachel confided.

Gaynor laughed. "My Greg is a bit like that but it works out well. I do hope I can give him a happy life. He has had his share of ups and downs.

"Today is definitely a high point. I know Greg will do his best to help the people who voted for him."

Other people were arriving now and Martin was busy pouring drinks. Rachel could see Dirk swimming strongly in the pool and went over to watch him. It was certainly a beautiful setting and great for entertaining. The Formans were very lucky people indeed.

Chapter 19

Madeline was out of bed early on Good Friday. She liked to attend the dawn morning church service and then with most of the stores closed, they would have a quiet day. Joanne heard her mother leave the house. She pulled the blankets up higher and settled back to sleep. There was no point in getting up too early.

She woke again about eight o'clock, had a shower and washed her hair. Jason was arriving later that afternoon and she wanted to look her best for him. She could hardly wait to see him again.

Her father was up before her and already in the dining room. "I'm lost without a paper to read," he complained. "Your mother should be back from church soon. I suppose we could make a start on breakfast."

Joanne took the hint and pulled a packet of cereal out of the cupboard and poured some into a bowl. She found yoghurt in the fridge and added some milk. "This will do for me. What did you have in mind?"

"That's no breakfast for a working man. Where's the bacon and eggs and toast? Come on Joanne, you could rustle up a feed for your poor old Dad."

"Okay, but you should really be watching your diet. You know Mum wants you to lose some weight." Joanne obligingly took out two slices of bacon and began to fry them in a pan. She added a slice of tomato and an egg, then put two pieces of bread in the toaster. She had to admit it did smell tempting.

"You're a good girl Joanne. You'll make someone a fine wife one day." Steve sat and ate his breakfast with relish. "You can keep your muesli rubbish," he muttered.

With a whole day to fill in, Joanne took her time tidying her room and putting a load of washing through the machine. Bradin had stayed at a friend's house last night and she knew he would have a pile of clothes to be washed. She may as well do those as well.

She wandered over to the O'Connors' house to see what time they were expecting the boys. Flo was baking loaves and a chocolate cake. "I'm not sure what time they'll be here, but I'm sure they will expect some fresh home baking."

Joanne went back to the house and picked up the local paper. She hadn't had a chance to read it that week. There were two stories by Rachel Saunders, one featuring the new bypass and another on the opening of a hall. They were well written but the topics were not the most exciting.

There would be more to write about next week with the new councilors in office. "Do you know who won the election? I know it will all be in the local paper next week, but did anyone see a list anywhere else?"

"They were all in the morning paper a couple of days ago. There were hundreds of names from all over the city and I didn't finish reading them."

Madeline was not particularly interested in council elections. As long as the rates didn't go up she was quite happy with the way things were. "The paper should still be around somewhere if you really want to read it. I think it came on Wednesday."

The week's papers were piled in a corner ready to be recycled. Joanne sifted through them until she found the page she wanted. Jason might be interested in the election results. "Great. We have a woman mayor and I think I voted for most of these new councilors. It's hard to remember."

"Did that Mr Forman get elected? I liked the sound of him." Madeline looked up from her magazine. "He was the one with the good looking wife."

"Yes, Gregory Forman got the third highest number of votes. Let's hope he can live up to his promises." Joanne remembered the article on Mr Forman. He was a very handsome man and had a strong business background.

She would keep the paper and discuss the results with her class next week. They could make a wall display using all the newspaper articles. That would be an interesting project.

Perhaps she should invite one of the councilors to come and talk to the children. Yes, that is what she would do. Children were never too young to learn about their town and the people who ran it.

****

After a late night at the tavern, Rachel and Dirk were still asleep at nine o'clock the next morning. Rachel opened her eyes reluctantly and looked at the clock. "Oh my God. Do you see what time it is? My mother will be here in a couple of hours and I need to tidy up this shambles."

"I'd better make myself scarce then. I'll take my things and leave you to bond with your mother. What time do you want to be rescued?" Dirk pulled on a pair of jeans and headed for the bathroom.

"Come back about four o'clock and stay for dinner. We will have to eat in as nothing will be open tonight."

"That's right. It's Good Friday. Your country does take it seriously. Even the pubs will be shut."

Rachel made some coffee and a slice of toast. Luckily she had shopped earlier in the week and there were steaks in the freezer and salad vegetables ready to prepare. The spare room where Julie had slept was ready for her mother but the living room and kitchen were littered with books and newspapers as well as jackets and shoes.

Maybe they should have come home a little earlier last night, but Rachel had felt like celebrating. All her stories had been written by deadline and Pete from the television company had contacted her.

"Sorry about the delay," he said, "but I wanted my boss from Wellington to see your tape. He is very interested and wants you to come back to the studio next week for another test."

"Wow. That's exciting. I'll have to take time off work but let me know when you want me to come in." Rachel had put down the phone and hugged herself with excitement. Dirk was thrilled when she told him the news.

She packed the plates into the dishwasher and picked up the clothes from the living room. A few minutes later the apartment was looking a lot tidier. A quick vacuum and it should please her mother's critical eye.

She shoved Dirk's clothes into the wardrobe and closed the door. She wanted her mother to meet him before she found out he was living here.

Rachel had just finished dusting the book shelf when she heard a car pull into the driveway. Marjorie got out and looked around her. She opened the car boot and began to unload the contents.

"Hi Mum. I'm glad you made it safely. Here, let me help you with that." Rachel took the bag from her mother and carried it into the apartment. Marjorie Saunders followed, carrying a pile of bags and boxes.

"Hullo Rachel darling. You do look well. The island holiday must have agreed with you. I've brought you a few goodies just in case you haven't done any shopping. It's most inconvenient that all the stores are closed today but we will just have to make the best of it."

Rachel smiled at her mother's exuberance. "This is your room. I do hope you will be comfortable. It's lucky that Julie has gone back to her parents otherwise it would have been a bit awkward."

"I do hope you are coping with the rent on your own. You must let your father know if you run short of cash. He does love to spoil his little girl." Marjorie looked around the room and appeared to be satisfied. "You can make me a cuppa while I unpack my things."

A few minutes later they were sitting down with a cup of tea and some hot cross buns which Marjorie had produced from one of the packages. "Now I want to hear all your news. I so dislike talking on the telephone. Are you still seeing that boy you told me about? I saw the article in the travel pages. He is very handsome and everybody said that you looked gorgeous. By the way, when am I going to meet him?"

It was difficult for Rachel to get a word in, but soon she had told her mother a little about Rarotonga, leaving out the more intimate details. She also told her about the television experience. "I go back to the studio next week for another interview. I'm not sure if that's the work I want to do but I feel it is time for a change."

"I agree. Your talents are wasted writing for that newspaper but it has been a good experience for you. I do hope we get to see you on the screen very soon."

Marjorie was quiet for a moment. She got off the couch and picked up a cardboard box from the counter. "I was sorting through the cupboards and I came across these old photographs. I want you to have them. We are planning on moving soon and the place we have in mind is much smaller than our home on the farm."

"You said something about moving but I didn't realise it would be quite so soon." Rachel was horrified. What would her father do on a small property? He did so love to drive around on his tractor checking the stock.

Her mother opened the box which contained an album and a bundle of loose photographs. "I must admit I shed a few tears when I came across these photos. Your father bought a new camera specially to take these pictures. You were so small and so precious."

Rachel looked at her mother curiously. It was most unlike her to show this much emotion. She turned the pages of the small black album. A much younger Marjorie was holding a tiny baby wrapped in a shawl, just a small face peeping out.

She turned the pages and saw herself at three months, six months and then at her first birthday party. A paper hat was perched on curly hair. Her eyes were enormous. She remembered the black and white cat and the large scruffy farm dog. There she was at five years old, her arms around the neck of a pet calf.

"It's so long since I've seen these photos. They bring back so many memories of happy days on the farm." The loose photos were mostly copies, but there was one shot which had her puzzled. A teenage girl, wearing a woollen cardigan was sitting between two small boys. Rachel didn't remember having a cardigan like that.

"Where was this one taken and who are those little boys?" She studied the photo more carefully.

"Rachel, this is what I have come to tell you about. There is something you should know about your birth. I kept putting off telling you this but your father and I adopted you when you were about two months old. Your mother died when you were born."

Marjorie stopped and moved closer to Rachel. "I was unable to become pregnant. As the years went by, I desperately wanted a child of my own. It wasn't until I was almost 40 years old that the opportunity came. Your father heard of a place that would arrange an adoption. It was all very discreet and the details would be kept secret."

"But why didn't you tell me years ago. Why have you kept this from me?" Rachel was shocked. She couldn't believe what her mother was saying. If Marjorie and James had adopted her, who were her real parents?

"You were kept at the children's hospital for several weeks because you were so small. We moved to the farm around the time we brought you home. We knew no-one, so all the neighbours assumed that I had given birth to you. For some reason I didn't want to tell them the truth."

"You could have told me when I was older. I wouldn't have thought any less of you."

"I know you are right and I can only hope that you are able to forgive us for holding back the truth. You were so beautiful and I was so proud of you. We just wanted the best for you."

Rachel was still holding the last photo. "This looks like me but I don't remember those little boys. Surely this can't be my real mother."

Marjorie sighed. "Somebody tucked the photo into the envelope with the adoption papers. We can only assume that it is your birth mother, as you are so much like her. I'm so sorry my dear. I know this is a big shock for you."

Rachel had never seen her mother look so distraught. There was no way she could be angry with her. She put her arms around Marjorie and held her tight. "Thank you for being brave enough to tell me the truth. I can't take it all in right now but I'm sure it won't make any difference to how I feel about you and Dad. Now I think this calls for something stronger than tea."

After a glass of brandy, Marjorie was back to her old self. "We are looking at a town house on the shores of Lake Taupo. It's all very modern and convenient, but there isn't much space. We will have to leave most of our large furniture behind."

"Who will run the farm if you move to Taupo, or are you planning on selling it?" Rachel couldn't imagine Marjorie parting with any of her precious antiques.

"We have a very good manager as you know and he will move into the big house. Farms aren't selling well right now so we will hold on to it until the real estate market improves."

There was so much to take in that Rachel's head was in a whirl. Her whole world had suddenly been turned upside down. She decided to call Dirk and see if he could come over earlier. They could go for a drive and show her mother some of the city highlights.

Dirk's friend called him to the phone and it was agreed that he would come over right away. They could drive to the botanical gardens and take in the old inner city homes. It would be good to get away from the small apartment and take their minds off the morning's conversation.

Marjorie was relieved that Rachel appeared to be taking the news of her adoption so calmly. She felt guilty that she hadn't shared the secret years ago but it was out in the open now.

Chapter 20

Unfortunately for Joanne, Jason and his friends arrived back so late that she didn't see him until the next day. She phoned Flo during the evening but there was still no sign of them. "I hope there hasn't been an accident. The roads are so busy on holiday weekends," she said. Joanne was beginning to panic, until Flo phoned back a few minutes later.

"You may as well go to bed Joanne. The boys are still about two hours away."

"Thanks for letting me know. Tell Jason I look forward to seeing him tomorrow."

She woke early and would love to have gone next door but resisted the temptation. Jason would come over when he was ready. She didn't want to seem too keen. It was after 10 o'clock before he appeared, unshaven and dressed in an old track suit which had seen better days.

In Joanne's eyes he looked very inviting and she was in his arms as soon as the door opened. "Whoa. That was a nice welcome. Don't bowl me over on my first day home." They laughed and looked at each other.

"You'd better come in. We're just finishing breakfast and Dad is happy as he has a paper to read." Joanne led the way into the living room where her parents were enjoying a leisurely cup of tea.

Bradin was still at the table finishing his breakfast. "Good to see you bro," he called out.

Madeline poured a cup for Jason and he sat beside Joanne on the couch. "It's good to see you back Jason. I know your mother has been counting the days. She really misses the two of you."

Bradin was now the proud owner of a station wagon and he offered to drive them into town later in the day. They knew they should take advantage of the last summer days before the cold weather set in.

"I'd better get back and sort out something decent to wear. Let me know when you are ready to leave?" Jason finished his cup of tea and headed for the door. He had clothes to unpack and laundry to sort.

Joanne watched him go reluctantly. At times like this it would be good to have your own apartment where you could have some privacy once in a while. They had been apart too long and she just wanted to feel Jason's arms around her.

Her mother needed to stock up at the supermarket and Steve was off to place some bets at the TAB. There were several race meetings around the country today and he wanted to be part of the action.

An hour later Bradin was ready to set off for their drive. Joanne phoned Jason who arrived almost immediately and they piled into the wagon. Bradin had removed a patch of rust and the vehicle needed a repaint, but he was delighted to have his own set of wheels.

"One of my mates can paint it for me. I just have to choose a colour." Bradin took off with a roar but drove carefully along the suburban streets which would take them to the motorway. Then he put his foot down and they were off, cruising along the outside lane and passing the slower cars.

"Don't drive too fast Bradin. You know there will be plenty of cops around today."

"It's sweet. I'm only 10km over. They can't get me for that." Jason wasn't so sure but didn't comment. They would be off the motorway soon and heading for the city.

Joanne didn't know where they were headed, but didn't mind too much. Soon downtown Auckland came into view and Bradin found a parking spot in a back alley near the harbour. "We can walk along the waterfront and if there is a ferry waiting let's take it to the other side," he said.

They were soon walking towards the ferry building where they bought tickets at the booth. "You've just missed a boat but there will be another along shortly," the operator said. They sat on the hard wooden bench drinking takeaway coffee and watched the crowd walk by. There were many family groups and people with dogs. Several of the passengers were wheeling cycles and wore helmets and jackets.

"I should have brought my bike," Jason laughed. "It's probably covered with cobwebs by now."

It wasn't long before they were walking up the gangway onto the boat and fifteen minutes later they were across the other side of the water where a long tin shed housed a variety of shops and stalls.

They crossed the road and followed the crowd through the shopping centre where baskets of specials were temptingly displayed along the pavement. Joanne bought a colourful scarf and Bradin chose some new sandals. Jason refused to be tempted.

Soon they walked back along the other side of the street then through a park to the sandy beach beyond. Children were splashing about in the shallow water and the playground was crowded with parents and noisy infants.

Jason held Joanne by the hand as they strolled together in the warm sunshine. He had arranged for them to have dinner with William and Jamie that night, even though he knew his mother would like him to dine at home.

Joanne was pleased. She had something to show Jason and she knew their friends would be interested too. The photograph was still sitting on Joanne's dressing table and she looked at it most days. Those features were etched in her mind.

Bradin had gone on ahead and was waiting at the wharf ready to take the ferry back to the city. "There's a boat just about to leave but I don't think we'll make it." They walked quickly to the end of the pier but the ferry sounded its horn and backed away.

As the craft turned to face the city, Joanne caught sight of a familiar face at the back of the boat. The girl from the travel article was leaning on the rail watching the wake which foamed out behind the boat.

She grabbed Jason's arm. "Look, there's the girl I keep running in to. The one who looks like me." The distance was now too great for Jason to see anyone. He put his arm around Joanne and gave her a squeeze. "We've got to sort out this mystery one way or the other. That was so close. You were almost on the same boat and you could have had a chance to speak to her."

Joanne was disappointed. "Yes, it would be good to meet this girl named Rachel. I'm sure a lot of questions could be answered.

****

Rachel's mother was enchanted with Dirk. His manners were impeccable and she loved the South African accent. After a delightful drive around Auckland's best suburbs they enjoyed a quiet dinner and Marjorie was ready for an early night. Dirk took his leave shortly afterwards promising to be back next morning to drive them to the waterfront where they planned to catch a ferry to the North Shore.

It was 10 o'clock when Dirk arrived. Once more he was on his best behaviour. He opened the car door for Rachel's mother and drove them smoothly through town. They left the car in a vacant spot in the parking building and walked across the street to the waterfront.

Dirk bought tickets from the booth and they boarded the ferry which was docked to the wharf. Marjorie had visited Auckland several times but hadn't experienced a ferry ride before so this would be a new experience.

"He really is a delightful young man Rachel. I know your father would approve."

"Really, mother. He is just my boyfriend. We have no long time plans at this stage. He's just as likely to go off on his travels again."

Rachel didn't want to give her mother any false hopes. She and Dirk had never discussed a future together, they just enjoyed each other's company right now.

The historic town of Devonport came into view and Marjorie was impressed with the historic buildings and heritage atmosphere. "I could live here. Look at those old villas, all in perfect condition."

"It is lovely. But you are moving into a new place soon. You don't need a century-old home at your age." They crossed the street and walked through the shopping centre where antique shops beckoned.

"Why don't you go and browse while Dirk and I have a coffee? We can meet you back here in about half an hour." Rachel didn't really feel like admiring relics from the past, but knew that her mother would be in her element. Besides, she wanted a chance to talk to Dirk. She wasn't sure whether she was ready to share her big secret just yet, but the opportunity might come up.

"That would be lovely my dear. And then I'll treat you to lunch if you can find a good restaurant." Marjorie went off happily while Rachel and Dirk sat down at a table on the pavement under a trendy black umbrella.

"You have made a good impression on my mother. She thinks you are the best thing that ever happened to me."

"She is quite right too. You've never likely to meet anyone nearly as perfect as me." A girl took their order and they sat back, enjoying the ambiance.

"My mother told me something really shocking yesterday. I don't know how to tell you about it." Rachel stopped, unable to go on. "In fact, I feel as though I've been living a false life. I'm not the person I thought I was."

"Come on Rachel. How could you feel that way? You are a beautiful, uncomplicated human being. You have great parents and you are very fortunate to have had a privileged upbringing."

"It might seem that way Dirk, but today I have found that I am not that person. I have no idea who I am."

"That sounds rather dramatic Rachel. Your mother is a lovely woman who brought you up well." Dirk was mystified. He could find no fault with Marjorie Saunders. If only he had a mother like that. How different his own life would have been.

The coffees and muffins were placed in front of them and Rachel didn't know where to begin. "The fact is that Marjorie is not my mother. She and James adopted me when I was an infant and brought me up as their own. I have only just been told this today. Do you wonder why I'm sounding a little bit strange?"

"Whoops. That's a big one to take on. How come they didn't tell you earlier?"

"It seems like they were so proud of me they wanted to claim me as their own and then after that, they never quite got around to it."

"Did they give you any idea about your real parentage? Have you any idea who your real parents were?"

"The only clue is this photo which they assume to be my mother. She died when I was born but someone put this picture in the file." Rachel pulled the photo from her bag and handed it to Dirk. "I'm sure that this girl is my real mother."

Dirk took one look at the old photograph and totally agreed. Except for the hairdo and the clothes it could have been Rachel. "Actually, I find this quite exciting. If this is your real mother, the two boys are obviously related and you have probably got a whole new family just waiting to be discovered."

"I just want to go back to the way I was. I don't need to know I have a whole lot of relatives out there. They mean nothing to me."

"You may feel like that right now, but I'm sure that once you get used to the idea, you will be anxious to find your real family. In the meantime, your mother will be back soon and we want to make sure she enjoys her afternoon."

"You are so right. It took a lot of courage for my mother to tell me the true story. I want her to enjoy her time with us."

As if on cue, Marjorie walked up and joined them at the table. "I've had such a lovely time. There are so many treasures in those stores, but now I think it is time we found something to eat."

They chose a restaurant in an old hotel with white tablecloths and a gracious atmosphere. The wine list was impressive and the menu extensive. Rachel realised she needed to relax and go with the flow. Dirk was right. She was privileged to have been chosen by Marjorie and James and she would always be grateful to them.

It was some time before they left the restaurant and they boarded the ferry moments before it cast off from the dock. Rachel found a space on the rail in the stern of the boat and watched the foaming water. She thought she saw a face she recognized. A young woman stood on the jetty. She looked exactly like the girl in the photograph that her mother had given her. It was all very peculiar.

****

Jamie was so pleased that Jason and Joanne were coming to visit. William had been in a strange mood ever since the day they walked together in the park.

She would ask Jason to talk to him and try to find out what the problem was.

Samuel was now toddling around and beginning to say a few words, but Jamie felt that she was ready for a life outside motherhood. There must be a way that she could go back to her studies that were interrupted by her pregnancy. Perhaps Samuel could go into part-time care while she completed her arts degree.

The menu had been chosen with care and Jamie knew that she would be able to relax and enjoy the company. William would barbecue the meat and the vegetables and salads were all prepared.

Jason seemed in good spirits and Joanne was obviously pleased to be with him again. They sat outside on the patio and enjoyed a quiet drink, only interrupted a few times when Samuel refused to go to sleep.

Joanne showed them the photograph that Flo had brought from the household in Hamilton. "I'm absolutely positive that this is my natural mother and these two boys are probably my uncles. I'm thinking about contacting them to see if they have any more information about poor Jennifer."

William couldn't get the memory of the grim adoption files out of his head. He had copied them, then returned them to the cabinet. He now had quite a record of events at the former nursing home. The more he thought about what they contained, the more disgusted he was with the firm of Barlow and Reid.

He had tried talking to Ted Baker about the safety of the records, but Ted had refused to discuss the problem. "Beryl will know what to do when she gets back," was all he would say.

William was puzzled. Betty Long was still running the office and there had been no sign of old Beryl coming back on the scene. Ted Baker seemed to scuttle in and out as if the whole place was about to fall apart. William's future with the firm was very shaky indeed.

It would have been tempting to share the information on the adoption papers with his friend, but William wasn't ready to do that just yet. Among the babies adopted during 1963, two names had practically jumped off the page. Their mother was Jennifer Blake, deceased, and he reeled with shock at the name of the father. He knew he was sitting on a time bomb. This was not the right time to disclose that information.

He looked across at Joanne who seemed so happy to be with Jason. He pushed away the dark thoughts and poured another round of drinks. "Come and help me with the barbecue. We'll leave the girls to organize the rest of the food." He ushered Jason from the room and out onto the deck.

"I've discovered some very controversial records about the adoptions. I'm really worried about what sort of information is contained in those old filing cabinets at the office. There could be a lot of trouble if it got into the wrong hands." Jason could see that William was stressed.

"Do you think you need to talk to someone outside the firm? I don't like you fretting about something out of your control. Ted Baker and his former partners are the ones who should be worried."

"You're right. I'll talk it over with a senior lawyer who works at the court with me. He will advise me on what I should do. In the meantime, let's get on with cooking these steaks or Jamie will suspect that there is something wrong."

Jamie was delighted to have Joanne to confide in. She had bottled up her concerns and now she had a willing ear.

"I've been worried about William lately. I know lawyers come under a lot of stress at times but I think the work is really getting him down. He's talking about finding a new job. His boss seems to have lost the plot and old Beryl is not around to hold things together."

"That's a shame. William seemed to be doing so well. Perhaps he just needs a break. Are you able to take a holiday? That would be the best thing for both of you."

Jamie smiled. "I'll do my best to persuade my hard-working husband that he doesn't have to be a martyr. Life would go on without the great firm of Barlow and Reid."

William was pleased to see the girls laughing when they came out to join them. Obviously, Jamie hadn't picked up on his dark mood. The steaks were served onto oval dishes and carried to the table, where the vegetables and salads were ready.

Jason kept them entertained with his stories of life in the capital city and Joanne shared her experiences in the classroom. "I've decided to invite a new councilor to talk to the children next week. We will collect all the information from the newspapers and turn it into a project."

"That sounds like fun. Which councilor are you thinking of?" Jamie asked.

"I would like to ask Greg Forman to come along. He seems like an interesting guy and he's seriously good looking."

William almost choked on a mouthful. He coughed and hastily took a sip of water from a glass. Jamie looked at him in alarm. "Are you okay? I think Mr Forman would be a good choice. He sounds like a good clean living sort of bloke."

"Yes. I'm sure Mr Forman doesn't have too many secrets to hide." William pulled himself together. He dished up another portion of salad. "Come on folks, eat up. I thought we'd play a game of poker after our meal. It's ages since we did anything like that."

They finished the meal and cleared the dishes away. Jamie found the playing cards and set some chairs around a small table. "You'll have to show me how to play. I've totally forgotten," Joanne said.

An hour later, Jason had won a pile of poker chips and the girls had totally run out. William was still putting up a fight. "Just a few more deals. I know I can win."

They were interrupted by the loud ringing of the telephone. Jamie got up quickly to answer it. "Hullo. What's that? Oh no!" She put her hand over the receiver and called out to William. "It's the police. Your office is on fire. They want you to go over there right away."

William jumped up and ran over to take the call. "How bad is it? Is there much damage?"

He replaced the phone and turned around. "The building is badly damaged. The brick walls are still standing but the interior and the roof are totally destroyed."

He rushed into the bedroom to get his coat. "You can't drive there. You've had a couple too many drinks." Jamie was taking charge. "Joanne, do you mind staying here with the baby and I'll drive."

"Sure. You should go too, Jason. I'll be okay here on my own." Joanne wasn't sure what she would do if Samuel woke up but it was important for the others to go straight to the office.

It only took fifteen minutes to get to the scene. The street was cordoned off so they parked the car and walked quickly to what was once the premises of Barlow and Reid. The fire brigade had extinguished the flames and columns of smoke poured into the air. What remained was a burned out shell. Stark blackened brick walls, gaping holes where the windows had been, twisted iron lifted from the roof.

William made his way up to the policeman who was holding back the bystanders. He introduced himself and was led over to the fire chief who was still holding a heavy hose.

"The building was well alight by the time we got here. We haven't been able to get inside so we've no idea what caused it."

William noticed a figure standing on the edge of the crowd. Ted Baker. He excused himself and rushed over to his side. "Ted, I'm so sorry. This is a terrible thing to happen. What could possibly have caused such a serious fire?"

Ted just gazed transfixed at the building. He didn't say a word. William realized that he was in shock and led him over to an ambulance that was standing by. "I think this man needs to rest for a moment. This was his life's work and he seems to be overcome at the extent of the damage."

The young attendant helped Ted into the ambulance and sat him down. William signed the paper work and went back to rejoin Jason and Jamie. "I'm not sure what we can do here. I've been having bad thoughts about this place but I certainly didn't expect it to be burnt down."

He thought about all the records inside the cabinets and wondered how many of them would have survived. He went back and spoke to the policeman. "There's nothing I can do here tonight. I'll come back early tomorrow and see what needs to be done."

"You're best to report to the police station in the morning. There will be many questions to be answered. " William went back to the ambulance to check on Ted Baker. "We'll keep an eye on him and drop him home later. If he doesn't improve he may need to spend the night in hospital."

Ted was sitting on the bed drinking a cup of tea. He didn't acknowledge William in any way. "He lives alone so it would be best to take him to hospital. He has had a few heart problems and I wouldn't like to see him left by himself."

It was a quiet trio that returned to the car. "Well, it looks as though my decision about changing jobs might have been made for me. I can't see Barlow and Reid rising from the ashes." William was overcome with weariness. He felt sorry for his boss who had looked so lonely and bereft. He must let Beryl Griffin know as soon as possible. She may be able to be of some comfort to him.

Chapter 21

The phone rang incessantly until Rachel could ignore it no longer. Who would be ringing her on Easter Sunday? She knew Dirk wouldn't be out of bed at this hour of the morning.

"I'm sorry to disturb you Rachel, but there's an urgent job I want you to do." It was Bill Osborne, Rachel's editor.

"Surely you don't need me on a holiday weekend. Can't it wait a couple of days?" Rachel was annoyed to say the least. If something was so urgent why hadn't Bill taken care of it.

"I'd do the job myself but I'm away up North. There was a big fire in the city last night. A legal office was apparently burnt to the ground. An old lawyer was running it and there was a younger chap working there too. See what you can find out. There could be a good human interest angle."

Rachel sighed. She realised she had no choice but to cover the story. She would contact Dirk and he could drive her there. She remembered her mother was still asleep in the spare room. She would probably be content to stay around the apartment for the morning and catch up on some reading.

She picked up the old photograph that had disturbed her so much and studied the face that looked up at her. If only she knew the girl's story. The news of her adoption had scarcely sunk in. It all seemed unreal and she wasn't sure how she felt about it.

After a shower and a cup of coffee Rachel was wide awake and ready to face the day. She phoned Dirk and he said he would come around soon. She asked him to bring his camera as she had left hers at the office. She hadn't planned on using it over a holiday weekend.

Rachel looked in on her mother as she was leaving. Marjorie was lying in bed and said she would look after herself until they returned. "Be sure to bring that delightful young man back with you," she said.

The streets of the city were unusually quiet. As they got closer, Rachel could see a plume of smoke still rising from the building. "What a mess. It doesn't look as though anything could have survived." Dirk looked at the scene in amazement.

They approached the nearest policeman and explained who they were. He had just come on duty and was far from pleased at being dragged out when he should have been home sharing Easter eggs with his family.

"There's not a lot I can tell you. The area is cordoned off until the fire department has finished inspecting it. The cause of the fire is not yet known but at this stage it isn't being treated as suspicious."

Dirk took a number of photos of the fire crew pulling sheets of tin from the roof. The supervisor was standing by and was willing to answer some questions. "No, they hadn't found the cause of the fire." "Yes, the building would have to be totally demolished." "It was hard to say whether anything could be salvaged."

"I still haven't got my human interest story," Rachel said dryly. "Let's try the police station. We might get something there."

It was a short drive to the station and the constable on duty was happy to talk to the press. He answered all Rachel's questions but couldn't really tell them anything they didn't already know.

They were just about to leave when there was a knock on the door of the interview room. "Excuse me Constable Bailey. There's someone here to see you about last night's fire. Shall I ask him to wait?"

"Yes please. I'll be right there." Rachel and Dirk were shown from the room and into the foyer where a tall sandy haired man was standing. He stared at Rachel. "Joanne, what are you doing here?" Then he realized his mistake. "I'm sorry. I thought for a moment you were someone I know."

"I'm Rachel, a reporter from the Chronicle. Could I ask you a few questions when you've finished here?"

William would not normally have spoken to the press, but because the girl looked so much like Joanne he agreed. He was also curious to find out more about this girl named Rachel.

"Sure. I'll catch up with you as soon as I have spoken to the police. It shouldn't take too long." He followed the constable into the office.

"Take a seat. Now tell me who you are and do you have any connection with the law office?" It didn't take long for William to give him the details but he was surprised that he was being questioned so closely. Constable Bailey was very thorough. He wanted to know who worked at the office, who had access to the premises and who was the last person to leave the building.

William had stayed on until about six o'clock on the Thursday night and Betty had left just before him. She said she had a nail appointment and he had wished her a happy holiday. He suddenly realized that he would have to contact Betty about the fire. She would be most upset as her precious computer had probably gone up in flames.

The constable wanted a list of all the people who held keys to the building. William was a bit vague about the details. He knew that a cleaning lady came in once a week and old Beryl still held a set of keys, along with himself and Ted Baker.

"Are you sure you weren't in the office on Saturday?" William assured him that he was home all day with his wife and son. They had gone shopping and bought Samuel an Easter bunny which he had taken to bed that night.

"Thanks for coming in. Sorry about all the questions but we just want to know if anyone was in the building over the weekend. We'll keep in touch and don't hesitate to get back to us if you think of anything that might help." Constable Bailey handed William his card.

The interview had gone on longer than William expected and he found Rachel sitting alone in the reception room reading an outdated magazine.

"I sent my boyfriend back to the apartment. My mother is staying over and she will be wondering what is keeping us so long. I'll give Dirk a call when we're finished here."

William introduced himself. "I think it would be more convivial for us to have a coffee. That's if there is anything open on Easter Sunday." Rachel didn't like their chances but wanted the opportunity to get a story about the fire. This young man named William was the best bet at the moment.

The only coffee they could find was at a drive through service station then William stopped the car a little further down the street. Rachel felt uncomfortable. "If you wouldn't mind driving me back to my apartment we could talk there. It's only a few minutes away from here."

William was only too delighted. He had found the elusive Rachel and didn't want to let her go. Dirk was surprised to see William arrive back with his girl friend but at least it had saved him a trip.

Marjorie was also taken aback to see her daughter with another young man, but once they were introduced she relaxed and carried on reading her book.

William was soon telling Rachel all he knew of the history of Barlow and Reid. "It's possibly the oldest law firm in the city, dating back to the early 1900s. The former partners are no longer with us and these days, Ted Baker is the senior lawyer."

Rachel noted down the name. It would be good to get some thoughts from the older man. She asked for his address and William told her that he might be in the hospital. "He was in total shock when I last saw him. I plan to visit him today to see if he is okay."

Rachel learned about Beryl Griffin and how she had been with the firm for many years. She was another person that William would need to contact.

"Do you think the records will be totally destroyed? There must be so much history filed away in your archives." Rachel could only guess at the number of stories those files contained.

William was keen to get back to his family and he promised to drop a photo into Rachel's office. "I should be able to find one with Ted and Beryl in it as well," he said.

Because he suspected that she was the missing twin, he wanted to help Rachel as much as possible. She was a lovely girl, a little slimmer than Joanne with shorter, fairer hair. The unusual grey/green eyes were her best feature. So like the old photograph of Jennifer Blake.

****

With the election behind him, Greg Forman was looking forward to a break before the council meetings were underway. Gaynor was feeling well, but he didn't want to risk taking her too far, even though the doctor was pleased with her progress.

He should really go down country for a few days to check on the factory. He was in touch with the manager several times a week, but it was good to put in an appearance once in a while.

He had just finished breakfast when Gaynor came out to say there was a call for him. He went inside and picked up the phone. It was a teacher from a school out in one of the suburbs. The children were studying the local body elections and would he be willing to come out and speak to them?

"I don't mind at all but wouldn't you be better with one of the experienced councilors? They know a lot more about the work than I do."

The young woman seemed determined that it was Greg that she wanted. "I've kept the newspaper clippings and I would really like you to come."

Greg found himself agreeing and a time was arranged for the following week. He could fit it in before he went away, but he wasn't sure what a class full of children would want to know.

When Gaynor heard about the arrangements she decided that she would like to go along too. "I'm tired of hanging about the house. It would make a nice change."

Chapter 22

After talking to William and Constable Bailey, Rachel knew she could start writing the article about the fire. She had time to get an update on the possible cause of the blaze before deadline and she would try to interview Ted Baker or the office assistant.

"I'll call the hospital and see whether Mr Baker has been admitted. It would be good to get a statement from the senior partner." Rachel was reluctant to work over the holidays but felt obliged to complete the task. Her mother was leaving today so Dirk would be moving back later in the afternoon.

The hospital receptionist was brisk. "Mr Baker was discharged this morning," she said.

Rachel wondered what she should do now. She didn't know where Ted Baker lived and she had no way of getting there until Dirk arrived. She may as well enjoy the last few minutes of her mother's visit.

"I've had a lovely time Rachel, but it's a shame you had to work over the holiday. I do hope you get good news from the television company. Your father and I would be so proud to see you on the big screen." Marjorie Saunders had not said another word about the adoption. It was as though she had got the matter off her chest and didn't want to have to deal with it any more.

"I'll let you know how the next screen test goes. I'm not getting my hopes up just yet." Rachel knew that her days with the Chronicle were numbered but she wasn't sure what her future would be.

****

William was just about to take Jamie and Samuel for a drive when the phone rang. It was the police station and the sergeant wanted to see him urgently. "Something has come up. I need to talk to you again," was all he would say.

"What a shame. I was really looking forward to going out together. I hope you won't be held up too long." Jamie was cross. It had been weeks since they last spent a day together, but the office fire had stressed her husband out and she would need to be patient.

The constable on the desk escorted William into the interview room where the sergeant and another man were seated. "Something serious has come up and we have brought in an investigator. This is Barry Giles." The men shook hands and William sat on the spare chair on the far side of the desk.

Constable Bailey looked grim. "The fire crew has discovered several suspicious items at the seat of the fire. We have reason to believe the blaze was deliberately lit."

William was shocked. Not many people had access to the building and why would one of them want to destroy it? He thought of the damaging information hidden away in the old filing cabinets. Surely Ted Baker wouldn't have burned down his own office.

The investigator took over. "Several of the drawers in the filing cabinets had been pulled open and accelerant poured in. Someone must have had a good reason to want to destroy those documents."

Once again, William could think of nothing to say. Why burn down the whole building? Wouldn't it have been easier for someone to simply remove the damaging papers?

The two men were studying him, noticing his unease. "Do you know of any reason why anybody would want to destroy those records? Have you any idea who would carry out such a task?"

William knew he would have to say something. "I've recently found a few papers that would be very embarrassing if they got into the wrong hands. I suspect there is a great deal of sensitive information in those filing cabinets involving well-known identities in this city."

Barry Giles looked at William with more interest. "How many people would have known about these documents?"

"I guess the former partners would have been involved but they are all dead and gone. The only one left is Ted Baker, and of course, his secretary Beryl Griffin. She was always very protective of those files."

"Do you have proof of any of this? Do you have copies of any of these documents?" William felt trapped. Should he share the adoption files with these men?

"I do have a few pages that I copied while I was working on a case. How badly have the originals been damaged? Is any of the material still readable?"

"Between the fire and the water damage, many of the documents are unreadable, but they will have to be sifted through to see if anything can be saved. I think we need to talk to Mr Baker again, and where can we find his secretary? Do you have a contact for her?"

"I know where Beryl Griffin lives but she's with her mother somewhere down country at present. I'm sure she was far from here at the time of the fire."

"Then they leaves Edward Baker. We need to pay him an urgent visit. Sorry to disturb your day. You'll be hearing from us again soon." The two men rose and William knew the interview was over.

If someone had purposely destroyed the building there would probably be no insurance cover. All the books and equipment he owned would be lost. He thought of the hours of work that had gone into the information he had gathered. His reference books had cost an arm and a leg. By the time he got home to Jamie he was in a very glum mood. He needed to talk to his friend Jason as soon as possible.

****

Moments after Rachel's mother drove away Dirk came roaring up the driveway. He jumped out of the car, grabbed his bag and came into the apartment like a whirlwind.

"I've missed you. That bed was so lonely without you." He took Rachel in his arms and hugged her tight.

"I missed you too, but right now I have to try and track down that old lawyer, then I can finish my story." Rachel held Dirk off at arm's length. They would make up for lost time tonight. She had found an address for Ted Baker but he had not answered his phone. She would try to catch him at home.

"Okay. I guess it will keep. I'll drive you to this guy's house and then we can go for a drink to celebrate my return." Dirk tossed his bag on the bed and picked up his camera. "I may as well bring this along just in case."

Ted Baker's home was in a leafy suburb where century-old homes stood behind high brick walls. They found the right number on the elaborate iron gate and parked the car on the opposite side of the road. "I'll try the small gate and if I don't come out in about fifteen minutes, come and rescue me." Rachel laughed nervously. She wasn't really keen on knocking on people's doors to get a story.

The gate was stiff as though it wasn't used much and a moss covered path led along the side of the house. Tall trees overhung the gardens where fuchsias and rose bushes bloomed.

Wooden steps led up to a covered porch at the back of the house and Rachel looked around for signs of life. Nothing stirred, except a breeze which rattled the verandah shades.

Rachel took a deep breathe and headed for the back door. Coloured glass panels were dingy with cobwebs and the potted plants were choked with weeds. This place could certainly do with a bit of a spruce up. She knocked on the wooden panel and waited. No answer. She tried again and was just about to give up when the door opened a fraction.

"Can I help you?" It was an elderly woman who peered through the crack in the doorway.

Rachel explained who she was and why she was there and the woman opened the door a little wider. She was dressed in a dark blue cardigan and straight black skirt and her hair was tightly curled. "I'm sorry, but Mr Baker is not seeing anyone. He has had a shock and is not feeling well at the moment."

"I would really like to speak to him, or perhaps you can help me. Have you any connection with the law office that was burned down?"

"I've worked there for many years but I'm not able to tell you anything. That place was our life's work and I don't know what we will do now." The woman was about to close the door but Rachel persisted.

"That law firm was possibly the oldest in the city. It would be good to learn a little about its history. It would be a shame to let it just quietly disappear." Rachel saw the woman hesitate.

"I don't suppose it would do any harm to talk about that, but I can't say anything about the fire. You'd better come in and sit down." The woman led the way into the house and through to a small sunroom at the back.

Rachel sat down on a hard couch covered with a floral pattern. There was a large window overlooking the back garden and crowded bookshelves lined the remaining walls. She waited for the woman to speak.

"I'm Beryl Griffiths. I've been secretary for the law firm for many years but lately I've been away looking after my mother who unfortunately had a fall. She's now in a comfortable rest home and I hope she will be happy there. I was all ready to go back to work when the fire occurred. I don't know what I'm going to do now." The woman looked distressed.

"Have you heard what caused the fire? The building looked as though it was totally destroyed. Was anything saved?"

"I don't think there is much that wasn't damaged by the fire or water. Someone will have to sort through the mess but we aren't allowed to go back there right now."

Rachel couldn't think of anything worse than sifting through piles of smoke damaged records. It would be so much safer once records such as these were kept on computers and copies stored away from the building. She knew that day would soon be here but it wasn't going to help poor Beryl and the rest of the Barlow and Reid employees.

She took some notes as Beryl told her more about the law firm and how many important clients they had dealt with. "Most of the history is in this magazine article that was written a few years ago when the original partner died. You can have this copy if it will be any use to you.”

Rachel gratefully took the magazine. She heard footsteps outside and caught sight of Dirk walking past the window. There wasn't much more to find out here so she thanked Beryl Griffin and joined Dirk on the porch.

“That was so depressing,” she said as they walked back along the garden path. “That poor woman seems really heartbroken and there was no sign of Ted Baker himself.

“Maybe we should call back at the police station and see if there is any more news and then I'll call it a day.” Rachel wanted to move on and enjoy what was left of the Easter break.

Constable Bailey was back on duty and showed Rachel into his office. “There is an update. You can say that the cause of the fire is suspicious and a number of people are being interviewed, but that is all I can give you at this stage.”

Rachel confirmed that she could use this information and thanked the constable. Dirk was waiting in the parked car and gave her a hug. “Come on. We have places to go and things to do.”

Half an hour later they were sitting in their favourite bar enjoying a glass of wine. A jazz trio was playing on the stage and the place was starting to fill up. “That wasn't exactly the holiday weekend we had in mind. It looks as though the only way to get peace and quiet is to go to Rarotonga.”

“Yes, how good it would be to sit on that soft white sand and watch the sunset.” Rachel agreed. “Everything has changed so much since we came back. I don’t seem to know who I am any more.”

Chapter 23

It was early on Tuesday morning when Rachel returned to work. The Chronicle had to be out on time and the story about the fire would make page three. William had supplied photos of himself, Ted Baker and Beryl Griffith, taken at a social gathering. That, along with Dirk's picture of the firemen on the roof of the building, would complete the account of one of the city's biggest fires in years.

The fact that the fire was considered to be suspicious was big news but Rachel knew the daily papers and television would already have covered that part of the story. She concentrated more on the way the event had affected the two long-time staff members whose life work was in ruins.

"Nice work Rachel. I couldn't have done it better myself. I'll keep you on." Bill was in a relaxed mood after a break in the Bay of Islands. He had caught a tuna and a photograph of that was no doubt destined for the sports page.

The phone rang at that moment and Rachel picked it up. It was Pete from the television studio. "Are you able to come in tomorrow? We want you to do another test."

Rachel looked across at Bill. "I think my boss owes me a few hours. What time do you want me?"

"How about 10 o'clock? And then I'll buy you lunch."

"It sounds like you're going out on a hot date. Anybody I know?" Bill was curious. With the paper finished for the week, tomorrow would be a quiet day and there was no reason for Rachel to be there.

"That would be telling." Rachel wasn't giving anything away. The television sessions would remain a secret at this stage.

****

It was just nine o'clock in the morning when William was disturbed by a loud knocking on the door. Who could it be at this hour? Standing on the porch were two burly police officers. "William Brown, we would like you to accompany us to the police station."

"What is this about? What do you want with me?"

"We have reason to believe that you were involved in the arson at the Barlow and Reid law office. We will need to ask further questions at the station."

William couldn't believe what he was hearing. Surely they didn't think that he would set the building alight. He called out to Jamie. "I need to go down to the police station. I'll be back as soon as I can."

Jamie was in the bathroom and didn't see William leave. What was so urgent that he would go without saying a word?

When William was escorted in by the two constables, Barry Giles, the special investigator was already in the interview room. He looked across at William and instructed him to sit down.

"We have received information to suggest that you were the one who started the fires that destroyed the law office where you worked. You aren't required to say anything without a lawyer present."

"That's a bit of a joke," thought William. "The only lawyer I know has probably set me up." He remained silent, waiting to hear what the investigator would say.

"We have a witness who says you entered the building on the evening of the fire. It seems as if you were the last person to be in the building."

"My wife can tell you I was home all evening with my family. There was no reason for me to be at work over the holiday weekend." William couldn't believe what he was hearing.

"The witness has also testified that you were seen taking confidential documents from the building." The investigator barely looked at William but his voice was slow and deliberate.

"I don't intend to comment on these ridiculous accusations." William could keep silent no longer. "I demand to know who is accusing me."

"You can go now but must be back here in the morning. The officers will drive you home." Barry Giles closed his folder and left the room leaving William numb with shock.

"What a load of bollocks," he managed to say as he followed the policeman to the patrol car. "I assure you that the last thing I would do is destroy the place where I work. Goodness knows where the next dollar is going to come from.”

The moment he arrived home he was on the phone to Jason. “I don’t know what’s going on mate,” he said, “but someone’s got their wires crossed.” He explained what had happened at the police station.

“I’ll be over right away.” Jason was able to borrow his father’s car and he was on William’s doorstep a short time later. “There must be someone who can help us. Let’s work out who has something to lose if the documents in the filing cabinets are still readable.”

“As far as I know it could only be Ted Baker or Beryl Griffin. I’m sure Miss Griffin was away when the fire started so that only leaves Ted.”

“What about that other woman who was working there? The temporary one. Are you sure she wasn’t hired by someone who wanted the place destroyed?”

William didn’t know what to think any more. He hadn’t given a thought to Betty Long, the new assistant. What if she had been secretly working for someone else?

“Maybe you need to take the papers you have to the police. Tell them that you suspect there was a lot of sensitive material hidden in the filing cabinets and you had probably only discovered the tip of the iceberg.” Jason couldn’t think of anything else to say.

He felt sorry for his friend but was returning to Wellington in two days so there was not a lot more he could do. There must be someone with influence that they could turn to.

When William returned to his home he didn't tell Jamie what had happened. There was no sense in alarming her over what was probably a big misunderstanding. He thought about what Jason had said about the new temporary assistant. She had just conveniently turned up to replace Beryl Griffin and they really knew nothing about her.

He remembered the name of the agency and asked to speak to the manager. When she replied he asked whether he could contact one of their employees named Betty Long. "She comes highly recommended," he said.

The woman sounded puzzled. "We have a number of very competent employees but I have never heard of Betty Long. You must have the wrong agency."

Now William was confused. He had personally made the request. Surely they had sent Betty Long to fill the position. "Did you send a temporary clerk to the law office of Barlow and Reid about a month ago? I made the request myself."

"Sorry sir. At the time we had no-one available. I did leave a message on your phone. I hope we can be of service in the future." The woman rang off and William stared at the phone in dismay.

Who was Betty Long and where had she come from? If she hadn't come from the agency who was she working for? He would have to talk with his old boss and see if he knew anything about the woman.

"Sorry to keep leaving you, honey, but I need to try to contact Ted Baker. I've had no luck on the phone so I'll drive around to his house." William took the keys for the car and headed out the door.

"Will you be back for lunch?" Jamie had put Samuel down for a nap and was ready to tackle a pile of laundry.

"I'm not sure. Don't wait for me. I really need to talk to Ted and then I might have to go back to the police station." He gave Jamie a kiss and hurried out. It didn't take long to reach the suburb where Ted Baker lived. William had visited him once before and pulled up outside his home, parking under a plane tree, its branches spanning over the pavement and dead leaves filling the gutters.

He opened the small gate and made his way along the narrow path, dodging the overhanging branches. As he came to the back of the house he was surprised to see Beryl Griffin sitting on the verandah in an ancient cane chair. She jumped up in fright when she saw him then sank back onto the seat.

"William, you startled me. What a terrible business. It is all most upsetting."

"That's not the half of it. The police say it was arson and they are trying to pin it on me." William was walking back and forth in agitation.

"Sit down William and tell me what has been going on. The police have been here and practically accused poor Mr Baker of setting fire to his own office. The man is so distressed he is not speaking to anyone. When I heard the news I came back to see if there was anything I could do and I've been here looking after dear Ted for the last few days."

William moved some boxes off a chair and sat down beside Beryl. "I am so worried, Beryl. I don't know whether the firm will survive and whether I still have a position there. We really need to have access to the files to see if anything can be saved."

"I was able to tell the police that I was at my mother's new nursing home at the time of the fire. I wanted to stay with her until she was settled, but I was so worried about Ted I felt I should be back here."

"So you have an alibi, and I know I was home with Jamie but the police don't want to believe me. What about Ted? Was he able to say where he was that night?" William was sure he could trust Beryl Griffin. Maybe he had found an ally.

"Unfortunately, Ted has not been able to account for his movements. He was at his club until 10 that night then left to go home. A nasty man named Mr Giles has spoken to him several times and practically accused him of burning down his own premises."

William was relieved that other people were being blamed for the fire. It must be the way this inspector worked, trying to shock people into making a statement.

"The person I'm confused about is Betty Long, the temp we hired to cover for you. I contacted the agency and they have never heard of the woman. I wonder who she is and how she knew about the vacancy."

Beryl thought for a moment. "I'm sure I didn't tell anyone about the job. It all happened so suddenly. Though, when I think about it I did mention it to my hairdresser and there were other people in the salon, and I suppose someone could have overheard when I asked the post office to hold my mail."

"Ted might have talked about it at his club. There are all sorts of possibilities, but Betty Long must have had a good reason to take your place. I wonder whether Ted knows any more about her."

As if on cue the sliding door into the kitchen opened and Ted Baker stumbled out onto the porch. William could see that he had lost a lot of weight and what was left of his hair was now completely white.

"Hullo Ted. It looks as though we are all being grilled by the police. Could you tell them where you were on the night of the fire?"

There was no answer from Ted who sat heavily on a seat and stared gloomily into space.

William tried again. "Do you know anything about that woman who came to work for us? She wasn't sent by the agency and we are trying to work out how she knew about the job."

There was a grunt from Ted. "I never liked the woman. Her finger nails were too long." Beryl looked at him in surprise. That was the most communication from Ted since she had come to his house.

"I'll go back and tell the police about this strange woman and then I'd better get home to Jamie. Young Samuel should be awake by now and I promised to go with them to the park." He thanked Beryl for taking care of Ted and promised to help out if there was anything they needed.

William was pleased to see Constable Bailey when he arrived at the station. The formidable Barry Giles had left. Soon he was filling the constable in with the new information.

"We have had no luck finding this woman either. We had a name and that was about it. No address or contact number. It is strange that she came without authority, but she might just have been desperate for a job."

William had to agree. The woman may have heard of the vacancy and made the most of the opportunity. "I know that Beryl Griffin was with her mother many miles from here when the fire started, but I'm not sure that Ted Baker has an alibi. The incident has affected him strangely. I wouldn't have thought that he would be capable of such an act, but there were many documents in those filing cabinets that he didn't want anyone to know about."

"The fire service and the police have lifted the protection order from the building so you should be able to go in and check out the damage. Any papers that are readable can be taken away and sorted. Would you be able to organize that?" Constable Bailey wanted the whole mater cleared so the building could be demolished. It would be a target for vandals the way it was.

With Jason's help William thought they could move any readable pages into his garage. It would mean leaving the car outside but it would be their only chance to salvage some of the documents before the building was bull dozed.

But how were they going to find the mysterious Betty Long? Her name didn't appear in the phone book but the police should be able to check bank accounts and licensing details. He remembered that she had mentioned going to the nail salon and the hairdresser in the nearby arcade. Perhaps they would know something about her. He would ask Jamie to help him with that and she could treat herself to a manicure and hair cut at the same time.

By the time he got back to his house he was feeling much more positive. Samuel was ready for his trip to the park and they set off in the brisk air, well wrapped up in track suits and hats.

****

Joanne was quite excited when she knew that Greg Forman would come to the school. She had cleared it with the principal who thought it was a splendid idea. "You can ask him about the new playground we are supposed to be getting at the local park. That seems to have been put on the back boiler."

"I'll make a list of possible questions and let the children ask them. I want them to feel really involved. I must remember to bring my camera along and get a photo of Mr Forman in the classroom."

When the time came, Joanne felt quite nervous. Several of the children had been given a slip of paper with the question they would ask. The stories and photos from the newspapers had already been glued to a wall chart so the room was ready.

When Greg Forman was shown into the room by the principal, Joanne was surprised to see Mrs Forman there as well. She really was very beautiful. Greg introduced himself and his wife to the class and it was a few moments before he turned and acknowledged Joanne.

"Thank you, Miss Bennett for inviting me. It is a real privilege to be here." He stared at Joanne as if he could hardly believe his eyes and for a moment was lost for words. His wife sat down on a nearby desk, her eyes wide with surprise.

"It was good of you to agree to talk to us. The children have some questions to ask you." Joanne was puzzled at the couple's reaction but moved smoothly on with the lesson.

Soon the pupils were firing their questions at the new councilor who answered most with ease. He wasn't prepared to commit himself on the subject of the playground, however, and said he would do his best to find out what progress had been made.

He and Gaynor agreed to be photographed and one of the pupils thanked him nicely on behalf of the class. It was time for the morning break, so Joanne was able to thank him personally. "I'm sure the children learned a lot today. Thanks again for taking the time to come here. It was good to meet you too, Mrs Forman."

She was surprised when Gaynor took her hand. "Look, you probably think I'm very rude, but when we saw you we got a bit of a shock. You see you look exactly like another beautiful young lady that we have met recently. Honestly, you could be taken for identical twins."

Joanne felt the blood drain from her face. These people knew Rachel, her elusive look alike. That was why they had looked so startled when they came into the room.

Greg turned and looked at her. "My wife is right. It was like seeing a ghost when we walked into the classroom. Rachel works at the Chronicle and she has written several articles for me. She has visited our home several times and we have grown very fond of her."

"I'd like to learn more about this person. Could we meet some time and talk about it. I have a few things I would like you to know." Joanne wanted to make the most of this unexpected opportunity.

"Please do come and visit us. I was planning to go away in the morning so maybe you come around later this afternoon. Do you have transport?"

Joanne thought quickly. She would like Jason to be there to hear what she had to say.

"My boyfriend can drive me over to your house. He knows as much as I do about the situation. We can be there around five o'clock if that's okay."

She showed them out and grabbed a quick cup of coffee before it was time to return to the classroom. Perhaps she would soon learn the truth about Rachel.

****

As he waited for Joanne and her boyfriend to arrive, Greg Forman was feeling anxious. He had only learned the truth about Jennifer six months ago when he was going through some papers after his father's death. He was horrified to find out that she had become pregnant and had died giving birth to the baby. Even though he had been just 18 years old, there was no way that he would have abandoned her if he had known the truth.

He assumed that the baby had not survived, but since meeting Rachel and now this other girl named Joanne, he was not so sure. He would need to learn their story. The resemblance to Jennifer was too strong to be ignored.

He had recently told Gaynor the sad story about Jennifer and she was horrified that Terence Forman had kept the truth from his son. Greg went off to business school, totally unaware of Jennifer's fate. The man must have paid the family to disappear and no doubt it was he who had footed the bill for the hospital expenses.

Gaynor sat down beside him. "Don't look so worried my dear. We are dealing with two very beautiful young women who happen to look alike. You say they also look a lot like the girl who died. Like three peas in a pod. It's probably just a huge coincidence. We may find that both girls were born to perfectly ordinary couples and there is no connection at all."

"I know. My imagination is playing tricks on me. Soon we will have a precious child of our own and I will be the best father ever." Greg touched the small baby bump affectionately. The danger period was past and Gaynor had never felt better.

Greg's son Martin was with his mother so it was Greg who set out the drinks while Gaynor prepared a platter of cheese and crackers. The weather was starting to turn cooler but they could still sit out on the patio at this time of the evening.

Joanne looked around in surprise as Jason pulled into the driveway. He had borrowed his father's car and was looking forward to this meeting with Greg Forman. He had read several articles about him and it would be interesting to meet the man himself.

This was certainly a palatial home. The chemical industry must be booming. They walked up the stone steps, bordered with white urns filled with elegant palms, which led to a massive wooden door.

A moment later Greg was there to welcome them and they were shown into a vast hallway and through a living area to the outdoor patio where Gaynor was waiting. "It's lovely to see you again." She smiled and invited them to sit on the comfortable lounge furniture which overlooked the pool.

"I feel as though I already know you as Rachel has been here twice already. Make yourself at home and Greg will pour you a drink." It felt really strange to be welcoming this girl who looked like Rachel and her boyfriend who was very different from Dirk. Jason was introduced and the conversation was general for a while.

Greg was first to broach the subject they had come to discuss. "We've met Rachel a number of times over the past few weeks and feel that we have become friends. I'm curious why someone else could possibly look so like her. If your hair was lighter, you would be identical."

Joanne wondered where to begin. "Yes, a couple of times lately I've caught sight of someone who looks just like me. She was also featured in a travel article about Rarotonga. In fact, one of my pupils brought the pictures to school because he thought it was me. A couple of people have mistaken me for a girl named Rachel so I'm guessing that is her name."

"Although we've met Rachel we know nothing of her circumstances. We don't know where she was born or who her parents are. That would be interesting to find out." Gaynor was intrigued by the whole mystery. "Now help yourself to some nibbles and Greg will fix you another drink."

"I've thought about meeting the girl and talking to her. I wasn't sure what I would say." Joanne was still not ready to tell the Formans the rest of the story.

"It's intriguing that you are so alike but even more strange that you both look like someone I used to know." Greg was also holding back. He was not ready to divulge the truth about Jennifer just yet.

"So tell us a little about yourself, Joanne. Where were you born and what is your family situation?" Gaynor wanted answers.

"My mum and dad are Madeline and Steve. We live about half an hour south of here and I have an older brother named Bradin."

"Rachel told me she was brought up in the country. She went to boarding school and has no brothers or sisters."

Jason had been silent until now. He was wondering where the conversation was going. He knew that Joanne was being evasive and he felt that Greg Forman knew more than he was letting on.

"Joanne, I think you should share a little more with Greg and Gaynor. You are keen to learn more about Rachel and this is probably the best chance you will have." Jason wanted the mystery solved one way or the other. Was Rachel the missing twin?

"All right." Joanne took another sip of her drink. "I was adopted by Madeline and Steve when I was a baby. I've always known that, but lately I found out that my birth mother died just after I was born.

"Our neighbours tracked down her parents who live in Hamilton. Her father is living with one of his sons at present. If this is true, I have a couple of uncles and several small cousins that I haven't met."

"That is a fascinating story Joanne. We would like you to come to dinner tomorrow night so we can get to know you better." Greg spoke quietly, showing no emotion.

Joanne felt drained after telling her story. She wasn't ready to share any more right now but would accept the invitation for the next night

As they left, Joanne felt quite shaky. "I didn't like to tell him the name of the girl who died and when I come to think about it I didn't tell them that I possibly have a twin."

Jason drove slowly out onto the street. "Greg wasn't telling us everything either. He seems to have a strong connection with that young girl who looked like you. I'm not sure what that's all about."

They drove a short distance and stopped at the edge of a reserve where children were playing on the swings and slides. There were climbing frames and jungle bars and a flying fox for the more adventurous. Jason put his arm around Joanne's shoulders and they sat for a time in silence.

"We must try to catch up with William and Jamie again soon. That fire has probably destroyed so much of William's personal collection. I know he had all his books and notes stored at the office."

"I feel so sorry for them. It would be good if they could take a holiday while he isn't working. William wasn't sure whether the office would reopen as Ted Baker was almost ready to retire."

"I can't see them getting away as someone will have to go through any files that were saved from the blaze. I wonder if they know how the fire started." Jason was worried about his friend who had appeared to be stressed even before the fire. He would phone him when he got back and see if there was anything he could do.

****

William was panicking. He had heard nothing more from the police and Ted Baker was not responding to his calls. He tried to contact Beryl Griffin but the phone number for her mother had been disconnected. She wasn't answering the phone at home either.

He needed to talk to someone. He wasn't sure if he still had a job and the mortgage payments would soon eat up their savings.

"I wanted to talk to my friend at the court but he has gone on leave for three months. Until they find out who was responsible for the fire, our whole future seems to be up in the air." Jamie had never seen William more despondent. They needed some answers and needed them fast.

"The only one you can talk to is Jason. Ask him to come around. He doesn't go back to Wellington for a few days and I'm sure he'll be able to help you." Jamie felt vulnerable. With a young child to care for she felt she could do little to ease the situation and returning to her studies was certainly out of the question.

Jason was only too happy to call on his friend. He needed the exercise so he would use his cycle. It had sat in the garage since the last time he was home. He found his helmet and leather jacket. The brisk autumn wind was a reminder that winter would soon be here.

He wanted to tell his friend about the strange visit to the Formans' home the night before. He was sure that Greg Forman was hiding something and that it involved Joanne.

William was alone in the house as Jamie had taken the car to the shopping mall He was keen to tell Jason that he had met the elusive Rachel and knew where she lived. He wasn't sure how much more he could share about the contents of the files.

"I want you to keep this to yourself, but the fire at the office was no accident. Someone deliberately lit it to destroy the documents in the filing cabinets. I've spoken to the police and they are talking to everyone who had access to the building." William looked exhausted.

"That's terrible. I imagined it would have been some electrical fault and the insurance would cover everything. You must have lost a considerable amount of material."

"I think so, but I won't really know until they let someone back into the building to sort through the mess. My files were not near the source of the fire and the cabinets could have saved them. But the main worry is that I don't know when I'll be returning to work, if at all." William was pacing up and down.

"To change the subject, you'll never guess who I banged into at the police station? I met Rachel, the journalist who wanted to interview me, and if she's not Joanne's twin sister, I'll eat my hat."

Jason did a double take. "That's a strange coincidence because Joanne and I were invited to Greg Forman"s home. I'm sure he knows more than he's saying about the girl who died at the nursing home. He keeps insisting that she looked exactly like both Joanne and this Rachel."

William took a deep breath. He knew the time had come to share more information with his friend.
"Okay, this is what I found out from the files. Two babies were adopted a few weeks apart. One went to Madeline and Steve Bennett and the other to a couple named Marjorie and James Saunders. The mother was Jennifer Blake, deceased, and the father was named as Gregory Forman. They were just two of the adopted babies on the document.

"The worst thing was that someone was making a great deal of money from the adoptions. The maternity services at the nursing home closed down just after Jennifer died but the circumstances have never been made public."

William took the document from his case and handed it to Jason. "I think this is one of many secrets hidden in those burned files. I kept a copy and returned the originals. Now I feel as though I'm sitting on a load of dynamite."

"Wow. What can I say? Greg Forman is Joanne's father? No wonder he was so fascinated with both the girls. He must have been a teenager when they were conceived and his family probably paid for the hospital treatment. Do you think he knew the babies survived?"

"That's something I don't know, but it's almost certain that Terence Forman took care of the details. He was on the board of the nursing home at the time and arranged the closure of the place soon after the tragedy."

William stood and took a bottle of whisky from the drinks cabinet. "I think we need this. I'm relieved to have shared the information but I still don't know where to go from here."

"Maybe nobody else needs to know apart from the girls. It really only concerns them and their father. Although I suppose the adoption details need to be kept somewhere safe in case anyone is looking for their birth parents."

"This is only one of several files. They listed adoptions over about 20 years. The rest would have gone up in smoke."

The two men sat in silence, the enormity of what William had uncovered hung heavily between them. They heard the sound of a car engine and a few moments later Jamie was in the room, Samuel clutching her hand as he tottered along beside her.

"Hi guys. I'll leave a little boy with his father while I unload the groceries." She handed the wriggling child to her husband and headed back towards the car. William picked Samuel up and tossed him in the air. "How's it going buddy? Did your mother buy out all the shops?"

Jason finished his drink and stood up ready to leave. He wanted to be home before the rush hour. "What you've told me today needs a lot of thinking through. I won't say anything to Joanne for now. We'll wait and see what eventuates. Take care now and try not to worry too much."

"Thanks. I feel better already at having shared the load. It would be good for you to meet Rachel then decide for yourselves how much you want to share. It could be a good result for everyone." William looked much happier as he followed Jason outside. Perhaps there would be a happy ending after all.

Chapter 24

Dirk had been sent away on an overnight job so after Rachel finished work she went home to an empty apartment. It was a good chance to catch up on some chores and have an early night. She was almost ready to go to bed when the phone rang. It would probably be Dirk wanting to say good night.

"Hullo Rachel. It's Greg Forman here. How are you?"

"I'm fine. I had a busy weekend as it happened and tonight I'm catching up."

"Rachel, there's something I want you to do for me. Could you come over for dinner tomorrow night? There's someone I want you to meet. It really is very important."

"I guess I can do that. But Dirk is away and won't be back until late tomorrow. I really don't have any way of getting to your house." What could possibly be so important that Greg wanted her to visit?

"I can call for you or better still, I can get someone else to pick you up. I have invited another person along you see, because I feel you might have something in common."

Rachel was mystified. She'd rather wait for Dirk to come back but knew that he wasn't due until later in the evening. She found herself agreeing to go along with the arrangements. It all sounded very intriguing and by then she would have completed her second screen test at the television studio.

She climbed into bed with a book. If the phone
rang, she didn't hear it. She was asleep almost as
soon as her head hit the pillow.

****

When Joanne asked Jason to drive her to Greg
Forman's house, he reluctantly declined. The car
wasn't available for a start and he had promised
William to help move the damaged files from the
office to his garage. He had managed to coerce
Geoffrey into helping as well and it had to be done
that evening as the building could be demolished at
any time and the remaining files would end up as
land fill.

Joanne was ready to cancel the dinner invitation
when her brother overheard the conversation and
offered his services. "It's okay sis. I can be your
escort tonight. I'd like to see how the rich and
famous lead their lives.'

Greg didn't seem bothered about who was escorting
her, but he asked them to call at an address to pick up
another passenger. He felt it was time to get the two
girls in the same room and see what eventuated.

It was after four before Joanne arrived home from
school. She wanted to have a quick shower and wash
her hair before going to the Formans' house. Gaynor
always looked so immaculate, she felt she needed to
upgrade her image to match.

Instead of the usual pony tail, her hair fell to her shoulders and she chose a trendy pant suit in pale green. "You do look nice, Joanne. Your brother had better be on his best behaviour to keep up." Madeline had insisted that Bradin wear a clean pair of jeans and a smart shirt.

Steve looked up from the newspaper and smiled. "You're a good-looking pair and no mistake. Make sure you bring you sister home safely." Madeline had baked a chocolate cake and insisted that they take it along. "You can't arrive empty handed," she said.

It took a while to find the address on the note that Joanne was holding. Bradin took a wrong turning somehow and they ended up on the wrong side of the highway. Joanne was studying the map and they retraced their route.

"This must be it. That block of apartments. Just turn into the driveway and I'll find the right one." Bradin parked the car and Joanne got out to check the numbers on the mail boxes. When she found the right address she pushed the buzzer beside the door.

A light came on and a few seconds later the door opened. The two girls stared at each other in amazement. Joanne imagined she was standing in front of a full length mirror while Rachel was mesmerized to see her image standing in front of her, the light shining on long shiny hair.

Joanne was the first to speak. Surely Greg could have warned her that she was about to meet her twin. This was a total shock. "You must be Rachel. I've

wanted to meet you for ages and it looks as though
Greg Forman has made it happen.'

Rachel pulled herself together. "Greg said he
wanted me to meet someone tonight, but I had no
idea it would be you. It is so weird that we look alike.
I can't imagine how that
could have happened."

"I guess it's just coincidence, but anyway, my
brother's waiting to drive us to the Formans' house
so we had better not keep him waiting."

Rachel locked the door and followed Joanne to the
car. Bradin did a double take when he saw the two of
them together. "Oh no. Not two Joannes. I don't
think I could cope with that."

For some reason they all saw the funny side and
dissolved into laughter. With Joanne in the front seat
and Rachel in the back, Bradin couldn't resist
playing the clown. "I want to drive us to the tavern
and show you off to my friends. They think my sister
is a babe. Imagine what they would say if I turned up
with two of you."

Joanne became serious. "Cut it out Bradin. Greg
and Gaynor are expecting us. We'd better not keep
them waiting." Rachel sat quietly in the back seat
watching the byplay. This was all new to her. How
much more crazy was her life to become?

The Formans' home was a short distance away and
Bradin acted like the grand chauffer as he opened the
car door and helped them out. "I hope you enjoyed

my grand limousine," he joked. "I'll try to bring the Rolls next time."

Rachel couldn't stop smiling. Although Dirk wasn't here to share the occasion, she had a feeling that the evening would be far from dull. She had visited the television studio earlier in the day and eaten lunch with Pete who was confident that she would be successful. "You'll be working with us before you know it," he told her as he dropped her off at the apartment.

Bradin continued to defuse the situation as he picked up a palm leaf and fanned himself. He knew instinctively that they had found Joanne's twin but the other girl seemed unaware of the situation. "Enter the temple of the master. Where do you think they keep the monkeys?"

Rachel was surprised when Martin opened the door. "Hi, I didn't know you would be here tonight." She walked confidently into the hall and through to the patio.

"We're in here tonight. It's too cold outside." Gaynor's voice came from the living room. "Do come in and make yourselves at home. Greg will be out in a moment.

Joanne was introduced to Martin who couldn't help looking from one of the girls to the other. "What is going on here?" he gasped.

Bradin was busy taking in the surroundings and trying to work out how much it had all cost. Being in the building trade made you think in those terms.

By the time Greg came into the room, Martin was pouring drinks and Gaynor was asking the girls how their day had been. Rachel and Joanne were sitting side by side on the sofa and he found it difficult to tell them apart. Their initial introductions must have gone well as the mood seemed positive.

"Thanks for coming here tonight. I'm sorry Dirk and Jason couldn't make it but it's good to meet you, Bradin. I probably should have warned you that I was going to spring something on you tonight and I'm not going to make any fancy speeches, but I just wanted to show you something." Greg reached into his pocket and took out a battered photograph.

"This is Jennifer. When I first met the two of you I couldn't believe my eyes. Jennifer suddenly went away and I only learned about six months ago that she had become pregnant but died when the child was born. I assumed the baby had died too but now I'm not so sure. In fact, I'm doubly not so sure."

He handed the photo to Joanne and as she looked at it her eyes misted over. "That's Jennifer. I believe she is my birth mother."

She silently passed the picture to Rachel whose eyes filled with tears. "But how can that be? My mother told me over Easter that I was adopted and gave me a photograph that had been left with my papers. I'm almost certain she's my birth mother."

"It looks as if this girl named Jennifer passed away as she gave birth to twins. Except for a couple of old photographs we really can't be certain that you are those children." Gaynor was trying to be practical. "But if you are those two babies, then I think it is a miracle that you have found each other."

Greg looked at the two girls sitting side by side in his living room. A feeling of joy began to sweep over him. It was as though Jennifer had returned from the grave. Surely his clumsy love making on that night so many years ago couldn't have produced such perfection.

Neither girl had moved. It was as though they were stunned. They looked at each other timorously, too choked up to speak. Joanne was the first to move. She flung her arms around Rachel and held her tightly.

"When I was a small child I was always reaching out for someone. It was as though something was missing," she sobbed.

"It was the same for me. I had an imaginary friend who I talked to all the time." Rachel pulled herself together. "Ever since I found out that I was adopted as a baby I have felt totally confused and unreal. To find I have a twin sister is even more unbelievable."

Gaynor had moved away to check on the meal which was in danger of over cooking. She turned the stove off and called Martin to join her. Bradin felt awkward so he followed them out of the room, leaving Greg and the girls alone.

"I think Greg needs some time with Rachel and Joanne. He may have something more to tell them." The boys followed Gaynor out to the patio where

Bradin lit a cigarette. "I hope you don't mind. This is all getting a bit too emotional for me."

Greg pulled up a chair and sat close to the two girls who were still sitting side by side. "Just before I left for business school Jennifer and I made love one evening and we went a bit further than we intended. We wrote for a time then the letters stopped coming. When I got back home my father told me that the family had gone to live up north. I tried to find out where they went but had no luck so I thought she had forgotten me.

"I did keep a photo that she gave me and carried it for ages in my wallet. I married and my son Martin was born, but we divorced shortly afterwards. Then I was lucky enough to meet Gaynor and we are very happy."

"So you say you didn't know that Jennifer became pregnant. She must have been devastated that you didn't keep in touch." Rachel could see where the story was leading but felt badly that the girl had been abandoned.

"After my father died about six months ago my sister and I had to go through his papers and we were horrified at some of the things we found out. Business dealings, hospital records, all sorts of transactions were covered up. That's when I learned that Jennifer had been treated at the Parkhaven Nursing Home and that she had died through lack of proper care.

"It affected my sister quite badly as she idolized her father and was proud of the family name. She was afraid that the documents would get into the wrong hands so together we destroyed them. Susan returned to Australia a disillusioned woman."

Joanne had been listening with bated breath but she could wait no longer to find out the rest of the truth. "So you are trying to tell us that you could be our father. But how do you know that she didn't sleep with anyone else?"

"Knowing Jennifer, I think that would be unlikely. Although she was very beautiful with her golden hair and flawless skin, she was actually quite shy and I doubt that she would have been with anyone else in that short time. But now that we have met, I would be very proud to be a father to two lovely girls like you."

At that moment Gaynor came back into the room. "I don't know about the rest of you but I'm starving. I think the girls have learned enough to digest for one night. Let's just relax and enjoy each other's company."

They all agreed. There were still a number of facts to be verified, but it looked as though Joanne and Rachel had truly found their other halves.

****

For Joanne it didn't take long for disbelief to turn into joy. She had been subconsciously searching for her twin for some time now and to finally meet this girl named Rachel was the answer to her prayers.

On the other hand, the news that she was adopted was still raw to Rachel and she had never known about a possible twin. It would take some time for this new information to sink in.

The mood was subdued as they sat around the dinner table, sharing the casserole which Gaynor had prepared. When it was time for Bradin to drive them home Greg gave each of the girls a hug. "You will need time to get to know each other. I'll always be available if there's anything you want."

As they got into the car Joanne asked Rachel if she would like to come home with her to meet Madeline and Steve but Rachel declined. Dirk might be back by now and she needed time to digest all that had happened.

"What about you and your boyfriend meeting us tomorrow night? We can have a meal and share our stories." Rachel was curious to learn more about this new person in her life.

She felt very much alone as she opened the door of her apartment. She knew that Joanne would be going home to share all the excitement with her family. It was too late to call her mother and Dirk had not returned. She was tempted to pick up the phone and call Greg's house. Her mind was racing.

Madeline and Steve were still awake when Bradin pulled into the driveway. They were full of curiosity about the visit to the Formans' home. Madeline pulled on her robe and met Joanne in the hallway. "How was the dinner? Did you meet some interesting people?"

"I think you need to sit down, mum. I've got so much to tell you I hardly know where to start." She filled her mother in on the events of the evening and how she had met Rachel.   "He showed us a photo just like the one Flo got from Hamilton and it turns out that Rachel has one too. I don't think there is any doubt that Rachel is the tiny baby who was born just after me, but she had no idea that she was a twin. It was a huge shock to her to learn the truth."

"The poor girl. Are you going to see her again soon? Now that you have found each other you will have so much to share. I'm looking forward to meeting her and I know Flo will be so excited. We will have to organize a big celebration."

Joanne didn't want to rush things. "I have to give Rachel time to get used to the idea. She has only just learned that she was adopted, let alone that she is a twin. I can't wait to tell Jason about our meeting, but it will have to wait until morning."

It was a long time before Joanne fell asleep that night, the events of the evening spinning around in her head. Tomorrow she would meet Rachel again and they would begin to fill in all those missing years.

Chapter 25

Gathering up half burnt papers from a bleak charred building was a most depressing job and William was tempted to leave it all behind and let the demolition crew take it away. He was pleased to find that most of his personal files were still intact as the fire-proof cabinet had shielded them. The books on the open shelves were totally ruined, however, blackened with smoke and soggy from the firemen's hoses.

"I wonder if it's worth salvaging anything." Geoffrey looked around in dismay. "Are you sure any of this is worth saving?"

"If someone went to the trouble of trying to destroy these documents there must be something of value. But you're right. It will be a soul destroying task." They pulled half burnt documents from the twisted metal and threw them into rubbish sacks. Soon the car boot was filled and they delivered them to William's garage.

An hour later they had retrieved several bags of paper and decided to call it a day. With no power, the building was now in darkness until the security guard produced a strong light as they gathered the last load.

Back home, William was ready for a shower to wash away all trace of the smoke and grime. He had dropped his friends off at their house and thanked them for their help. "I'll contact the police in the morning and tell them we have taken all we can from the building. I guess the wreckers will be in as soon as possible. It's a sad end for the once great firm of Barlow and Reid."

Flo had kept a meal for Jason and Geoffrey She was curious to learn that Joanne had been invited to the Formans' home for dinner. "I wonder what that's all about?" she asked. She was disappointed that she had heard nothing back from the Blake family in Hamilton. She thought that one of Jennifer's brothers might have been in touch by now.

Jason would love to have driven Joanne to the Formans' home, but now he knew Greg Forman's secret he would have to be careful not to let the cat out of the bag just yet. It was up to Greg to enlighten the girls when he was ready. He heard Bradin's car return and half expected Joanne to arrive on the doorstep. He would have to wait until morning to find out what happened.

With just two days to go before they were to return to Wellington, Jason was anxious to help William in any way he could. Who could have wanted to destroy the documents in those old filing cabinets so badly that they would have burned down the whole building?

He suspected the old lawyer Ted Baker. He probably had the most to lose if the papers got into the wrong hands. He had also been acting strangely since the fire, not communicating with anyone. Beryl Griffith the secretary was also under suspicion but she appeared to have a water tight alibi if she had been with her mother many miles away.

He was sure that William was innocent as he and Joanne had been with him that evening and what possible reason would he have to destroy documents when he didn't even know what they contained? He wondered about the temporary secretary Betty Long. The fact that she had turned up out of the blue was suspicious but what motive could she possible have?

****

After tossing and turning for an hour, Rachel got out of bed and heated up some milk. She was relieved to hear Dirk's car pull into the driveway and she met him with open arms when he came through the door.

"That's a nice welcome. I meant to be back earlier but it was hard to drag myself away from paradise.

Dirk had spent the previous night at a new resort which would cater for the ski season. He had been treated to a night of luxury with a spa treatment and five course dinner so he certainly wasn't complaining.

"You'll never guess who I met tonight. My twin sister. I'm not kidding. I actually have a twin sister." Rachel sounded hysterical. "A week ago I was an only child with two perfectly normal parents and now I have a bunch of strangers, all claiming to be my long lost family."

"Hey. Slow down and tell me what's going on. I can't keep up with you." Dirk led Rachel to the couch and sat beside her. "You mean that girl who looks like you is actually your twin? How can you know for sure?"

"She has a photo exactly the same as mine. The really weird part is that Greg Forman has one too. They are all photos of a dead girl named Jennifer. You're not going to believe this bit, but it looks as if Greg is actually my father. He made love to Jennifer when he was a teenager and it seems that Joanne and I are the result."

"Greg Forman? Wow! But you could do worse. He seems like a really good bloke and he's very rich." Dirk was intrigued by the whole scenario. It was as though a screen play was unraveling before him.

Rachel was still confused. "It's so weird. I guess I should be overjoyed as I always wanted a sister, but I don't have any feelings for these people. They are like strangers to me."

Dirk went to the cupboard and brought out a bottle of red wine. He poured two glasses and handed one to Rachel. "Here. Let's just sit and talk about it. These people are strangers to you. You have only just met them and it will take a while to get to know them. I hope you've arranged to meet up again soon."

Rachel confirmed that they would meet the next evening. "I've invited Joanne and her boyfriend to dinner. We could eat here or go out somewhere. What do you think?"

"It might be easier to meet at a restaurant the first time and take it from there." Dirk knew of a quiet place where they could relax and chat. He would phone tomorrow and reserve a private booth.

It was such a relief to have Dirk back that Rachel felt much more relaxed. She had seldom let anyone get close to her. Was it too late to start now?

****

As soon as he had finished breakfast, Jason excused himself and headed next door to Joanne's house. With the boys home, Flo had insisted on a full meal of bacon and eggs. "Goodness knows what you will eat when you get back to Wellington. And don't forget to make sure all your washing has been put in the laundry." The boys were leaving next day and she wanted them to start off with clean clothes. They were due to fly out in the evening and Stan was to drive them the short distance to the airport.

The Easter break had provided an unexpected chance to see her sons and they would be home again at the end of the term which was only a few weeks away.

Joanne was reading the morning paper and jumped up as he opened the door. "Hi. I was hoping you would come over. How's the packing going?"

"I haven't really started as my mother insists on washing and ironing everything. We've got all day tomorrow before we fly out." Jason went to sit down but Joanne felt restless.

"Let's go for a walk. It's a lovely morning and I have so much to tell you."

"In that case, I'll get my jacket and meet you outside."

A short time later they were strolling arm in arm along the quiet street towards the park. Apart from a few people walking their dogs the streets were deserted. Joanne wasn't sure where to start. She had so much to share with Jason and so little time before he went away. The parting would be easier than last time as he would be back in a short time and Joanne would be on a welcome holiday.

It was hard to believe that she had finally met the twin she had been thinking about for months. She would have to tell her friend Tracey all about it. They hadn't got together over Easter as Tracey had been staying with Mike at his parents' beach house. Things seemed to be getting really serious in that relationship.

Jason described the unpleasant task of moving the half burnt papers into William's garage. "I'm sure the building will be bulldozed this week. They won't want to keep a security guard there any longer than they have to. But tell me, how did your dinner at the Formans' house go? What did Bradin think about it?"

"You'll never believe who Greg asked us to pick up. It was Rachel, the girl I keep seeing who looks just like me, and it seems as if she really could be my twin. She has a photo of Jennifer just the same as mine. Someone left it with her papers when she was adopted."

Jason was quiet. He knew the truth about the twins' adoption but he wanted to wait for the right moment to share it. William might find all sorts of new information about the birth and nursing home when he looked through the papers in his garage. He would wait and see what Joanne had to tell him first..

They came to a walking track through the park where the trees were shedding their autumn leaves making a colourful, crackling pathway. A small stream ran alongside the track, rippling over the smooth pebbles and shining in the sunlight.

Jason stood and watched the water flow by. He would be back in the busy, bustling city of Wellington soon and would miss the time with his parents and Joanne. Especially Joanne. It just felt so right to be by her side.

"We've been invited to have dinner with Rachel and her boyfriend tonight. I hope you can come along. I do so want you to meet her. I keep getting this excited fizzy feeling in my stomach every time I think about her. There is so much I want to ask her."

"I would have preferred a night out just with you, but I must admit I am very curious about this girl named Rachel. Just think, you were born together and then separated. You've been brought up in different environments. I can't wait to learn how it has affected your personalities."

"It sounds as though you are doing a case study on us, but you're right. We should have been brought up in the same household, made to wear the same clothes, gone to the same schools, but it sounds as though our lives have been quite different."

"I know my mother is over the moon that you have found each other. She always does like a happy ending. She wants to go back and visit that woman in the rest home and let her know what has happened."

Joanne thought about old Marie. It was because of her that they had got this far. She may not remember telling them the story, however. Her mind was very disturbed and it was hard to know how much of what she said was true.

She had hardly given school a thought but would be back in the classroom tomorrow with new lessons to prepare. The wall chart about the council elections had been completed along with the photograph of Greg. She still hadn't accepted the idea that he may be her father. Jennifer could easily have slept with someone else after he left for business college, but if it could be proved, Martin would be her half brother with a sibling to come.

It was arranged that Dirk and Rachel would call and collect Joanne and Jason about five o'clock. This would give them time to meet Joanne's parents for a quick drink and it was almost certain that Flo would pop in out of curiosity. Joanne once again took extra care with her appearance. Her hair was glossy and make up perfectly applied. She didn't want to look like the ugly sister in the children's story.

The nervous feeling in Joanne's stomach had turned into full fledged butterflies by the time the car pulled up in the driveway. Madeline was just as excited. How would she feel about meeting the twin of the child she had raised?

Steve opened the door and smiled in welcome. "Come on in. We've been looking forward to this day for quite some time." He led Rachel and Dirk into the living room where the others were waiting. There was a flurry of introductions and glasses of drink were poured. Bradin had one up on the others as he had met Rachel the night before. He thought it was all a bit of a hoot. Maybe life back in New Zealand wasn't so dull after all.

Madeline took Rachel by the hand. "You're just lovely my dear. I'm so happy to meet you. Come and sit beside me and tell me about yourself."

"Give the girl a chance, love. She's probably totally confused at meeting us all." Steve was his usual genial self. He turned his attention to Dirk who was standing by the window taking in the scene. "You look as if you should be playing for the All Blacks. A good strong fellow like you."

"I doubt it sir. If I played rugby it would be the Springboks I would choose. That's the best team in the world." Dirk smiled at his host. It was a long time since he had played the game of rugby but knew everyone in this country was crazy about it.

Joanne caught Rachel's eye and shrugged her shoulders. "You'll get used to my family after a while," she said, apologetically, but Rachel was enjoying herself. "No seriously, this is fun. I'm not used to a family. My parents have always been a little too formal."

She found a seat beside Joanne and they glanced at each other. They had both taken a glass of Chardonnay and they sipped it slowly as Jason and Dirk shook hands and stood together behind the couch.

It didn't take long for Flo and Stan to join them, Flo barely able to control her excitement. "Oh my goodness. Just look at the pair of you. What a happy day this is." Her eyes filled with tears as she squeezed Rachel's hand. "That strange woman at the rest home was right. Poor Jennifer did have two babies just like she said."

Jason led his mother to a chair. "Sit down Mum and don't embarrass the girls. They are just getting used to the idea themselves. Welcome Rachel. I've been looking forward to meeting you. I leave for Wellington tomorrow night but I'll be back in a few weeks for the winter break."

Joanne finished her drink and rose to her feet. "We'll need to be getting away soon. Do you want to see my room?" She looked at Rachel who nodded in agreement.

There was a moment's silence as the two girls left the room. Madeline was fighting back the tears. "If

we'd known there were two of them they need never
have been separated. We would have found room for
two little babies."

"I know love. It would have been a bit of a stretch
but we would have managed." Steve choked up.

"They're together now and have a lot of catching up
to do. Let them take it slowly. It will take some time
for them to adapt." Jason could see that everyone was
getting very emotional but he knew that they needed
to stay calm.

Rachel looked around Joanne's bedroom which
probably hadn't changed since she was a child. One
of the single beds had been exchanged for a larger
one, but apart from that, the floral duvets, the old oak
dressing table, writing desk and book case belonged
to a much younger girl. She thought of the apartment
she was now sharing with Dirk. What would Joanne
think of the Queen-sized bed and the stark modern
furniture in the living room?

She stood beside Joanne as she applied fresh
lipstick. The two faces in the mirror were reflected
back and they couldn't help smiling. Joanne pulled
her hair over her face in the same style as Rachel's
and they laughed aloud.

"It would be fun to dress alike and get the same hair
do. We could fool everyone, but I'd have to lose a
few pounds." Joanne looked ruefully at her curvy
body.

"You look fine. Maybe I need to gain weight, then
we would be equal." Rachel admired Joanne's

curvaceous figure. She would love to look like that. She noticed the photo attached to the mirror on the dressing table.

"It's so weird that we both have the same photo. My mother gave it to me just a few days ago, when she told me that I was adopted. I think she was worried that I would meet you and find out the truth."

"I have always known that I was adopted but the story about our birth mother is new to me as well. Jason's friend William is trying to find out more, but he's been distracted by the horrible fire."

"I met William when I was sent to the burned building to do a story. The police say it was arson but I don't think they have found out who was responsible. I didn't know he was a friend of yours."

Madeline put her head around the corner of the bedroom. "Are you girls going to stay here all night? I think the boys are ready to take you to dinner." She was pleased to see the pair so deep in conversation. The awkward moments appeared to be over.

It didn't take long to say their goodbyes and drive away. "I hope you like the restaurant. It has a great atmosphere, almost French, and I've booked a quiet table." Dirk had everything under control.

Joanne was happy to sit so close to Jason in the rear seat. Tomorrow she would be back at school and he would be leaving for Wellington. It would be a long, lonely time until the next break.

****

Antoines Restaurant was a great success. They were shown into a booth with soft leather couches and a chunky wooden table. The menu was extensive with many dishes new to all of them. Dirk ordered a plate of escargot cooked in garlic herbed butter and laughed at the look on the girls' faces when large snails were placed before them. They had to admit that they were delicious, but no-one could persuade them to try the frogs' legs.

A bottle of red wine was soon empty and they started on a second as they dined on the finest steak, veal and chicken dishes, subtly flavoured with sauces and herbs. Jason was a little nervous about the price, but knew it was a very special occasion and a night they would always remember.

"It's a pity you're leaving tomorrow. We could have done this more often." Dirk was enjoying Jason's company and was keen to get to know him better. The girls had gone to find the toilet and they were alone.

"I have seen more details of the girls' birth details and William is still searching for information in what's left of the files from the law office. But I think they have enough to handle for the time being." Jason was not ready to tell them about the adoption papers. Although they suspected that Greg Forman was their father, they had no real proof.

It was after midnight when Dirk drove back to Joanne's house. The girls had arranged to meet for a drink on Friday night. Joanne hoped that Bradin would give her a ride into the city and Rachel had offered her a bed for the night. "The spare room is nice and tidy right now because my mother has just left. It's not always like that, I can tell you."

Joanne and Jason lingered over their goodnight kisses. It was decided that Joanne would go with them to the airport when she got back from school. It would be a bit of a squeeze but she wanted to be there. The parting was not as difficult as before, as Jason was due back in four weeks for the winter break.

Joanne let herself quietly into the house. She felt elated after such a magic evening and this was only the beginning. Three days of school and then she would stay at Rachel's apartment. There was so much she wanted to learn about her new sister.

Chapter 26

A week after the Easter break William received some good news. He was offered a job at a major law firm which was expanding into the suburbs. He came off the phone and called out to Jamie. "Hey, I think we can afford that holiday after all. I've just had a call from Thompson and Brent and they've offered me a job."

"Oh boy! That is exciting. Where will you be based and when do you start?" Jamie rushed over and gave William a hug.

"They're opening a new office in Henderson which is only about a half hour drive. I'm to start in three weeks time. Pack your bathing suit. We're off to Rarotonga." William had been tempted by Dirk Kloeten's travel article and knew it would be a perfect place for a break. He would call at the travel agency and make the arrangements.

Jamie felt like dancing around the room and Samuel picked up on the mood and began to wave his arms about in excitement. William picked him up and twirled him around. "You'll be able to swim in the warm sea, little buddy, and run on the sandy beach."

William had called at Ted Baker's house several times and the old man was beginning to show signs of improvement. Beryl Griffin had moved into his home and taken over the role of housekeeper.

"We're still no further ahead with finding out who lit the fires. Maybe it was just some street kids wanting to make trouble." William could think of no other solution. Neither he nor Jamie had had any luck tracing the mysterious Betty Long. Jamie had chatted with the staff at the hair salon but they knew very little about her.

They looked up the name in the appointment book. "This woman came in one day and wanted her hair dyed blond and styled. She certainly looked different when we had finished with her and we suggested that she would need brighter lipstick. She didn't make another booking." The girl was most helpful, but couldn't tell her any more.

The nail salon produced another dead end. They didn't recall any particular blond with long finger nails. Most of their clients looked a lot like that.

William didn't tell Ted or Beryl that he had salvaged some of the files. As far as they knew the whole lot had been destroyed and the building bull dozed. He had begun the unenviable job of sifting though the charred remains but had found nothing of interest. He would try to complete the task and dispose of the bags of rubbish before they went away.

The agency called later in the afternoon and confirmed that bookings had been made for air flights and seven days' accommodation. They would be leaving in just five days, so Jamie was in a spin, pulling out suitcases and sorting the summer clothes that had been packed away.

She held up her flimsiest summer dress. "Do you really think it will be warm enough to wear this?" Shorts, t-shirts, light trousers and sandals were soon spread out in the spare bedroom. Samuel had almost out grown his summer clothes but Jamie managed to find enough that still fitted. "We'll get him an island shirt and one for you as well," she laughed.

After all their recent problems, it was so good to have something to look forward to. The police hadn't interviewed William again, but he did call and tell them about the woman having her hair dyed blond. She was obviously keen to change her appearance.

"We haven't had any luck tracking down this woman. She didn't appear to have any bank accounts in that name and no postal address or telephone." Constable Bailey was keen to trace this mysterious woman. At this stage the chief suspects were some young people who had been caught vandalising a school building, but no-one had been charged.

"I'll just go outside and check a few more files. I want to get that job done as soon as possible so we can have our garage back." William left Jamie to prepare lunch and went out to the single bay shed which sat on the lawn a little way from the house. It would be good to have a larger garage built on to the house at some stage, but it was one of the plans that had been put on hold.

He took a folder from the bag and emptied it onto the trestle table that he had set up to make the job easier. Most of the pages were intact and he read through them one by one and threw them into a large cardboard box which was already half full.

He found himself looking at a cash ledger, the columns all carefully filled in. The wording at the top was partially obscured but the words and numbers on the page were clearly visible. He was looking at a bill for a medical procedure. Surgeon, anesthetist, hospital charges and a whole list of equipment and dressings.

He picked up the next page and found the same thing. The procedures seemed expensive but it didn't state what they were. The patients were not named and neither were the doctors. Surely one of these papers would name the hospital and explain what type of operations were being carried out.

He placed the pages in a separate pile. These wouldn't be going into the recycling until some questions were answered. They were probably just routine operations on people who could afford private hospital care, but if that was the case, why would someone want to destroy them?

He heard Jamie calling him in for lunch, but his interest had been aroused and he would get back to the garage as soon as he could. Jamie had other ideas as Samuel needed a new pair of sandals and her bathing suit was totally ruined. "I wore it while I was pregnant and it's gone all out of shape. I really need to go to the mall to find a new one."

It was rather late in the season to find a bathing suit but after a bit of searching they found a store that had some left over from summer. The best thing was they had been reduced to half price and Jamie found one that she was happy with.

The shoe store was the next stop and they emerged with cute sandals for Samuel as well as a pair each for Jamie and William. "Just as well I'm starting work soon. We're getting through our savings fast." William sighed, but he was in a cheerful mood. Life had taken a turn for the better.

****

The newspaper office was busy as the last stories were laid out on the pages. The typesetters had made up all the advertisements and added them to the dummy. As Bill Osborne placed the last page into the box to take to the printer, he turned to Rachel.

"We won't be doing it this way much longer. I've had a call from head office and we'll all be working on computers before we know it."

"That should be interesting. It'll take a while for us to learn how to use them and the girls in production won't be very pleased." Rachel had been given a few computer lessons during her training and knew that big changes were in store.

"The printers' union has already called a meeting for later in the week. They don't want journalists taking over typesetters' jobs. Well. I'd better be off. These pages will be on the printing press tonight."

It was an hour's drive to the printing company which produced the newspaper and sometimes Rachel made the journey in the company car. How much easier it would be just to send the pages over with the push of a button.

She tidied her desk and ate the last of the bread roll she had started at lunch time. Her phone rang and it was Joanne. She was waiting for Jason's family to leave for the airport and just wanted to catch up. "That was such a good night and I'm looking forward to staying at your place. It will be a great chance to talk."

"You must miss Jason when he's gone. I'm sure getting used to having Dirk around." She couldn't imagine being apart for all those weeks. It must be hard to keep the relationship alive.

She knew their friendship could be on shaky ground. She couldn't see Dirk staying around writing travel articles for much longer. He was a wanderer at heart and would soon be off looking for the next great adventure.

She suddenly remembered that she should be at a council meeting. They were voting this afternoon on the new bypass and she needed to catch up with the result. She would stay for a short time then pick up some fresh food and cook a meal for Dirk tonight. After that she would make up the spare room ready for Joanne. They could go through her photograph albums and compare notes. That would be a good way to fill in those missing years.

****

The council meeting was in full session and Greg was trying to focus on the discussion taking place. All this talk about bylaws and terms and conditions was a bit mind boggling. Why couldn't people be allowed to just get on with what they wanted to do?

He knew the new bypass would be a death sentence for the half a dozen small businesses that struggled to survive on the highway, but they would be compensated and able to move to a better location.

He would certainly be voting in favour of the new route to the city. He opened his wallet to check whether he had brought along the parking permit he would need to visit the transport office on his way home. His eye fell on the photograph that he always carried.

His mind went back to the dinner he had shared with Jennifer's daughters just two nights before. It took his mind back all those years to the time he last saw her. She was heartbroken that he was leaving and wouldn't be back until the end of the term. She said she would write and would love him forever.

When her letters stopped coming and he found that her family had moved his pride was hurt. How could she go off without a word? His father told him to forget her and move on. "There are plenty of suitable young women for you to partner. Our family has many influential friends with beautiful daughters."

They had held dinner parties and invited many suitable young girls to the house. Tennis games were arranged and barbecues, but Greg had been bored with them all. Jennifer, with the soft hair and glorious eyes was the only one he craved for.

He came out of his day dream with a jolt. The chairman was calling for votes on the new bypass and the councilors voted in favour by a wide margin. A crowd of spectators had gathered for the session and several stood up and applauded the result. A larger group left the chambers, muttering their disproval at a decision that would change their lives.

He was surprised to see Rachel emerge from the press bench. He hadn't seen her earlier and went across to talk to her before she left. Her face lit up when she saw him and there was just time for a quick word before the next item on the agenda. "I had a great time catching up with Joanne last night. She is staying at my apartment on Friday night which should be interesting."

"I'm so pleased for you. Do come and visit at any time. Gaynor and I would be happy to see you." There was no time for further words and Rachel left to go back to the office.

One of the other councilors looked across at Greg. "She's a bit of all right that one. Is she a friend of yours?"

"You could say that. Yes, she's a very special friend." He smiled as he took his seat. How good it would be to stand up and claim the girls as his own. That would be a very proud day indeed.

As she was leaving the council building, Rachel noticed the crowd standing outside the door. They were gathered around a woman who was speaking in a loud voice, protesting at the decision that had just been made. "Don't they realise that highway will completely ruin our neighbourhood and all our local shops will go? What's wrong with these people? Don't they have a heart?"

Rachel introduced herself and began jotting down the concerns of the objectors. She wrote down a few names and got permission to quote them. There were two sides to every story and she needed to maintain a balance of opinion.

Outside on the pavement a television crew was waiting. Rachel recognized the reporter and waited, fascinated to see what she would do. The woman stood there, blond hair smoothed down with just a few strands escaping to blow across her face. She was reading from a board with the cameras focused upon her, then she turned to an angry bystander and asked him some questions.

The whole scene was over within minutes. The reporter hung about looking bored while the gear was packed into a waiting van. Rachel noticed one of the cameramen who had been involved in her trial at the studio. "Hi. So this is how you fill in your day?" The man recognized her and stopped for a moment.

"Has the studio got back to you yet? They really liked your work. You should be hearing from them soon." He climbed into the van and drove off. They had to interview the shopkeepers who would be affected by the new road and be done in time for the six o'clock news.

Rachel stood and watched them as they drove away. It would be very flattering to be accepted for television, but was that the type of journalism she wanted to be involved in? She would be sure to watch tonight's news bulletin to see the result.

****

It was several hours before William got back to sorting the papers in the shed. He soon had a small pile set aside, all relating to hospital expenses which he would look at later. He sifted through more files, but they were so badly damaged by water that they fell apart as he tried to open them.

A thick file, secured by a charred string caught his eye. He could just make out the label - Vitex Industries. He remembered that this was the name of the company started by Terence Forman and now owned by his son Greg. The papers seemed to mainly deal with submissions about discharging water from the factory onto neighbouring land.

A small creek had been polluted and the environmentalists were up in arms. There were documents from lawyers wanting the factory to be closed down and reports from experts claiming that banned chemicals were being manufactured there.

William was puzzled. This had all happened about 10 years ago but he had never heard about it. Surely it would have been big news at the time. He would search through old newspapers to see what he could find. Big money must have changed hands to keep this episode out of the press.

He would also need to find out more about Vitex Industries. Perhaps a visit to Greg Forman would be in order. He was yet to meet the man he had heard so much about.

He took a note of the dates on the pages and decided to pay a visit to the library right away. Jamie was sitting in the living room engrossed in a book, while Samuel was taking his afternoon nap so he would make the most of the opportunity.

The librarian recognized him at once and was only too pleased to find the newspapers he needed. They had been reduced in size and he was handed a magnifying glass to peruse the pages.

He had the reading room to himself as he sat and skimmed through 10-year-old news. The 1970s seemed to be all about long hair and pop music. The Vietnam conflict was over with the US pulling out its troops, abortion was legalized in the US and New Zealanders were protesting against French nuclear testing in the Pacific.

He turned over the page and read that colour television arrived just in time for Princess Anne's wedding to Captain Mark Phillips, the Domestic Purposes Benefit was available to solo mothers and Fred Dagg was introduced to the public. William smiled. It had been a good time to be a teenager in New Zealand.

Vitex Industries was mentioned a number of times on the business pages, with share prices rising and changes in management. One lengthy article described the company's plan to create a clean, green environment and offered a prize for the best recycling ideas.

William made a note of this item and would follow it up with Greg when they met. He also noted the names of the CEOs around the time. If there had been a problem with pollution, it didn't appear to have been publicized and the company had gone out of its way to make amends.

He was just about to give up when a name hit him in the eye. It was a clipping out of a newspaper. 'Daughter of Terence Forman involved in shoplifting scandal. Susan Forman was stopped outside a bottle store with a cask of wine hidden under a shawl. She became aggressive when apprehended and will undergo a psychiatric report.' A photo of Susan Forman appeared on the page and William stared at it long and hard. The woman had brown curly hair and a solemn expression but if you looked closely, her facial features were very much like those of the missing secretary, Betty Long.

He would certainly be visiting Greg Forman now, to find out all he could about his sister Susan. Could this woman be the answer to the mystery of the horrendous fire?

Chapter 27

With the children well settled after the Easter break Joanne's days were busy. Everyone had stories to tell about the holiday and Joanne encouraged them to write a few sentences and illustrate their work. She hadn't prepared much in the way of worksheets but the days passed busily enough.

Every now and then she glanced at the photograph of Greg Forman which was prominently displayed on the notice board along with the rest of the council election project. The children were still talking about the visit from the councilor and Joanne found it hard to believe the events that had followed.

If Greg hadn't come to the classroom that day she may never have met her twin. He was the catalyst, the turning point in her life. He had loved Jennifer all those years ago, and now he could be part of her daughters' lives.

Joanne felt guilty that she had been neglecting her old friend Tracey. She would phone her tonight and arrange to meet for a much needed catch up. It seemed so long ago that the four of them had enjoyed that wonderful camping holiday in Coromandel. So much had happened since then and she wanted to share it.

The trip to the airport had been uneventful and Flo was quiet on the way home as she had got used to having her sons back in the house and missed them when they were away.

"They'll be back before you know it, eating us out of house and home." Stan tried to comfort her.

As she sat in the staff room sharing a cup of coffee with the rest of the teachers, Fiona sat down beside her. She looked exhausted from her busy day dealing with five year olds, and knew she had another hour's preparation ahead of her before she could go home.

'Those kids finish everything too quickly. Their attention span is so limited." She sighed and slumped in the chair.

"I'm pleased I chose to teach the next age group. At least they can tackle more complicated tasks." Joanne was feeling confident. She knew she was doing a good job and the children were responding to her whereas Fiona obviously needed more guidance from the senior teachers.

But now she needed to get home and decide what to take to Rachel's house. Bradin had promised to drive her there, before meeting some friends while Joanne spent the night at the apartment.

When she walked in the door, Madeline was sorting through a box of old photographs. "I thought it would be nice if you took a few of these with you when you go to Rachel's house. You were such a cute baby with your pretty curls and huge green eyes." She looked nostalgically at the photo she was holding. "And here you are taking your first steps."

"Rachel probably has photos too so I'll just take a few. We don't want to spend all night comparing baby pictures." Joanne hadn't seen most of the photos for some time and was soon caught up in the past, remembering herself as a small child then going to school and celebrating birthdays. There was one formal photo taken with Bradin. She had loved that red dress with a sailor collar and white cord knotted in the front.

She selected half a dozen photos and put them in an envelope. Rachel could see the rest some other time. The phone rang and it was Tracey, wanting to meet over the weekend. Joanne felt guilty once again that she couldn't be there for her and pulled a chair over to the phone to have a long chat. It would take some time to fill her friend in on all that had happened since they last met.

"I finally met the girl who looks like me and we were right. She really is my twin." Half an hour later they were still talking until Madeline called Joanne in to dinner. Tracey would drive over to see her next week. She and Mike were still an item and the family holiday had proved interesting.

"Mike's family is something else. Her father has remarried and his new wife and Mike didn't really get on. His two sisters were behaving like brats and ended up sulking most of the time. All we could do was walk on the beach to get away from them."

"I guess I'm lucky with the family I have. Rachel certainly seems to think so as her parents sound rather stuffy. I don't think she has been as lucky as me." Joanne was beginning to appreciate the people she had taken for granted all her life.

With the task of sorting through the damaged papers almost complete, William kept aside the pages that interested him and threw the rest into rubbish bags to take to the recycling depot. He thankfully piled the bags into the back of the wagon and headed for the dump.   There was no charge for recycled paper which he heaved into a giant bin in the yard which was overflowing with bottles and cans.

He had placed the newspaper item in a folder, along with the environmental and hospital reports and adoption papers. Now it was time to pay Greg Forman a visit. He pulled up outside the downtown office block and took the elevator to the eighth floor.

The receptionist looked up from her desk and pushed the buzzer to alert Greg Forman who opened his door and came out to meet William, shaking him firmly by the hand. Although he had no idea why William had come, the new councilor was always willing to speak with the residents of the area.

William sat down in the pristine office, noting the subtle décor which contrasted with the bold modern print hanging over the desk. He wasn't sure where this conversation was going to lead but started by explaining who he was and how his office had been destroyed by the recent fire.

"Someone deliberately set fire to the documents in several of the filing cabinets and we are trying to find out who would do such a thing. The only reason would be that there were sensitive papers in the files that this person wanted to destroy."

Greg listened with interest but wasn't sure what all this had to do with him. "Have you any idea what the documents contained?"

"That's why I'm here. There was quite a lot of information about your father's business affairs. I managed to rescue some of the papers, this one for example." William pulled out the charred pages reporting Vitex Industries and the pollution claims and handed them to Greg.

"If there was any substance to these accusations there could be good reason for someone to try to cover up the truth."

Greg gave a wry smile. "The environmentalists have always tried to close us down but my company is careful to maintain high standards. I admit my father was careless on that occasion but he made amends by supporting a major campaign that has resulted in a much cleaner, greener environment."

"That sounds fair enough. I can't imagine anyone burning down a building over that, but how about this one?" Greg found himself looking at an agreement signed by his father. His face turned pale as he read the contents. His father had agreed to cover up the death of Jennifer Blake when the hospital could have been charged with malpractice. And worse still, her parents had been paid to keep it quiet.

William sat silently waiting for Greg to react. Did he already know the truth about Jennifer's death after giving birth to twins and the closure of the hospital?

Greg didn't say a word, but reached across the desk and picked up the phone. "Cancel all my appointments for the rest of the day. Something important has come up." His hand shook as he replaced the receiver.

"This is the first I've known about much of this. We need to go somewhere and talk. I only found out recently that Jennifer had died from lack of proper care. I didn't know that the baby had lived, let along that there were twins. But to find out that my father was so closely involved in a cover up shocks me to the core."

They agreed to meet at Greg Forman's house in 20 minutes time. William thanked the receptionist who was looking most annoyed, and took the lift to the ground floor. He had a general idea where Greg lived from what Jason had told him, but it would be easier if he could follow his car.

A short time later he drove behind Greg's car and parked in the driveway. Greg opened the front door and ushered him inside. Gaynor had a doctor's appointment and wasn't due home for some time, so they had the house to themselves.

"I seem to be meeting a lot of new people lately but usually under better circumstances. I know that you are a friend of Jason's and you obviously know quite a lot about his girlfriend Joanne. Tell me what you have found and I'll try to help you as much as I can."

Greg offered William a drink and poured himself a whisky. He sat down on the leather couch and took a sip from his glass. At least the document he had just read proved that there were twin babies, but he didn't know for certain whether they had lived or died.

He tried to recall Jennifer's parents and justify why they would accept payment. They had recently arrived from Scotland and his father had arranged their work visa as he needed an engineer at the factory. It was likely that their housing had been provided as well and young Jennifer's pregnancy back in the 1960s would have brought disgrace to the family.

William spoke quietly. He could see that the news had shattered the other man. He told him all he had found out about Parkhaven Hospital and the large amounts paid for surgical procedures. "They must have had adequate equipment in the operating theatres, but not in the maternity section where Jennifer perished."

Greg was astounded at the list of operations and the costs involved. He knew his father was chairman of the board but thought he had little to do with the running of the hospital. He was too busy building up the chemical business at the time.

There was still one more page that William was concealing. It held the proof that Greg was looking for. He had only shared this information with Jason, the list of babies who were adopted and their new parents.

Chapter 28

As soon as Bradin arrived in from work on Friday, Joanne was ready to leave. "What's the hurry, Sis? We've got all evening." He didn't take long, however, to shower and change and soon they were heading for the city.

The traffic was thick as there was a major concert being held at the events centre that evening. A 1950s' band was coming to town. Dirk's car was parked outside the apartment and for a moment, Joanne wished that she could have Rachel to herself. But that wasn't fair. She knew that Jason would probably be with her if he wasn't back in Wellington.

Rachel was casually dressed in dark blue jeans and a floral shirt with her blond streaked hair tied back in a knot. She showed Joanne where to put her bag and Dirk poured them a wine as they settled on the black leather couch.

The décor was certainly very different from Joanne's cluttered home. Wooden crates had been painted bright green and served as shelves and a coffee table, while balloon shaped lamp shades hung from the high ceiling. Bright cushions in orange and shocking pink brightened the armchairs and a large screen television dominated one wall.

Joanne was envious. It would be very cool to have her own apartment and decorate it as she wished, but she knew it would be some time before she could afford it. She remembered the photographs and went into the bedroom to get them.

"My mother brought my album last time she stayed. Let's compare notes and see whether we have always looked alike." Rachel pulled her book down from the shelf and they opened the first pages together.

Dirk left them to it as he had an article to finish. Baby photos weren't exactly his thing and he would be better off working at the desk in the bedroom.

The early photos showed a big difference in their looks. While Joanne tended to be chubby, Rachel was petite which made her eyes look much larger.

"The lady I met at the rest home said you were just a little scrap of a thing and she wasn't sure whether you had survived. I wonder how long they kept you in the big hospital?"

"My parents have never told me about that. I guess they didn't get me straight away." Rachel realized there was very little she knew about the circumstances of her birth. It was a bit of a shock to learn that she had been frail. No wonder her mother had guarded her so carefully when she was young.

As they looked through the pages of Rachel's album, alongside the few photos that Joanne had brought, they could see how the likeness between them grew. By the time they were a year old, they were almost identical and by their two-year-old birthday, it would have been difficult to tell them apart.

"Far out! It's so weird to see pictures of myself in someone else's photograph album. Imagine what fun it would have been to grow up together. It's so sad that they kept us apart." Joanne was beginning to feel emotional. It seemed as though so many years had been wasted.

But now Dirk was ready to hit the road. They were off to the tavern where the girls had first glimpsed each other. This time they would be together and Dirk could hardly wait to see what the reaction would be from the regulars. The whole situation was like a movie plot and he couldn't wait to find out what would happen next.

Rachel shrugged. "That's Dirk. Always Mr Action Man, but he makes life interesting." They laughed as they picked up light jackets and followed Dirk to where the car was waiting.

It was several months since Joanne had last been in the tavern and she was surprised to see such a large crowd. It had become a popular meeting place and they were lucky to find a table with high wooden stools. The girls hung their jackets over the back of the seats while Dirk went to the bar to buy drinks.

They could see him talking animatedly and pointing in their direction. "Oh dear, it looks as if we are on show. I guess this is what twins have to put up with all their lives." Rachel tried to look inconspicuous.

"I don't mind. I think it's wonderful that we are finally being acknowledged for who we are." Joanne was all smiles. When Dirk returned he had another young man in tow.

"This is Steven. He wants to meet you, Joanne." The newcomer grinned. He was good looking in a relaxed, casual kind of a way.

"Hi, I've always told Dirk that he is lucky to have met Rachel, and now I see there are two of you. Do you mind if I join you?" This was a new situation for Joanne, as for so long she had only dated Jason. What harm was there in sharing the evening with someone else?

"Sure," she found herself saying. Steven gave her a warm smile. He dragged up an extra stool and placed his beer on the table. "I work with Dirk at the paper, except I cover sport while he's off to exotic places. Have you told them where you're going next?"

Dirk looked uncomfortable. "Nothing's confirmed yet, so I haven't said anything, but now that my friend has let the cat out of the bag, they want me to cover a tour through China. I could be away for six weeks."

Rachel was startled. She knew that Dirk would be off travelling again some time, but hadn't expected it to be quite so soon.

By now several of the regulars were coming to their table and introducing themselves. They all wanted to hear the story of the twins finding each other. "It was Greg Forman who introduced us. He knew our mother, Jennifer, and has only recently learned that we are her daughters."

The girls were caught up in explanations, and excitement grew as the patrons heard their story. "You should sell that one to a women's magazine. They'd pay big bucks for that story," one person suggested.

All the attention was getting quite exhausting. Rachel looked at Joanne and they slipped away to the privacy of the toilets. "I can't get my head around the fact that Dirk could be gone for so long and hasn't got around to telling me. Sometimes I don't think I know him very well."

"You'll know how I feel when Jason leaves. I always miss him so much."

Joanne was sympathetic. She knew that her sister was in for a lonely few weeks.

They rejoined the boys who decided it was time to leave and find somewhere quiet to eat. They headed for a Thai restaurant and it seemed natural for Steven to accompany them.

Joanne had never eaten Thai food before and the boys were hilarious as they tried to use chopsticks. "I'll starve to death if I have to use these in China," Dirk said, as he dropped another piece of chicken onto the table. Luckily a spoon and fork were also supplied.

It was almost midnight before they returned to Dirk's car and made their way back to the apartment. Steven had his own car and thanked them for a great evening. "Hope to see you again," he said as he left.

Joanne was glad that he hadn't been more insistent. He was a fun person but she didn't feel right about dating someone else right now, when Jason was due back so soon. It would be good to go out in a crowd though. There would be no pressure that way.

They were ready for bed by the time they got home. There was all day tomorrow to be together and learn more about each other's lives.

****

When she woke next morning it took a few minutes for Joanne to remember where she was. The double bed was comfortable and she pulled the duvet up higher to keep out the chilly morning air.

They had nothing planned so Dirk suggested a drive to the hot pools just north of the city. Rachel had a spare swimsuit for Joanne to wear so they set off over the harbour bridge and along the highway until they arrived at the sleepy little village of Waiwera where the famous pools dominated the town. Being Saturday, the pools were crowded with family groups but the adult only pools were almost deserted and they soon lowered themselves into the hot water and relaxed in the heady, steamy atmosphere.

Dirk swam a few lengths in a leisurely manner but the girls were content to float and feel the bubbles from the jets cascading onto their skin. They stayed in the water a little longer than the recommended time as they knew the temperature would be cold when they got out.

They made a dash for the changing sheds and dressed quickly into warm clothes and dried their hair. "Ahh, it's freezing," Rachel gasped. "We'll need to find a warm place for lunch. A plate of hot soup will do nicely.'

Dirk drove back to the larger town of Orewa, with its long sandy beach, and it didn't take long to find a café where they ordered soup and garlic bread. Joanne felt as though she was on holiday as she rarely ate out, but it seemed to come naturally to Dirk and Rachel. Being at home with her parents had certainly led to a sheltered life, compared to her twin.

Although she had work to prepare for Monday, it was decided that Joanne would stay another night. Dirk wanted to watch a rugby match on the television and they would order in pizza for dinner. Joanne envied them their free and easy lifestyle and enjoyed being part of it.

She flicked through a magazine while Dirk and Rachel sat together watching the game. They seemed so content in each other's company and she would love to have Jason here to share the experience. There always seemed to be people around when they were together.

Dirk opened a can of beer while Rachel made coffee. The game was almost over and the excitement was building. The local team was winning by three points but one penalty goal could even the score.

There was a great cheer from the crowd when another try was scored and time was up on the clock. The conversion went over and the referee blew his whistle for the end of the game.

"Great match. A good win to Auckland. Steven will be hard at work now interviewing the captains and writing an account of the match. I'm pleased that I'm not the sports reporter." Dirk drained the can and gave Rachel a hug.

"When will you know about the trip to China? Six weeks is a long time for you to be away." Rachel had been thinking. She turned to Joanne. "How about sharing the apartment with me while Dirk's gone? I know it would be further for you to go to your school but the bus service is good and I'd really like the company."

Joanne didn't take long to make up her mind. "If Dirk is definitely going to be away, then I'd love to come and stay here. I'm sure my parents would like the idea too."

It would be a great chance to make up for all those lost years and really get to know her new sister.

****

William was about to share the final page of information with Greg when they heard Gaynor's car pull up in the driveway and the sound of the garage door being opened.

"If you don't mind, I'd rather my wife didn't know about any of this right now. She's going through a risky pregnancy and the less stress she has, the better." Greg was concerned for Gaynor, even though she was now in good health. The baby was due in four months time and the scan had shown normal development.

"There is just one more thing I'm curious about." William was not quite ready to leave. "I believe you have a sister named Susan. Where does she live?"

Greg was surprised that anyone would want to know about Susan. "Why do you ask?"

"It's just that I think I may have met her. Does she happen to have blond hair and very bright finger nails?" William knew he was grasping at straws.

"That doesn't sound at all like the Susan I know. Mousy hair, short finger nails, very little make up. No, my sister shuns the spotlight."

"I must be mistaken then. The woman I'm thinking of worked at our office for a short time just before the fire. She seems to have disappeared into thin air and we are trying to locate her."

"I'm sorry I can't help you. Susan went back to Australia after our father died. She helped me go through his paperwork before she left and we destroyed a large number of documents. Some contained confidential information about the company and she was worried that they would get into the wrong hands. My poor sister was always so proud of the family name and would hate to see it tarnished. Some of the files you have shown me would upset her greatly." Greg looked very concerned.

William still had his suspicions about Greg's sister, but this was not the right time to voice them. He rose to go, and shook Greg by the hand. "It's great news that the dead girl's twins have found each other. They owe you a huge debt as it was you that saw the likeness and brought them together."

"Thank goodness some good has come out of all this mess. I was very fond of Jennifer all those years ago. You could say that she was my first love. In the meantime, I'll do some digging to try and find out more about the hospital closure. Some previous members of the board must still be alive."

After seeing William out, Greg went to find Gaynor who was surprised to see him home so early. "The doctor said I'm doing well and the baby is growing nicely. You look a little tired, my dear. I thought I would have a rest and then cook you an early dinner."

Greg sat in the small living room which opened onto the deck during the summer. It was some time since he had heard from his sister and he had been too busy to be concerned about it. He picked up the phone and dialed her number. The dial tone showed that the line had been disconnected. That was strange. Susan always made sure that he could contact her.

He phoned information and asked them to check the connection and after what seemed an age, a woman got back to him to say the number was no longer available. Greg was stunned. Why would his sister have the phone disconnected? Perhaps she hadn't paid the account. She shouldn't be short of money as she had been well provided for in their father's will.

All sorts of worrying thoughts were whirling around in his mind. Susan had always been a bit unstable. There was that crazy episode when she was young and for some reason stole a flagon of wine from the liquor store. She had created such a scene when she was apprehended that the doctors put her on tranquilizers.

At times she had become depressed and wasn't able to maintain a relationship, resulting in a series of unsuitable male friends. She had loved the idea that their father was rich and powerful and she lived like a princess, obsessed with the honour of being a Forman, a name that came from aristocracy in ancient times.

Should he report his sister as a missing person? The police probably wouldn't take him seriously as she was probably safely in her apartment on the luxurious Gold Coast. The best he could do was write a letter and if he had no answer he would take further action. Yes, that was what he would do.

Chapter 29

After a fun night of rugby and pizza, Joanne wasn't in any hurry to leave the comfortable bed in Rachel's spare room. It would be good to stay here while Dirk was away on his travels, but her parents would miss the board money which she would have to pay to Rachel instead.

Dirk had offered to drive Joanne back to her parents' home and they were all invited for lunch so they set off just after 11 o'clock and drove through the quiet streets. Apart from churchgoers no-one was up and about.

Rachel had brought along her photo album for Madeline to see and they were soon comparing it with the rest of Joanne's pictures. "You were just like a little doll with those big eyes and curly hair." Madeline was fascinated at the difference in size between the two girls. As they grew up they became more alike and she agreed it would have been difficult to identify them once they reached their second year.

The hair styles were different with Joanne's long fringe hanging over her eyes, while Rachel usually had her hair pulled back. As they were eating lunch, Joanne broached the subject of staying with Rachel while Dirk was gone.

Although Joanne's board money helped pay the bills, Madeline knew they would cope. After all, their children wouldn't be living with them for ever. Bradin was talking about a new contract in the South Island once his current roofing job was done. She and Stan would learn to get by on their own.

"That sounds like a good plan. Joanne has been a bit spoiled living at home, although she does know how to cook when she has to." Madeline was encouraging. "You will have to take your bus fares into account. Travel is not cheap."

Stan was fascinated that Dirk would be travelling through China. It wasn't the sort of place he would be comfortable in with all those people and crowded cities. Give him good old New Zealand with its open spaces and clean air.

Rachel was still waiting for a call from the television studios and she had almost given up hope. She described the interviews and how it wasn't as glamourous a job as it appeared. "Most of the time you are hanging about waiting for the camera crew and trying to keep your hair tidy."

"We'd love to see you on the television screen. It would make our day." Steve thought it sounded very exciting. "You could become the new Lotto girl."

"I hope not. I do enjoy following up stories about people and major events. Wearing an evening gown and reading out the lucky numbers each week would bore me to tears."

Dirk and Rachel left soon after lunch and Joanne decided to spend the afternoon in her classroom. She had work to mark and lessons to prepare and she wanted to mix some paints ready for an art project she was keen to try. They were going to create a jungle scene and the children would paint animals and glue them onto the leafy background.

She had found some animal templates and photocopied these for the class to cut out and paint. Some of the children would probably like to create their own jungle animals and this would be encouraged as well.

The paper would be pegged to a sturdy string that ran across the room. The children would like to see their work displayed so boldly.

She wouldn't be able to get to the school so easily once she was at Rachel's apartment, and being in the city, there would be more exciting things to do. She was really looking forward to living away from home for the first time.

Joanne knew she was a real home body compared to her sister, who had gone to boarding school and now had her own apartment. And what if Rachel became a TV presenter? Everyone would think it was Joanne on their screens each night. Her pupils would be really confused.

She arrived home two hours later, just in time to get a call from Jason. He was feeling the cold down in windy Wellington and looking forward to the next break. Joanne told him all about her stay at Rachel's apartment and how she would be living there for a few weeks.

"That's great news, Joanne. Maybe you could find room for me too when I'm back in Auckland." Joanne thought about the double bed and smiled. That could be an interesting possibility.

****

Rachel's week started off quietly. After the stories on the new bypass with the protestors' reactions and the coverage of the law office fire, the biggest news was the opening of a new Hospice building. The Prime Minister himself would be there and Rachel hoped to talk to some people who were involved with the Hospice programme.

She was just about to get in touch with one of her contacts when the phone rang. "Rachel, this is Pete. The big boss from Wellington is here for the day. Would you be free to meet her? She is very interested in talking to you."

Although she had been expecting the call Rachel felt anxious. Did she really want to be on public display several times a week? She agreed to meet Pete at the studio in a hour's time. It was just a short bus ride and she could make up the time later.

Pete's boss turned out to be an attractive woman about 50 years old with a vivacious personality. It was easy to imagine that she would have been a television star herself. She greeted Rachel warmly and looked her up and down.

"Mmm. You look every bit as good in the flesh. I was very impressed with your audition tape and would like to offer you a job. It just happens that we have a vacancy coming up as one of our presenters is leaving to have a baby."

Over the next half hour they discussed contracts and working conditions. When the salary was mentioned, Rachel gasped with surprise. She would be earning twice as much as she was now. Poor old Bill Osborne would never be able to offer that sort of money and would always have to rely on a junior reporter.

"You will be supplied with clothing while you are on the job. Quite a nice label I might add. Do tell me you are interested."

Maggie Davies was most enthusiastic. She knew that Rachel had the right looks and the voice to do the job. All that she lacked was confidence.

Rachel felt herself responding, especially when Pete came over and added his encouragement. "Come on Rachel. We'd love to have you on the team."

"I guess I've had plenty of time to think about it and I'd like to give it a go. When would you want me to start?" She knew that she would have to give Bill Osborne a month's notice so it was agreed that she would join the network at the beginning of May.

Everything familiar was changing, which might be stressful, but she felt a surge of excitement and she was optimistic about the challenges that lay ahead.

Chapter 30

The woman on the bed stirred and opened her eyes. She looked around in a dazed fashion, unsure where she was. A nurse in a blue uniform was hovering. "How are you feeling, my dear? You came in last night a bit disorientated so we put you to bed. Are you feeling any better now?"

Susan Forman tried to remember what had happened the night before. She recalled the motel room, the bottle of wine and the handful of pills. Had she taken them? She couldn't remember.

"You arrived in a taxi with no luggage, but you are in safe hands here Susan. Do you want us to get in touch with anyone?"

Susan paled at the thought of letting her brother know where she was. She had sought out this safe haven many times in the past. It was very discreet, and the doctors and nurses all knew who she was. She would rest here for a few days and then fly back to Australia.

She accepted the warm drink that was offered and sat on the edge of the bed. The medication she had received was making her feel warm and fuzzy and she found herself relaxing.

She knew she would have to send someone to collect her belongings. Who could she trust? She thought of the woman who had worked in the law office where her father's records had been stored.

Perhaps Beryl Griffin would show her usual discretion and help her out once again.

Yes, she would tell the nurses to contact Beryl and ask her to collect her few belongings and bring them to her then she would be able to make her way to the airport and leave this crazy city behind.

It was all a nightmare. Her father's reputation would be in tatters if anyone read the documents in those filing cabinets. They had to be destroyed. There had been no other way out. It was all very confusing. She lay back on the bed and let herself fall into a deep sleep.

****

Greg Forman was deeply worried about his sister. She had behaved oddly in the past, disappearing once in a while without any explanation. He had received no reply from his letter and decided to contact the police station in the Gold Coast town where she lived. They could call at her apartment and see if there was anyone there.

Rachel had phoned and told him the result of the television interview. "It looks as though you will be seeing me on your screen any time soon," she said.

'That's good news, Rachel. I think it's time you and your sister came here for dinner again. There is so much I want to share with the two of you."

Greg was having a busy time with his council obligations. There were endless meetings and so many hurdles in the way of achieving the things he had set out to do. He had talked to a few people who were involved with the Parkhaven Rest Home and they were confident that the place was well run. No-one seemed to recall the old days when it was a maternity hospital.

"There must be someone who was involved back then. I just need to talk to one of the board members and find out why the place was suddenly closed down." Gaynor was patiently listening. She was pleased that her baby would be born in the big hospital which had a very good reputation.

"The death of Jennifer may have been an isolated problem. It was probably a very respectable place apart from that."

"I'm still not sure what types of procedures were being carried out there. William found some interesting statistics but we can't be sure what was going on. I would like to talk to a doctor or nurse who worked there at the time."

William was still in Rarotonga having a well deserved break with his family and wouldn't be back for another few days. Greg would just have to be patient until he returned.

****

With a weekend coming up, Flo O'Connor decided it was time to pay another visit to the Blake family in Hamilton. She called over to Madeline's house and said that she wanted to persuade Joanne and Rachel to go with them to visit the family.

"I want to shock them. When they see the two girls together they are sure to realise that they are Jennifer's long lost daughters. Even the old man, Donald Blake, might be there. I'd love to see his face when he finds that his daughter produced two beautiful children."

"I don't suppose it would do any harm. We'll have to see whether the girls are prepared to meet their family. I'll talk to Joanne tonight and get her to ask Rachel whether she would agree to come along." Madeline was curious to meet the Blake family. It would be interesting to see their reaction if they met the twins.

When Joanne arrived home from school she agreed to phone Rachel and ask her to go with them to Hamilton the next day.

"It's a bit scarey but I guess we have to face them sooner or later. Dirk can drive us there if you don't mind being jammed in the back seat of his car. It's a while since I was in Hamilton and I don't think Dirk has ever been there." Rachel was intrigued. Her life was full of surprises lately so a few more wouldn't make much different.

It was early afternoon when Dirk's car pulled into their driveway and everyone piled in. Madeline sat in the front seat as she was the heaviest, while Flo and the two girls squeezed into the back. There was a bit of a problem doing up the seat belts but soon they were driving along the highway in the direction of Waikato's biggest town, which was about two hours away.

They decided to arrive unannounced. It would save a lot of explanations but there was a chance that no-one would be home, However, as they pulled up outside the house, they could see the four young children playing in the yard.

Rachel and Joanne looked at each other. They were about to meet these strangers who should have been part of their lives. Flo was the first to get out of the car. She called out to the children and asked if their father was home.

"Hey Dad," the oldest boy called out. "There's some-one here to see you." A young man with shaved hair and wearing a rugby shirt appeared at the door. He stared hard in their direction and came towards the gate.

"It you're those religious guys I'm not interested."

"No, it's not that. Are you Donald Blake?" Flo opened the gate.

"Yeah, that's me. What can I do for you?"

By this time the others had got out of the car and were following Flo along the path towards the house. Donald's wife had heard the voices and appeared at the door drying her hands on an apron. She recognized Flo and went inside to call Donald's father.

"Dad, it's that woman I told you about. She said she knew you years ago. Come out and be sociable."

By now Flo had reached the front porch and smiled at Barbara. "Hi, I guess you remember me. I didn't tell you the truth last time I was here but I think it's time you met Joanne and Rachel. They have quite a story to tell."

Dirk had stayed in the front yard with the children and was soon occupied kicking a football across the lawn while the small boys chased it enthusiastically. The little girl was staring at the visitors. She couldn't take her eyes off the beautiful ladies who she thought she had seen before. Who could they be?

She followed the group into the house and saw them stop and look at a photo on the wall. Then they went into the living room and sat on the chairs and couches.

"What is all this about?" The young man looked ill at ease. What were these strangers doing in his house? Why were they so interested in the old photograph on the wall?

He noticed his daughter and told her to go outside and play with her brothers, but she stayed in the room and clung to her mother. "I want to stay with the pretty ladies," she whimpered. Her big green eyes were wide and questioning.

"It's okay, Michelle. You can stay with me." Her mother took the little girl on her knee.

Everybody sat, looking at each other, no-one knowing where to begin.

A door opened and an old man was standing there. He looked around at the gathering and entered the room. He stared from Flo to Madeline and then his attention moved to Rachel and Joanne who were sitting close together, holding hands.

"Who are you? What do you want?" He looked very anxious, as if a great truth was about to be unveiled. Two girls who looked exactly like Jennifer. How could that be? Jennifer had died in that hospital all those years ago and her memory had been erased from their minds, apart from that photograph that Barbara had recently hung on the wall.

Young Donald could see that his father was visibly upset. He had also seen the likeness to the photograph and couldn't understand what was happening. His sister had disappeared one day and they had never seen her again.

"Can someone explain to me what is going on here? Barbara, how about making us a cup of tea and showing our guests some hospitality." He went over to where his father was still standing and led him to an armchair.

It was Joanne who spoke first. "We are here because of that photograph on the wall. Both Rachel and I have the same picture in our possession and believe it is our mother who died when we were born."

Rachel took up the story. "I recently discovered that I was adopted and then found out that I had a twin. Our mother's name was Jennifer Blake and we have tracked you down as her family."

Donald could not believe what he was hearing. His sister had given birth to twin babies and this was the first he had heard of it. Why had his parents kept it such a secret? He remembered hearing arguments all those years ago and then they were suddenly taken out of school and moved to Hamilton. He hadn't even said goodbye to his friends and he had been very upset.

"Well, this is a bit of a turn up for the books. Do you hear that dad? You've got two more grandchildren that you knew nothing about." He called Barbara in from the kitchen. She had heard the conversation and was very excited.

"That's wonderful news. Did you hear that, Michelle? These beautiful ladies are your aunties. What do you think of that?"

Donald's father still hadn't spoken. His mind went back to that terrible time when they learned that Jennifer was pregnant. His boss had been very angry and said they would have to move away. "I will arrange for you to work in Hamilton and there will be a house for you there, as long as no-one finds out about this disgraceful situation. My son has a great future and I won't let this indiscretion destroy his life."

"We knew about Jennifer's pregnancy, and Terence Forman offered to take care of everything. We had recently arrived in New Zealand and were totally dependent on Mr Forman's charity at the time. We were shocked to hear that our daughter had died but we never knew about the babies. There hasn't been a moment when I haven't felt guilty that we weren't there for her and that her boyfriend Greg wasn't told."

The old man was so distraught that Joanne felt sorry for him. She went over and put an arm around his shoulder. Rachel hesitated for a moment, then followed suit. Flo and Madeline were crying and Barbara busied herself with the tea cups.

Little Michelle was dancing around with excitement. She raced outside to tell her brothers the news and they came running into the lounge with Dirk close behind. There was bedlam for the next few minutes as everyone began talking at once and hugging each other.

Young Donald decided to take charge. "I'll call my brothers and tell them the news. Ron lives close by and I'm sure he will want to meet you. Unfortunately, Alan is in Australia."

Barbara settled old Donald at the table with a soothing cup of tea and gave the girls a hug. "Welcome to the family. Come and help yourself to a cuppa and some cake." She instructed the children to sit on the porch with their drinks and soon order was restored.

Rachel looked across at Joanne and smiled. What a great day this was turning out to be. After spending her life as an only child, her family was growing by the minute.

Flo was relieved that everything was going so well. She sat beside old Donald and explained about the story she had told Barbara the first time she had come to the house. "I couldn't think of any other way of meeting you and we really wanted Joanne, and now Rachel, to meet their birth family."

"I'm pleased that you did tell a little white lie. Seeing those two lovely young ladies is like having our daughter back. I wish my Jean was still here to see this day. She's only been gone a few months you know."

Madeline felt sad that the woman had never known about her grand daughters. She looked around at the happy scene. Young Donald had opened a beer and was sharing it with Dirk while little Michelle had come back into the room and was gazing at her new aunts with those huge green eyes.

A station wagon pulled up outside the house and a younger version of Donald came into view, followed by a plump woman and three small children. Joanne and Rachel began to feel like movie stars as they were hugged and poked and questioned.

"I was twelve years old when our sister died so I remember her well. The last time I saw her she looked exactly like you, but with shorter hair and no make up." Ron couldn't believe his eyes. His wife Margaret introduced their children.

"Jamie, Mark and Billie, these are your new aunties. See, that's their mother in the picture on the wall."

The children were too young to take much interest and followed Barbara into the kitchen where she poured drinks and cut slices of cake. Soon they were sitting out on the deck with their cousins who were excited at this unexpected party.

Young Donald opened a bottle of sparkling wine that had been saved for a special occasion. "May this be the first of many happy meetings," he said, as everybody raised their glasses and drank a toast to Joanne and Rachel and remembered their mother, the long-lost Jennifer.

Chapter 31

Beryl Griffin had returned to her own home and was feeling quite lost without her busy life at Barlow and Reid. Ted Baker was doing much better and had employed a part-time housekeeper.

They still shared dinner twice a week and Ted had invited Beryl to lunch and the movies on Tuesday, which Beryl was looking forward to very much. She was arranging a few flowers in a vase when the phone rang and for a moment she was puzzled

. The voice sounded familiar but she couldn't quite place it. "Miss Griffin, I wondered if you could do me a big favour. I need someone to call at the Grange Motel and pick up a bag for me."

"I'm sorry, who am I speaking with?"

"It's Susan Forman. I haven't been well and I'm staying at the usual retreat. The motel has been paid up until the end of the week and the room number is eight. Are you able to help me?"

Beryl was shocked when she realized who she was talking to. Susan Forman was supposed to be living on the sunny Gold Coast in Australia. She had only returned to New Zealand when her father died to help her brother sort through his papers. Now all those files had been destroyed in the terrible fire.

She hadn't heard from the police for several weeks. The last she heard they were trying to find the mysterious woman who had taken her place at the office. She smiled when she thought of Ted Baker's impression. "Her hair was too blond and I didn't like those long finger nails."

Carrying out Susan's wishes wouldn't be easy as it would mean catching a bus to the motel and hauling a bag into town, then catching another bus to the well hidden retreat just north of the city.

She was tempted to refuse but Susan was very convincing. "You are the only one who knows about this place. Even my brother is unaware that I stay here when life gets too difficult for me. It is somewhere to relax and be looked after until all the bad thoughts go away."

Reluctantly, Beryl agreed to the younger woman's request. She knew that Susan suffered from a nervous condition and was quite unstable at times. Terence Forman had been one of their best clients and had paid good money for their services. She felt she owed him a favour.

With the whole day ahead of her she may as well take a bus into town and try to find the motel. As the weather was cool, she dressed warmly in a woollen coat and hat and walked the short distance to the bus stop.

It wasn't long before the crowded bus stopped to allow her to board. The driver was impatient as she fumbled to find the correct change and drove off before she could sit down. Luckily a young woman gave up her seat and she thankfully sat and looked nervously out the window. Susan had explained that the motel was on this road but she wasn't sure exactly how far she would have to go.

"Do you know where the Grange Motel is?" she asked the man who was sitting beside the window.

"Not really, but I'll look out for it," he replied. A few minutes later he saw the sign and Beryl pushed the buzzer. The next stop was a short distance away and it took Beryl a few minutes to walk back up a steep hill to the long brick building with the illuminated sign.

The woman behind the desk was very helpful. "Ms Forman phoned to say you would be picking up her belongings so I've got them here ready for you. She said to take a taxi to the destination and she will reimburse you when you arrive."

Beryl heaved a sigh of relief. She hadn't been looking forward to carrying a heavy bag onto the buses. It would certainly be much easier to call a taxi and go directly to the retreat.

She sat down thankfully on a cane chair to wait while the woman ordered a taxi. The foyer was decorated with travel posters which showed tempting pictures of tropical beaches and snow-capped mountains. It would be nice to take a cruise or join a travel group. It would be even better if Ted Baker could be persuaded to join her. They certainly deserved a break after all they had been through.

A black taxi cab pulled up outside the motel and the driver carried the suitcase and put it in the trunk. She gave the address and he looked at her curiously. He probably thought that she was booking into the exclusive retreat.

It was a twenty minute drive through a leafy suburb and then along a narrow driveway bordered by tall trees until a long wooden building came into view. Beryl paid the taxi driver from her dwindling bundle of notes and pressed the bell on the closed door.

A tall woman in a blue uniform came to the door and asked who she wanted to see. The door opened silently and Beryl was ushered into a luxuriously furnished lobby complete with palms and a water feature.

"Ms Forman isn't receiving visitors, but she gave me this envelope for you. She is very grateful for what you have done for her." The woman took the bag and handed Beryl a thick envelope, then showed her out through the door.

Beryl felt very annoyed. Surely Susan Forman could have taken the time to speak to her. She stood for a moment outside the door and looked inside the envelope. It contained several hundred dollar notes. She knew she was being paid to say nothing about Susan's whereabouts.

She walked along the side of the building and peered through a large window into a spacious lounge. Several people were sitting around reading or just staring into space. One woman was standing, staring at the door through which Beryl had just left. She looked familiar, except that her hair was coloured a streaky blond. Susan Forman didn't have hair that colour, but apparently the missing woman Betty Long was known for her distinctive blond hair.

Beryl felt sick in the stomach. Had she stumbled upon the truth about the mysterious woman who had worked at the law office, then vanished without a trace?

****

William and Jamie walked out of the airport to face the chill of autumn after a week of tropical sunshine in Rarotonga. As they waited for the shuttle to drive them to where their car was parked, they both wished that their idyllic holiday could have lasted longer.

Samuel had loved wading in the warm sea and trying to catch the tiny coloured fish that darted about in the shallows, while Jamie had made the most of the sun and hoped her tan wouldn't fade too quickly.

In two days, William would be working with the new law firm and was looking forward to the challenge. He knew that several of his former clients would probably be in touch as the old firm of Barlow and Reid no longer existed.

After driving around the small island, the motorway into the city seemed busier than normal, but William knew it wouldn't take long to adjust. Samuel had slept on the four-hour flight and was full of energy so Jamie was kept busy handing him toys to distract him from trying to climb out of his car seat.

They would go straight home and unpack, then they would need to stock up on food at the supermarket. Jamie hadn't cooked a meal all week and wasn't looking forward to getting back into household chores. She was still in holiday mode.

It didn't take long to unpack their bags and throw a load of washing in the machine.

"I'd better check my answering machine before we head out," said William, not really too anxious to face reality. There were several messages but most could wait. The last one caught him by surprise. It was from Beryl Griffin and she wanted to speak to him as soon as possible. What could Beryl want that was so urgent?

The phone rang several times before she picked it up. "William. Thank goodness it's you. Something has happened that I think you should know about. It's supposed to be confidential but I really need to share this with someone. I think I've found the woman who called herself Betty Long."

"You're kidding. Where did you find her?" William could hardly believe his ears. He listened in amazement as Beryl told him of her visit to the retreat.

"I believe that Susan Forman and Betty Long are one and the same person. I was the only one that would have recognized Susan and of course, I was away helping my mother. The woman I saw looked like Susan but her hair was blond."

"That's what I thought when I saw the news clipping about Susan Forman. She looked a lot like Betty Long except for her hair and make up, and the long finger nails. So you think that Ms Forman disguised herself in order to take the job at the law office. Why would a wealthy woman want to work as a secretary? She certainly didn't need the money. What other motive could she have had?"

William was ready to spring into action. "I think it's time to pay Greg Forman another visit and see what he has to say. Then we will need to let the police know what you have found out."

****

When Rachel told Bill Osborne that she was leaving, he was horrified. "Rachel, you're the best journalist I've had working here. I'll have to train someone else and that is not an easy task."

"I'm sorry about that, Bill, but this chance has come up and I'm certainly not going to turn it down." Rachel was remorseful, but determined to make the most of this opportunity.

"That's okay, girl. I'm just disappointed, that's all. I'm really excited for you and will be proud to see you on the television screen."

Dirk had taken a number of photographs at the Evans' house and after work they had a great time going through them and trying to work out who was who. Little Michelle was the only girl but all the boys looked very much alike.

Rachel held up a group shot with all the grandchildren gathered around a very proud Donald Evans senior. "I know he'll love to have a copy of this one. We will be visiting them again very soon, I'm sure."

Dirk would be departing in a week's time for his trip through China and offered to leave his car for Rachel to use in his absence. She knew she would miss Dirk but with Joanne staying in the apartment and a new job to get used to, time would go by very fast.

"Let's drive over to Greg's house and show him these photos. I know he would be interested to see my new family." Rachel wanted to share the happy occasion.

As they pulled into the driveway, Rachel recognized William's car. "It should be alright to go in. William probably knows more about the situation than anyone."

Gaynor answered the door and invited them inside. She was looking very well and her pregnancy was now quite obvious. "My dears. Do come in. It's Rachel, isn't it. I'm never quite sure any more. Greg and William are just discussing something in the office. They looked very serious, but I'm sure they'll be out any moment."

She poured them a glass of wine and they settled on the long couch in front of a gas fire. Rachel looked at it and laughed. "The first time I saw one of those it took a whole three days before I realised it wasn't a real log." She pulled out the packet of photographs and soon Gaynor was sharing the excitement of the family meeting.

"I love the little girl with the big green eyes. That must be something that keeps occurring in your mother's family."

"She's a little cutie and wouldn't leave us alone. I think she would have come home with us if we'd let her." Rachel felt real affection for the little girl.

It was some time before Greg and William emerged from the office and when they did come out, they both looked very serious. "It's great to see you, Rachel, but something has come up. William and I need to pay someone a visit."

Gaynor was puzzled. Where did her husband need to go at this time of the evening? She knew he was worried about his sister but he couldn't do much as she was in Australia. It was up to the police to try and track her down.

Dirk and Rachel thanked her for the drink and drove away. They would eat out tonight somewhere closer to home. There was so much to celebrate.

****

The two men drove through the streets towards the northern suburb where Beryl had seen the mysterious woman. Greg was horrified to hear that his sister had checked herself in to this retreat without informing him. No wonder she wasn't answering her phone in Australia. It was all very worrying.

Beryl had given William a street address, but the roads were unfamiliar and the canopy of trees made it difficult to identify the numbers. It took some time to find the right driveway and Greg pulled up outside the front door of the long wooden building.

It was almost dark and a security light came on as they approached the entrance where Greg pushed the button beside the door. It took some time for anyone to respond but the door was eventually opened by a solidly built man wearing a security uniform.

"Visiting hours are over. You'll have to come back tomorrow," he said and was about to close the door when William stepped forward and showed him a card.

"We need to see Ms Forman who is staying here. I am her lawyer and this is her brother. The matter is most urgent." William hoped his bluff might work. The man looked puzzled, then opened the door wider and let them inside.

"I'll have to call the manager. Please wait here until she answers her phone."

Greg and William glanced around them. From the décor, it looked as though Susan had chosen a very expensive place to stay. If it hadn't been for Beryl Griffin they would never have found her.

The security man put the phone down and told them to wait where they were. The manager would be with them shortly. He sat back at his desk and shuffled some papers, glancing at the two men from time to time.

Ten minutes went by without any sign of the manager. Greg was getting impatient and began walking around the foyer picking up brochures and reading the notices on the board. This place was big on natural remedies, with spa treatment, massage, relaxation, and de-tox diets all being vigorously promoted.

A few minutes later two women came into the foyer. An attractive brunette in her 50s was accompanied by an Asian woman wearing a nurse's uniform who looked somewhat distressed.

"But I saw her just a short time ago and left her a menu. She said she would come down to dinner. How could she have left without anyone noticing?" She stopped when she saw the two men.

The manager came up to Greg and held out her hand. "Good evening Mr Forman, I believe. I'm Leonie Giles and I can confirm that your sister has been our guest. I sent the nurse to check her room and Ms Forman seems to have disappeared. Most of her belongings are still there but we believe a small bag has been taken, along with her wallet and some items of clothing."

"It doesn't sound as though your security man was doing a very good job. How could someone just walk out without anyone noticing?" Greg was very annoyed.

"This isn't a prison, Mr Forman. Our guests are entitled to come and go as they please, but I didn't really consider that your sister was well enough to leave us yet. I would have advised her to stay longer."

William sprang into action. "How long ago was Susan last seen? Are there any vehicles missing? We must try and find her as soon as possible."

Ms Giles began to issue instructions. "You go and check the cars, George, and Anna, call the other nurses and look around the grounds. There are many places where Susan could be hiding."

"I'm sorry about this, but Susan could have slipped out during the staff changeover. She would have to walk down the driveway to the road and then wait for a bus which is very infrequent."

Ms Giles poured them a coffee from the machine in the foyer and went out to check the rest of the rooms.

Greg and William drank the coffee and asked to see the room where Susan had been staying. The top drawer of the dresser was open and the contents spilled over onto the floor. Obviously, Susan had left in a hurry. The large suitcase that Beryl had brought from the motel was still in the cupboard but Greg knew she usually carried a matching bag which was nowhere to be seen.

"Let's look in the suitcase. She may have left some clue as to why she was staying here." Greg pulled the case from the cupboard and threw it on the bed. Several light trousers and tops were still folded in the case along with a large bag of make up.

William opened the bag and pulled out a bright red lipstick. This could only have belonged to the mysterious Betty Long. A bottle of blond hair dye confirmed his suspicions.

Greg opened the top of the suitcase and pulled out a brown cardboard file. He opened it with trembling hands. William recognized the familiar letter head at the top of the pages.

"So, she did take some of the files from the office." Several newspaper clippings fell out onto the bed, including accounts of the fire and also Greg's election stories, taken from the Chronicle.

They returned the papers to the file and closed the suitcase. They knew they would have to find Susan as soon as possible.

Leonie Giles was back in the foyer and the security guard was once more behind his desk. "There's not much more we can do here. I'll keep in touch and let you know if Ms Forman returns. You will need to collect her belongings and settle her account if she doesn't come back."

Greg unlocked the car door and they sat for a few minutes trying to decide what to do. They could call the police but what could they tell them? Susan Forman was free to come and go as she liked. She may have checked into a different motel but that could be anywhere in the city.

"Maybe we could check the airport. She could be flying back to the Gold Coast as we speak."

William was anxious to get back to Jamie and Samuel. They had only just returned from their romantic holiday and he was abandoning them already. "If you don't mind, I would prefer not to go to the airport. My wife will wonder where I've got to."

"I suppose you're right. Even if we did go there, we wouldn't be able to get into the departure lounge. If Susan has returned to Australia I'm sure I'll hear from her soon."

William didn't want to say too much but he strongly suspected that Greg's sister was the one who had started the fires in the law office. It was too much of a coincidence that she had turned up at their office as Betty Long, only to disappear after the fire. He would pay Constable Bailey a visit in the morning and tell him of the new developments.

They drove back to Greg's house in silence, each with their own thoughts about their visit to the retreat.

Chapter 32

Jamie was far from happy when William finally arrived home. She had waited for a time, then driven her own car to the supermarket to buy enough food for dinner and breakfast. Much to her embarrassment, Samuel had been cross and had started screeching in the store. There were curious stares as she tried to placate him.

"Here, give him a cracker biscuit. That works every time and won't spoil his tea." One woman was most helpful. Jamie took the biscuit and offered it to her son. He stared at the woman with big eyes, then smiled and munched on the cracker.

She got through the check out without any more outbursts and transferred Samuel to his car seat as she loaded the groceries into the trunk. Why couldn't she be back in calm, peaceful Rarotonga?

Samuel was fed and a meal prepared by the time William's car pulled up outside. "This had better be good," she thought as she met William in the hallway. Seeing the look on his wife's face, William decided he had better tell her the whole story.

"Greg Forman's sister has been here all along. She was staying in a retreat but has disappeared. I'm certain that she worked at the office as Betty Long and that she was the one who lit the fires in the building."

"Wow. That's quite a statement. How can you be so sure?" Jamie was surprised that her husband would make such an accusation. He was usually so careful about what he said.

"We found Betty's make up and a file of papers from the office in her bag. She must have left the retreat just before we arrived. No-one knew she had gone."

"Then shouldn't you call the police? I'm sure they would like to know who the mysterious Betty Long really is."

William collapsed into a chair. "I'll certainly call at the station and tell the constable of my suspicions, but it can wait until morning. Even if Susan Forman is planning on flying out, there is probably not enough evidence to stop her at this stage."

"Okay. I must admit I was annoyed that you left me to do the shopping alone, but I can see how it happened. I'll put the dinner on now and we can relax with a drink while we're waiting, just like we did all week on that beautiful sandy beach."

Jamie gave her husband a hug and went into the kitchen to turn on the stove. She poured two glasses of white wine from the fridge and carried them into the living room. Samuel was amusing himself on the floor with his toys which he hadn't seen for a week.

"It might turn out that Susan wasn't in her right mind at the time of the fire. In that case, the insurance company may pay out after all." William wasn't sure but thought there was a chance he could get some compensation for his books and office gear.

"It'll be good to put the whole sad event behind us. Here's to your new career with Thompson and Brent." Jamie raised her glass and smiled at her husband. Their future was suddenly much more secure.

****

Susan Forman sat tensely in the departure lounge at the Auckland International Airport. She looked anxiously at the clock. Only ten more minutes until they started boarding. Surely no-one could stop her from flying out, back to her secure apartment on the sunny Gold Coast, and thousands of miles from the burnt out office block.

It had been a mistake to check in at the retreat and let that Griffin woman know where she was. Maybe the police were after her. They could have worked out by now that she had masqueraded as Betty Long to retrieve the documents from the office files.

No-one must learn the truth about the procedures that were carried out at Parkhaven Nursing Home. Babies were delivered in secret, then sold to the highest bidder and worst of all, her own precious child had been stolen from her.

She was just eighteen when she realized she was pregnant from a stupid one-night stand with a boy she didn't even like. When her parents found out, she was quickly booked into the nursing home. Before she knew what was going on, she was drugged and by the time she woke up, the baby was no more.

She knew she was too young to look after a child, but she was given no choice. A living fetus was destroyed. From then Susan suffered from panic attacks. Medication did little to control them. Therapists didn't help much either. She should have hated her father for what he did, but in spite of his business connections which at times were shady, she was proud of the family name and didn't want anything to tarnish it.

She pulled herself back to the present. They were being called to the plane now. In a short time she would be flying far above the clouds and away from her nightmares. She would phone her brother as soon as she was back in the apartment and he need never know she had been back in Auckland.

****

Constable Bailey was busy on the telephone when William was shown into his office. He beckoned him to sit down and a few minutes later welcomed him with a smile.

"I'll just get your file. It won't take a moment." He disappeared and came back carrying a wad of papers.

"Nothing fresh to report, I'm afraid. We drew a blank trying to locate Ms Long. It was almost as though the woman didn't exist." The constable looked rueful.

"That's because there was no Betty Long." William sounded triumphant. "We believe the woman was Susan Forman, Greg's sister, and she had good reason to want the documents in the office destroyed."

He went on to describe the visit to the retreat the night before and how Susan Forman had disappeared, leaving some damaging evidence behind.

"We think the woman is either hiding out in a motel somewhere, or already on her way back to Australia."

"I wish you had come straight to me last night. We might have stopped her on suspicion of arson." Constable Bailey was annoyed. "But on the other hand, we wouldn't have enough evidence to detain her until we check out your story."

"Ms Forman's belongings are still at the retreat and she could well return for them. The toilet bag was the biggest giveaway. Greg says his sister would never wear makeup like that and I certainly recognized that bright red lipstick."

Constable Bailey thanked William for the information. "Maybe you should consider taking up detective work," he said. "You seem to have got to the truth quicker than we did."

William felt light hearted as he left the police station. A new job and a fresh start awaited him next week and he had helped bring two sisters together. Even though Jason was back at school he should call at Joanne's house later in the day and find out how the reunion was going. Jamie loved an excuse to get out of the house so she and Samuel might come along with him. Yes, that's what they would do.

****

Rachel finished work early on Monday night and found Dirk already in the apartment when she walked in the door.

"I'm too excited to stay home. Let's call and see Joanne and tell her that I'm going to be a TV star. She should be home by now."

Dirk was only too happy to oblige. He was glad that Joanne would be sharing the apartment with Rachel while he was gone and wanted to get to know her better.

As Dirk drove into the driveway, William's wagon followed close behind. "This is becoming a habit. We seem to be following each other around," Dirk laughed.

Rachel was pleased to finally meet Jamie and Samuel and by the time they reached the front porch, Joanne had the door open. "Come on in. Mum and Dad are still at work but they should be back soon."

It was the first time William had seen the girls together and everyone was right. They really were very alike. He felt quite emotional to see how well it had all turned out. If he hadn't rescued those papers before the office was burned, the truth of their birth may never have been discovered.

Jamie's eyes were brimming with tears. It was such a beautiful story and it appeared to have a very happy ending. Joanne and Rachel worked together to find some drinks and potato chips while Dirk told William about his upcoming trip to China.

Samuel played with some old wooden blocks that Madeline had never had the heart to throw out. "They'll come in handy for the grand kids," she often said.

There was no mention of poor, sad Susan Forman. That information could wait for another day.

Joanne looked at the mail which was piled on the bench and there was a letter from Jason which she would read later. There was also a large red envelope and when she opened it, she pulled out an invitation to a birthday party.

'Michelle Blake invites her beautiful new cousins, Joanne and Rachel, to her fifth birthday party. Please say you will come. Love, from Michelle.'

Joanne held the card out to Rachel and the two of them threw their arms around each other, tears of happiness in their eyes. They were no longer two isolated little girls, but members of a large welcoming family. Their new life was just beginning.